One Tiny Cry

ALSO BY CHRISTINA DELAY

ONE TINY CRY

CHRISTINA DELAY

JOFFE BOOKS

Joffe Books, London
www.joffebooks.com

First published in Great Britain in 2025

Cover art by Nick Castle

ISBN: 978-1-80573-277-8

For Granny, for always being the light

CHAPTER ONE

You gotta cut away the dead for a chance at life. Dad's long-ago words whisper in my ear as I trim away the dead undergrowth of an azalea. I push my hair back from my forehead, leather glove scratching against skin. Despite the lowering sun, it's still hotter than a picnic in hell. At least it's dry; humid is worse.

My favorite landscaper is waiting in his truck for his mulch order, his muffler rumbling in the North Texas heat. Diego never questions my advice when it comes to plants and nutrients, and that, in my book, is a prime quality in a man. The loader throws the last bag of mulch into Diego's truck bed, the last pickup of the day done and dusted.

"See you next week, Miss Carter," he shouts to be heard over the crunch of gravel under his tires as he leaves. Once his truck disappears from view, I walk back to the employees-only nursery. A row of my potted patients — plants with brown leaves, spotted leaves, no leaves — sit on a long, skinny planting table. At one time, the table may have had a coat of varnish, but now the wood is worn smooth, color leached from fertilizers and water, nicks and splinters caused by potting knives and heavy containers and heavier years.

It's like an ICU ward in here, or a shelter for the abused. A curtain of weighted silence divides this greenhouse from the rest of the gardening center, as if a loud noise could be the thing that strangles the last breath out of a struggling life.

One of my patients, an oakleaf hydrangea, suffers from an extreme case of root rot. I gently lift her out of her too small home, dry dirt crumbling against my chewed-to-the-quick nails, and rinse the soil away to expose the rot. I take my scissors — Dad's, once — out of their diluted bleach solution, and cut away the affected roots. The engraved metal warms against my palm, lately about as close as I get to having my hand held.

A soft whir of an electric car drags my attention through the yellowed greenhouse windows. A black Mercedes passes the Turning Leaf Nursery sign, turns into the parking lot, and a knot forms inside my chest. The car doesn't have a lick of West Texas dirt on it, and it belongs in my place of work, my safe haven, about as well as a turd in a punch bowl.

"Not here for you, not here for you," I mutter, doing my best to steady my hands and take deep breaths.

The driver door opens, and out steps a tall man wearing business slacks, a fitted white shirt, and shoes as black and shiny as his car. Odd clothes to wear to a gardening center, which only confirms my suspicions. Locals don't wear that type of costume — dirt leaps off these tables like a desperate barfly at closing time.

"Darla," Larissa calls out, her normal boss bitch tone teetering on the edge of apprehension. "Someone's here to see you." I've warned her of this moment, the inevitable second my past would come calling, and I would have no choice but to follow, kicking and screaming.

I force myself to breathe, and trim away the dead leaves of the plant in front of me, taking more time than I need, while my thoughts whirl around my escape room brain — only there is no escape. I've lost the key.

"Tell him I'll be there soon," I say over my shoulder, then turn back to my plant patient and try to calm my breaths as

2

I pat the soil around the stem of the struggling I-can't-even-remember. My hands go through the motions, but I can't think of anything other than, why now?

"No need, I'm here." His deep voice fills the room, my arms tense, and the plant under my fingertips seems to shiver in response.

His inability to respect boundaries speaks volumes about the man. I glance at him through the mirror, then turn my attention back to my work.

"How can I help you?" I say without turning around, my tone so flat it's almost convincing. I take my time and scoop my personal mixture of soil, sand, coffee grounds, and a dash of Epsom salt into a new pot, anything to keep from facing this man. Maybe he's just another client. Maybe he needs the plant doctor.

Maybe I'm in denial.

"Well, I'm not sure if you can or not," he drawls. "You work here long?"

I make room for the root ball and gently place the hydrangea in her new home, despite curdling dread stiffening my muscles. "'Bout six years," I respond.

"Six years, seven months, from what I understand. And before that, the QuikMart in San Saba, am I right?"

I freeze, and it's as if his words are beating me from the inside out. Turning me black and blue before I can recover and run.

In the mirror, he opens a brown folder, checks the contents, and locks his sky-blue eyes on me. "If I've done my job well, then that would make you Darla Caraway."

My breath kicks into the back of my throat, and I can't help it, I look for hiding places. Under the skinny potting table, behind the diseased sago palm, camouflaged in the bamboo stalks . . . there are none. It's a little girl's response, hiding, but also the only defense I have left.

Running away was always a temporary option.

I turn around.

3

He taps his folder against his open palm, waiting for me to respond. But I can't.

He shifts closer, and I'm breathing in nothing but instinct and silent prayers. I take a step back.

"You *are* Darla Caraway?" And suddenly the drawl is gone from his tone, and in its place is an icy professionalism.

Darla Caraway, carry me far away, give me your hand, I'll be your man.

The greenhouse rocks from a stray prairie wind, and the fluorescent lights sway overhead, out of sync on their long, metal chains. The part of my heart that hasn't yet let go of home hears the whisper of the East Texas Piney Woods, smells the scent of cut grass and decomposing leaves, feels the stickiness of the air, tastes snow cone-flavored kisses, and explores the curves of a younger girl who didn't know better.

Who had too much life, much too soon.

A bug buzzes into the bug zapper, and the pip-pops shake me back to this man, with his distant Clint Eastwood accent, this man, who is saying things he should not know.

I shake my head, realize I'm rubbing my belly, and yank my hand to my hip. "No. Carter. Darla Carter." I sound like I'm seventeen again, practicing my new name in front of the bus station's bathroom mirror.

He smiles, an unassuming, disarming, handsome smile. "But you used to be Darla Caraway. I was hired to find you and deliver a message."

I dart a look at Larissa, but she's got her head cocked and her forehead crinkled, and she's holding herself as still as a squirrel in front of a speeding truck.

He hands over the folder, turns on his shiny shoes, and leaves. A piece of paper slips out of the thin package he's shoved into my hands, and I catch it before it hits the dirt-dusted concrete floor. The symbol of a haloed white bird at the top is about as familiar and distant a memory as my mom's voice, with about the same amount of guilt and regret tacked on.

Larissa watches him go, then stares at me, waiting for an explanation.

But I can't. Because I'm drowning in the words scribbled on the back of the Church flyer announcing The Feast.

It's happening again. Come home before she dies, too.

CHAPTER TWO

My heart's rhythm is all off. I sink to the potting stool, dig my nails into my knees, and feel, more than see or hear, Larissa staring at me.

"Darla?" Larissa kneels in front of me and gently pulls my hands away from my knees.

Before she dies, too.

How does this person know when I'm not even sure myself? When I thought I was the only one who could have suspected . . .

Flashes of Caitlin's last few months hit me like sharp slaps across my irregular heart.

The smile that stopped reaching her cheeks, the bags under her eyes. Her insistence that she was fine, everything was fine, that I was paranoid.

Then that note, shoved into my hand as we passed each other between classes — *Meet me after school. You were right.* With that piece of notebook paper, torn in half, folded into an origami square, filled with coupled letters and lines.

That final look in her eyes, as her gaze held mine, promising the truth.

She was never seen again.

I try to talk, to take a deep breath, but there's a sharp pain in my chest, and I can't seem to get away from it.

"I can't go home." The words push through me as if they're roots pushing through new dirt.

A trapped bird chirrups by the ceiling and flits around the room, trying to escape. Through the dust-coated greenhouse roof, the sun sinks below the prairie sky and sprays deep reds and light pinks across the clouds, like splashes of petunias in a winter garden. Larissa holds my hands until I'm forced to look at her. The gray in her hair has gotten more pronounced over the past few years, and her skin is starting to get that soft, well-loved look of older women with happy lives.

All the questions she wants to ask run around the mirrors of her green eyes. Only, they're reflecting me. And I look like I'm drowning.

"When's the last time you talked to your momma?"

Of course, she assumes that my hesitation is from a fear of returning to the home I ran away from. I take a deep breath.

"It's been a while." At her raised eyebrows, I amend, "A long while."

Sixteen years long.

"Honey, that don't matter to mommas." She's never called me honey before, and it makes me feel young, loved, and riddled with guilt. She gives my hands a squeeze and groans as she stands. "Don't worry about your job, you hear? It'll be waiting for you when you come back."

She dusts off the back of her pants, walks toward the exit, and calls over her shoulder. "And take Percy with you."

She says about the only thing she *could* say that could make me snort at a moment like this. Percy. My baby avocado tree, parked in a prime position next to my workstation. My very dependable, not-needy pet plant.

Outside, the sand kicks up and patters against the panes of the greenhouse while I trace the edges of the manila folder and dig deep for a seed of courage. The name of the man, Stone Adams, Private Investigator, is embossed on the front in glossy, navy-blue ink. Who would've hired a private investigator to find me? Where I came from, no one had that kind of money.

My breath clings to the back of my throat, but I've been through worse. I flip open the folder. The first piece of paper is a paid invoice for one grand with a note that it was paid in cash and signed by *a concerned member of the Church*.

"Great," I say to Percy. "Now we owe some do-gooder a favor, and they want us to know just how big."

He looks back as if to say, *what's this "we" business?*

"Hey, we're in this together," I retort. Percy doesn't answer, which is just as well. I'm fairly certain talking to plants, and expecting them to talk back, is a sign of insanity.

I flip the page and study the flyer. It's a typical church flyer, printed on cheap, colored paper with an abundance of bad clip art images. The Feast, otherwise known as the Church Revival, is taking place on August first, as it does every six years. Everyone's invited to celebrate the milestone and also support the teenage youth group's initiation to becoming full-fledged church members, so the flyer says.

It's written in Pastor Abe's voice, and his threat — one of the reasons I left home, intending to never return — echoes through the typed print.

Initiate into the Church, or I'll run you and your Momma out of town.

But despite Pastor Abe's threat, despite my fear and guilt over returning home, it's the words on the back of the flyer that have caused my panic. The writing is scrawled, childish even, with the letters in print and varying in size and angle. It looks as if someone learning how to write has copied the letters, poorly, off the chalkboard.

How could this person know?

I push the flyer to the side. Taped to the inside of the folder is a picture, turned around so the back is facing forward, but I already know what it is.

My fingertips go numb, and a freezing sensation threatens to envelop my chest. My nail hovers above the handwriting on the back, the names of my closest friends written in my high school script, back when I took the time to add flourishes like hearts to dotted *i*'s. I blink a few times, but it doesn't change anything — that's a picture taken off the photo wall in my childhood bedroom. A dust-covered memory I thought I could leave behind.

I don't need to flip the photo over — I have the picture etched into my brain — but I do. We're standing under the bridge at Suicide Rock. Shelly and Emmie are riding piggy-back on Karl and Ivan. Tristan has his arm around my waist, and Caitlin's elbow is on my shoulder, with her side-swept smile that could be mistaken for a grimace. She's the only one of the seven of us who's staring directly at the camera, and it feels like even then, she knew something the rest of us didn't.

I feel light-headed, like I'm not quite here. Someone was in my childhood bedroom. Is this a threat? A message from whoever sent this that they have access to my home and my mother? Or is it simply another guilt tactic to get me home? Why that picture? Why include it at all?

The questions whirl through my head as I move through the motions and rinse away the day's dirt from my tools, scrub at the grime under my cuticles, fold Dad's gardening scissors back into themselves, protecting the sharp points, and slide them into their permanent spot in the side pocket of my cargo pants. My locker contains only a few personal items, and it takes less than five minutes to empty it of six years — and apparently seven months — of my work life. Larissa said my job would be waiting, but I recognize the empty feeling curling around my chest.

My plant patients, all twelve of them, stare at me as if I'm condemning them to death which, if I leave them here, I likely am. Larissa's already left for the evening, so I jot a quick note to explain that I've taken them under my care. It's not stealing — our clients know they might not get their potted plants back. And if I surprise myself and ever do come back, I'll bring them with me, healthy and alive.

I dust off the ever-present tarp in the back of my ancient Honda Accord, eye the space — it'll be tight, but they should all fit — and load everyone up. In the back seat, I buckle in a box full of African daisies for Mom's garden — not that flowers work as a stand-in for an apology — and into the front seat goes Percy, the seatbelt tucked tight around his terracotta home.

Old habits die hard, and my high school backpack, reutilized as my go bag, is in its permanent spot in the front passenger floorboard, and it's all I need — toothbrush, change of clothes, cash, a few mementos I never could let go of. The apartment is paid up until the end of the month, and nothing there is worth driving across town for. I pin the folder under Percy's pot, securing it to the seat while keeping it out of sight. The spare set of keys Larissa made me for the store weighs heavily in my hands. I drop them into the front pocket of my gardening apron, take the apron off, wrap it up, and find a safe spot for it in the glove compartment.

I slide into the driver's seat and slam the door shut, and in the silence, I try to convince myself that the only reason I stayed away was because of Pastor Abe's threat. That, after all these years, his threat still holds weight. Instead, I hear her. The real reason I can't go home. Because the pain was too much, the burden too heavy.

The distant cry of my newborn daughter, so weak I'm still not sure if what I heard was real, especially when I was told she didn't survive.

CHAPTER THREE

Percy is buckled into the front passenger seat, and his wide green leaves blow in the miraculously still-working air conditioner. I've raised him from an avocado seed, and in ten to fifteen years, he'll be ready to grow his first avocado. First, though, he'll need a place to plant permanent roots.

"There's the prison, Percy." I point to the super-max prison on the other side of the lake. "Our claim to fame." The sun is setting at our back, and it seems as if we're driving into darkness. Déjà vu creeps across the two-lane highway and my childhood plays over once-familiar landmarks. Memories on repeat of me and Dad, me and Mom, me and my friends. Memories that jam up my muscles, but I keep on driving.

I'd spent the past nine hours and forty-five minutes debating whether to turn my mom's car back around, but at this point it seems like tempting fate. It hadn't been a young car when I'd stolen it, but Mom had been young. Hadn't seemed it at the time though. I do quick math in my head — never could remember her exact age, but she had to be in her mid-fifties now.

I turn off the main road, slow my speed, and take the county road to my hometown. No streetlights out here, and

11

the trees and hills block the sunset. Dusk in East Texas always happens about twenty minutes before official dusk. I flip on my headlights and roll the windows down, and the decaying floral scent of night jasmine and the whirring songs of crickets flood my senses. In the ditches, fireflies dance like little twinkling lights, leading me home.

"Almost there," I tell Percy. "Just have to cross the river." I pat his pot, and my fingers graze the manila folder he's weighing down.

The folder's crumpled around the edges, bent and prodded from my obsessive flipping. Mom couldn't have been the one to hire the private investigator. After Daddy died, we lived paycheck to paycheck, and sometimes not even that.

My birth name, Darla Caraway, and my alias, Darla Carter, are smeared at the top. It shouldn't have been so easy to find me. Not since I changed my name and made up a new past. Not since I stopped looking back.

Darla Carter is from Houston. She got her GED, has a resume littered with part-time jobs, and finally landed on her feet in a gardening center in North Texas, almost at the Oklahoma border.

Darla Caraway is from a small town outside Livingston, Texas, and she's done nothing but run.

Darla Carter is a fixer-up. Darla Caraway is a screw-up.

My throat tightens as if a hand is clamped around my windpipe, thumbs digging into my hard-hitting pulse. I can't go home. Not now. Not in the dark.

The small, two-lane bridge crossing high over the Trinity River rises up before me. I turn on my blinker, though no one's around, and pull off the road to the packed-dirt edge. My throat relaxes, my shoulders drop. The old trail is still there, nothing more than an opening into the woods. Easily missed unless you know where to look.

I suck in a deep breath, and grab my flashlight from the glove box. "I'll be right back." I make sure Percy's still secure, get out of the car, and step into the forest.

The flashlight glints against a thousand gnats and moths and mosquitoes, but keeps me safe from the various sticks and ivy and tree roots on the worn footpath. I definitely should have put on mosquito spray, but I don't have any, and even if I did, I wouldn't want to take the time. I feel an urgency to see the river again, the beach, the place where I started running, all those years ago.

It's not an official spot, no park benches or parking lots, but growing up, it was our spot. A pair of sneakers dangles from a tree overhanging the river and throws me back to summers filled with bonfires by the water, cheap beer and bad guitar, and dancing with the fireflies under the moonlight. Tristan got drunk one night, took off his shoes, and threw them up there to prove a point. Sixteen years later, and I doubt anyone remembers the point, but the sneakers are still there. His or, likely, someone else's. The trees part and my flashlight stumbles onto the packed dirt of the riverbank, the remnants of a campfire, the tall, chain- link fence across the river, where the Atakapa tribe land begins. It had been part of the appeal, back then. Our way to safely rebel.

My light sweeps back up the river to the abandoned railroad bridge. From here, you can't see the bridge to town, and even better from a teenage-me perspective, no one driving across the bridge can see the beach.

Up until the day Caitlin died, this place always felt safe. Surrounded by my friends, slightly tipsy, lulled by the sound of the river and music, it was my bubble. But here, today, after being gone for so long, I can hear the ghosts.

Suicide Rock juts out of the river, just below the bridge. Or Murder Rock, depending on who you talk to.

I make my way down to the riverbank, keeping a sharp eye out for water moccasins and alligators, and swat at the mosquitoes honing in like vultures over roadkill. Rocks slide under my feet, the ground mushy from recent rains, and the river rushes wildly below. Caitlin had been one of my best friends, but I wasn't sure if I was one of hers. She was one of those bright lights, drawing everyone to her like a Venus flytrap. She'd offered a sticky friendship, and we'd all been happily stuck.

Suicide or murder. Probably still depends on who you ask. The police ran out of theories long ago, but rumors are hard to kill in a small town. Harder still when her body was never found, even if blood and hair were recovered from the rock.

A strong swell of nausea rises in my throat, and hot tears burn the corners of my eyes. "Not your fault," I whisper to myself, only for the sixteen-hundredth time, and wrap my arms around my middle, as if I can somehow find comfort within my own skin.

The river gurgles around the giant rock jutting out of its middle, gurgles and laughs, taunts. I pick up a termite-eaten stick at the river's edge and throw it as hard as I can. It hits Suicide Rock dead center with a dull thud and breaks apart into rotten splinters that scatter in the river and float away into the darkness.

CHAPTER FOUR

There's a crick in my neck when the sun glares through my front window. I pop the reclined driver's seat back into driving position, get out of the car to stretch my legs, and step behind a tree to relieve myself. Under the trees, the forest is cool, and the damp air is almost refreshing. I leave the shadows and immediately regret my decision. The day is already baking.

It's not until I'm about to climb back into the car that I notice them.

Two small piles of twigs sitting on the hood of the car.

I inch closer, but what I'm looking at still doesn't make sense. They're dolls. One is standing, arms raised in the air as if they are making a point, wearing a tie made of dried grass. The other is curled on her side, with an outstretched arm tied to another twig with green leaves sprouting from the top.

It looks like . . .

Me and Percy?

I'm frozen in place as I process what this means. Someone was here while I slept. Someone was watching me. Someone watched me long enough to make this and leave it for me.

The nerves in my fingertips buzz, but I pick one of them up.

It's not tied with string. It's tied with hair.

My fingers go weak, and I almost drop the figurine.

Generations ago, the Atakapa tribe lived all throughout these woods. Once the town was established in the early 1800s, mostly by settlers from Ireland, the Atakapa retreated to the woods. They're the reason the Church was formed about two hundred years ago — fears of the tribe escalated after rumors of cannibalism. The rumors were just that, though — rumors. The fears in the community remained, deep and hard, like old scar tissue. Mainly because of instances like this.

I turn the twig figure over in my hand. It really is quite elegantly crafted.

There's no sign of anyone else — no car, no tire marks, no footprints. I climb back into my car, close my door and lock it, and only then do I examine the dolls further. The hair is thick, maybe horsehair, not human hair. By the light of day, the figure looks more like a still life.

I place them in the cupholder, buckle Percy's seatbelt, and turn on the ignition. Mom's car sputters to life, just as the distant sound of familiar bluegrass music reaches through the small gap at the top of my window.

I bat at a mosquito and check the date on my phone.

"It's Second Saturday," I groan and wince at Percy. "Flea market day."

The one day of the month our small town swells to twice its size. Shoppers from all over the area swarm the field next to the cemetery, and most of the town gets involved, selling old junk as unique finds, Celtic-branded tchotchkes — a throwback to the town's Irish heritage — olive oil rebranded as miracle snake oil, homemade jam, smoked brisket, and cherry pies.

Mom should be out there selling homegrown vegetables and bouquets of flowers from her garden, but I have no idea what she's up to these days, or if she even still gardens. Guilt surges through me, almost makes me turn the wheel left out of town, but I tighten my stomach muscles and turn right.

The sign to the Church of Elevated Souls creeps up sooner than I'm ready for it. The old wooden sign has been replaced with something shiny and obnoxious, like it's gone through a bad HGTV remodel. The church is half hidden on the other side of the hill, but its tall steeple stabs the sky like it's trying to pierce the clouds. Cars are parked all along the side of the county road and the drive up to the church, and colorful pop-up tents litter the field in front of the hill. The scent of slow-smoked meat fills the air, and I can almost taste old and innocent days.

I roll up the window, turn on the radio, and flip over until I find the local station run by the high school. They're playing the same old playlist, with a couple of newish additions. Tristan and I used to put George Strait on repeat and make out in the small, makeshift radio station. I never knew if I'd gotten pregnant there or in the bed of his truck. I'd always hoped it was the radio station. Less cliché.

"Almost home, Percy."

It's been a while since I shared living space with someone. I'll have to remember not to talk to him so often once I'm at Mom's house. Talking to a furry pet is one thing. Talking to a plant is something entirely different.

A faded banner stretches from lamppost to lamppost across Main Street, announcing the highlights of Second Saturday. This town used to seem like it encompassed the entire world, but there's only six buildings on either side of Main, and half are empty.

But my house — Mom's house — is at the end of this road, a block away from Main, in an old ranch style with a sagging roof line. That house has chased me, has made me look over my shoulder since I left, never quite catching up but breathing that last image down the back of my neck. Mom rushing out the front door, not understanding why, but understanding enough to know I was leaving.

The closer I get to home, the louder the memories scream, memories I'm not sure I can trust.

Ms. Delaine had said my baby was a stillbirth. Dead on arrival. And then that one tiny cry . . .

I yank the car to the curb in front of the antique store, the steering wheel groaning under my hand at the sudden movement, and I can't breathe. I open the door, fall out, brace my arms on my knees, ass pressed against the rusty car. Cigarette butts and takeout bags litter the cobblestoned street, weeds poke through the stones, and I swear the dandelion growing in the gutter is the same one I saw the last time I walked this path.

Sixteen years is a long time away, and I feel like a color-blind person whose vision has been corrected. Emotions fly at me like colors, and I don't have the words to define them.

"Darla?" A man's voice runs over me, stopping my heart entirely and setting my fingertips buzzing with long-ago adrenaline.

Give me your hand, I'll be your man.

"You have got to be kidding," I mutter, straighten, and whip around, attempting to fluff out my car hair in that short time span.

On the other side of the car is a little family. Two girls, one holding a balloon and the other sucking on a pacifier. And one of my high school friends and ex-boyfriend, holding their hands.

My heart flatlines, my cheeks heat, and nervous sweat prickles the crooks of my arms. "Tristan? Shelly? So good to see you," I squeal, all everything-is-just-fine. Not like I walked out of their lives and never looked back.

They stare at me, shell-shocked.

"You two got married? That's so great." It's not. I hate that they're together, that Tristan didn't get out of this town, that it should be me holding his daughter's hand.

He doesn't even know she existed.

"What are you doing here?" Shelly speaks up finally, drawing closer to her family as if I'm going to hurt them.

Tristan hasn't stopped staring. He's aged well, but he's gone dull around the edges, losing that chiseled quarterback

18

shine. His dark hair has lightened at his sideburns and thinned on top, and his cheeks have started to go leathery. But he's still wearing his typical outfit. Tennis shoes — no socks — sports jersey, cargo shorts.

He clears his throat. "Did you come back for the Feast?" Confusion fills his every word.

I can't help my frown. "You know I never got into church stuff." I shrug, lock the car, and attempt to look like seeing him hasn't given me the jitters. "Town looks the same."

Shelly wraps an arm around her oldest, picks up her youngest, and presses her hip into Tristan's leg. She's dyed her hair blonde, put on about thirty pounds, and is still gorgeous.

"Well, it's not. And with it being the bicentennial Feast this year, everything's about to get a big spruce-up." She eyes Main Street like it's a room she needs to redecorate. Behind us, the door to the antique shop dings as it opens.

Shelly's gaze flits between me and the door, and her eyes shoot wide open.

"You kids ready for nap time?" A familiar voice says behind me, and Tristan's mother comes into view around my car, arms outstretched for her granddaughters.

"Mom," Tristan says, "guess who we just ran into," and nods his head at me. I'm not sure what to make of his tone, but it doesn't matter. Running into your ex-boyfriend's mother, who hated you before you broke his heart by leaving suddenly, is not an experience I ever hoped to share.

She whips around, an expectant smile already on her face, pastor's wife mask locked in.

"Hey, Mrs. Smith, good to see you." I force my hands from their crossed arm position and drop them to my side, doing my best to look comfortable when this situation is anything but.

Her mask changes, hardening from confusion to something else in less than a second. "Darla Caraway, well look at you." She looks me up and down, taking her time, and, like Shelly, shifts closer to Tristan and his family as if she needs to protect them. "What's brought you back to our little town?" There's a frost to her words that, in this heat, is impressive.

Does she know that her husband threatened me?

"Just time to come home, I guess."

She *hmms* and narrows her eyes. "Your mom will be glad to see you, I bet. It was hard on her when you left."

"Mom—" Tristan begins, a warning in his tone. His girls are looking from me to their dad to their mom and grandma with tiny, concerned expressions on their poreless cheeks.

Mrs. Smith blinks, breaking her hard stare. "Well, I need to get these two down for a nap. I'm sure we'll be seeing you around town. Just how long you planning on staying for?"

"Not sure," I say, trying to keep my words light and airy.

She *hmms* again, picks up her smaller granddaughter, and walks away.

Shelly picks up the other one and shifts to follow her mother-in-law. "It was great seeing you, but we have to go." She nudges Tristan with her elbow, and he finally rips his gaze away from me and nods.

They leave without saying another word, and it's nothing more than I deserve.

CHAPTER FIVE

The antique shop has added a small restaurant, and it's as good a spot as any to readjust to my hometown and recover from the shitshow that just occurred on the curb.

The safety I'd clung to — being no one, invisible — twists tight in my gut, then frays at the edges. It's like I've been losing threads since the PI hunted me down, threads that I wove together over the years to bind my secrets.

I find a bathroom, a safe space I had always searched for when I was homeless. Living on the street had been hard, but I'd learned how to survive, to take care of myself. I wash my face and spray dry shampoo into my lifeless hair, a home-made hack job shoulder-length cut. I pinch some color into my cheeks, sweep my hair into a ponytail, and leave the small sanctuary.

A waitress's tray nearly clotheslines me as I round the corner. I duck out of the way with a yelp, and the tray tips, dumping a full pot of coffee onto the floor and all over the waitress's shoes.

"Shit," she yells, then slaps a hand over her mouth. "Crap, crap, crap," she mutters again as she whips a stained rag off the back string of her apron and wipes off her shoes, then starts on the floor.

I bend down to help, pick up a shard of glass from the shattered coffee pot, and place it on her tray. "Baking soda will help that come out. And a replacement pot is like three bucks. No biggie." I'd made an even worse waitress than a cashier. Gardening was the only thing I'd ever been good at.

She sniffs, blinking back tears. "My mom will think it's a big deal." She dabs at her shoes again, her dark hair falling over her shoulders.

I nod, fully understanding how a ruined pair of shoes can be a big deal when you don't have money for replacements. "What size do you wear?"

She looks up at me then, green eyes going wary. "An eight."

It's a look I recognize well from years of barely surviving, of being used to people offering something in exchange for *what's in it for me*. A look I've worn well.

I press my lips together. *The only way forward is through.* One of Mom's favorite sayings. "Perfect. I'll make you a deal. You brew a fresh pot of coffee, and I'll give you the spare pair of tennis shoes I've got in my car. Barely worn. Bet your mom won't even notice."

"Why would you do that?"

Because I've been a disappointment to my mother before, too. I shrug. "You seem like you could use a break."

I'm back within minutes, and the girl already has an empty coffee mug sitting on a warped, wine-barrel table that looks out a window. I set the shoes on the spare chair next to me. The antique shop is musty, the air thick with dust and old things. Not the best spot for a café, but small towns can't be choosy.

The waitress returns, fills my coffee mug, and sets the new coffee pot on the table. She picks up the shoes, takes off her ruined, soaked ones, and ties the new ones on in a big bow. She stands, wiggles her toes, then sits back down. "They fit. Thank you."

I nod, doctor my coffee to get rid of the bitterness, and take a grateful sip.

"I'm Kathy." She holds out her hand. "Everyone calls me Kat, though."

I almost jerk my hand back, then force myself to take hers. *Kathy*.

I had wanted to name my daughter Kathy.

Kat's bones are like a bird's, delicate and tough. "Darla," I force out. "I had a friend named Caitlin that went by Cat, too. We used to swap shoes — you remind me of her."

"Did she live here?" Kat gestures out the window at the town, a grimace reshaping her mouth.

I do a slow nod and hope to God above that sadness isn't spilling out all over my face.

"Did she leave?" Her words are typical teen sarcasm — old enough to have an attitude, young enough to let the hope bleed through.

"Um . . . yeah." *If death is leaving, sure.* I take a grounding sip of my coffee.

"Lucky. I can't wait to grow up, start a family. Maybe even travel and do missions or something." She stands and places her hand on my arm, the cross at her neck swinging slightly on its chain. "Thanks again for the shoes. Guess you're on your way to Dallas or Houston or something."

"Nope. I'm staying for a few weeks, visiting family."

"Oh, you're from here?" She brightens when I nod. "Well, since it's summer break, I'm scheduled for almost every day. If you want to stop by again, that is. It's nice to talk to someone who left town, had new experiences, you know?"

"I do know. I'll see you around, Kat." I place a ten on the table and get up.

Ten dollars and a pair of shoes? My most expensive coffee yet.

I roll back my shoulders, clamber into Mom's car, and shift the car into drive. I can't delay the inevitable any longer. The car grunts and groans, and there's a burning rubber smell the maintenance guy at work has been itching to get his hands on for the past week, but my itty-bitty income wasn't enough to pay for parts, even with no labor fees. She starts up, and my breath hisses between my teeth. I could have walked home and been there in ten minutes, but I need to return the car to Mom. Then I didn't steal it; I borrowed it.

I grit my teeth. It'd been a hell of a lot easier to leave.

I'm trembling by the time I push down on the gas, and the road seems to have transformed into a conveyor belt, speeding me along. In a few minutes, I'm turning into the packed-dirt driveway.

The house had always looked better at twilight. But now, under the high-burning morning sun, it's hard to imagine it had good days. A coating of green mold matches the roof's sagging middle. One end of the sitting porch is held up with what looks like broom handles tied together. A few shutters are missing, and some siding has fallen off and lies rotting in the weed-filled yard.

My mother never allowed weeds in her yard.

My heart beats in my throat, little flutters tipped with worry.

I turn off the engine, and the car makes a new kind of groan that makes me really doubt she'll start back up again. I sit there, hands frozen to the wheel, and lose a few more minutes. I've lived a long time without my mother, but I always knew she was here, in this house, this town, this life.

How could she ever forgive me?

The front door opens. It sticks a bit midway through the swing. Foundation's going bad too, it seems. My mind whirs to the practical, because the woman standing in the doorway cannot be my mother.

She's a hunched skeleton figure in an old nightgown, braced against the doorframe for support, who then pushes herself forward in a falling step to the front rail of the sun-stripped porch.

"Darla?" A gravelly voice calls out, weak and wispy and not my mother's. She falls to her knees and reaches toward the car, all while cold regret slams through my veins.

24

And somehow, I'm there. On the porch, grabbing her arms, helping her stand, and saying words like "I'm here, Mom. I came back. I'm here." I still don't know this woman, this person who is more skeleton than flesh, with her falling-out hair and patchy-colored skin and unwashed odor. But I wrap an arm around her too-thin waist and guide her back inside as she sobs, and tears threatening to pour down my face, and I promise to stay, and how could sixteen years do this? It was only sixteen years, not a lifetime, not enough for this to be my mother.

As soon as we're inside, she turns in my arms, grabs my neck, and pulls me down with a strength I wouldn't have guessed, a strength that is all too familiar, and holds me tight, patting my back, telling me everything will be all right. We stand there, and she hugs me for as long as I need. Or maybe, as long as we *both* need. My heart settles back into a rhythm it had forgotten.

I'm home.

CHAPTER SIX

The house looks the same, and yet somehow not the same. The pink and purple painted candy bowl I made in kindergarten holds court on the old coffee table, but the hard candy has melted against the sides. The green velvet sofa has a new blanket spread across the top, a small, microfiber throw that looks like a Black Friday special from the local pharmacy. The corner curio cabinet hosts the set of grocery store China and the frosted brandy glasses we've never used, but the light in the top has gone out, and a fine layer of dust has settled over everything.

But the medical equipment is new.

A walker with tennis balls on the feet stands in the corner, next to a medical-grade cane and an oxygen tank, and I still don't know what is wrong with my mother. Or how she paid for all of this. Mom's career as a mail carrier for the post office hadn't been lucrative by any stretch. After paying off the medical bills we'd racked up because of Daddy's cancer, there hadn't been much left over for things like bread, milk, and shoes. Definitely not for a teenage mom and her baby.

Doesn't look like much has changed, except for the name of the patient on the medical bills.

I settle Mom on the couch and sit next to her. We stare at each other for a long time without saying a word. Remembering each other's features, memorizing new ones.

She lifts a trembling hand to my face, and I steel myself for the accusations, the blame, the words of pain I'm owed. "How did you know to come home?"

I take a deep breath, because I know she's gonna find my next sentence hard to believe. "Someone hired a private investigator to find me and tell me to come home."

Her forehead crinkles. "Why would anyone do that?"

"I . . . I don't know. They sent a flyer about the Feast and said I needed to be here. Maybe because you're . . . you're. . ." I can't say it, not until I know. She's sick, but did the message refer to her? Is she the one who is going to die?

Her eyes dart from side to side, as if she missed some clue or someone's spying in the shadows.

I dig the folder out of my bag and hand it to her, the pilfered photo and flyer tucked inside the back pocket of my jeans. No need to worry her needlessly, not in her state.

She takes the folder, her hands trembling — from anxiety or the disease, I can't be sure — and studies the invoice. Her skin looks like she's gotten an oddly shaped tan, but it doesn't look as if it's from wearing gardening gloves.

"Any idea of who it could be?" My forehead crinkles, and I push away at the wrinkles. Barely thirty, and I've already got worry lines.

"I don't have a clue, but I'm not going to question a gift horse, *mmhmm*." Mom's nervous verbal tic interrupts the flow of her words, and the sound — annoying to a teenager — is vastly comforting to an adult with no home. "You're here now, and that's what matters. You must be hungry." She pats my knee and tries to get up, but falls back to the couch, her breath suddenly coming short and labored.

"Mom, I'm fine. Relax, okay? I'll get you some water." I pat her hand. Her skin is cold and paper dry.

I make my way to the kitchen, taking the opportunity to check out Mom's true situation. There's little food in the refrigerator, some meals pre-cooked in nicer dishes than we've ever owned, and a bottle of half-drunk blush wine — that, unless my mother had a lobotomy, is definitely not hers. The lights work, so that's good, and the tap water is running clean.

Someone's been taking care of Mom's essentials.

I fill a glass with water for her and check the rest of the house for signs of a roommate. I peek in my old room, and it looks the same as when I left, but with the sewing machine in the corner. Mom's room is down the hall from mine, and so much of it remains the same — the curtains, the wooden memory box she keeps on her dresser — but now, there's a hospital-grade bed in place of her and Daddy's old brass four-poster. I stand there for a moment, take in a shuddery breath or two . . . or three.

My mother is sick. And this no longer feels like home.

Each time I see new evidence, the truth plows through another hard layer I didn't know existed, insisting on being heard. By the time I make it back to the living room, Mom has fallen asleep. Turned on her side, her bones protrude at every angle, from her ankle bones to her hips to her sharp shoulders. I pull the blanket off the top of the couch, cover her, and watch her breathe for a few minutes. Only once I'm convinced she's not dying right at this moment, I leave her to unpack the car.

Outside, the sun blazes in a cloudless sky and a heavy wind begins to blow, rippling the trees one by one, as if the wind is trailing lazy fingers through the treetops. The metal of the trunk of the car is already blazing hot. First order of business is getting my patients some water. I pop the trunk and lug all twelve of our guests and the African daisies to the front porch. Percy comes in last, as he's the most resistant to the heat, and the healthiest. "Let's get you inside and get a big drink of water. I bet you're thirsty." I mentally slap myself. "Stop talking to the plant, Darla."

Percy looks sad after hearing that.

"I'm sorry, I didn't mean it," I whisper, and lift him out of the car.

I set Percy on the front porch with everyone else, give them all a quick shower from the hose and, before I second-guess myself, take the two twig dolls out of the car and gently place them on the old stool on the front porch. They're growing on me — could be cute as garden decor; my customers would have bought them right up.

I go back inside to check on Mom, catching the front door before it squeaks. She deserved a better daughter than what I'd turned out to be. But I'm here now. Resolve burrows deep in my gut like stubborn dandelion roots. I'll make it up to her. She's still fast asleep on the couch, so I head back to my room — muscle memory helps me avoid the creaky floorboards throughout the house — and throw my go bag on the bed.

My room smells unused, the air thick. Dust motes dance in the sunlight from the window. There's a pile of boxes stacked in the corner, and bits of medical supplies strewn across my old dresser. I pull the photo out of my back pocket and tack it back on my photo wall, in the empty space it was nicked from. Snapshots of me and Tristan, me and Caitlin, me and the rest of the gang — Shelly, Emmie, Karl, Ivan — from awkward middle school days to the beginning of junior year. After that, after Caitlin, we stopped taking pictures.

Before old feelings have a chance to surge up and suck me down, I find a dusting cloth and start cleaning, changing out the cloth three times before the end. Our one hallway is so covered in old photos framed in Dollar Store frames that I can't see the wall. I give each of the frames a good dusting, pausing at my sophomore cheerleading picture. That girl behind that smile had no idea what was coming, and the urge to reach through the dusty glass and shake her is strong enough that I clink my nail against the frame. The bathrooms are next, and though I'd pay good money for a hot shower,

I don't know Mom's bill situation, and until I do, it's army showers. But first, the bathrooms need a deep scrub.

"Darla?" Mom's weak voice drifts in from the front of the house as I finish cleaning her bathroom. I try not to be concerned with the flecks of blood and vomit I've scrubbed off the floors and around the edge of the toilet, but it's impossible.

"I'm in here," I call out, pull off my gloves, wash my hands, and meet her in the living room, where she's sitting on the couch, looking dazed and sleep-worn. I'm struck again with the feeling that this cannot be my mother. My mother, who never learned how to sit still, who boiled over with energy, who made me tired by watching her.

The worried look on her face erases as soon as she sees me. "I thought I dreamed you. Thought I'd finally lost my mind."

I sit next to her, take her hand, convince her I'm real. An apology I've been practicing for the past sixteen years gets stuck in my throat, and no matter what I do, I can't push it out.

"I'm here now, Mom." I hate how rehearsed I sound. "I shouldn't have done that to you. I should have called or come back to visit or—"

She gives my hand a squeeze and looks me square in the eye. "Yes, you shoulda called at least. But you didn't, so that's that." She swallows and blinks quickly, and I get a glimpse at a fraction of the pain I've caused her. "I've always wondered what finally pushed you to go, but bottom line — I knew you'd go. You were built for more than this town. Wish you'd waited a year or two, but you're here now, and that's what matters. Can't change the past." Her gaze loses focus, and she sinks back against the couch.

I don't like how tired she is, how this disease is eating away at her health.

"Now don't look at me like that, *mmhmm*. They've given me three to six months, and I plan on beating that by a good measure."

Three to six months.

30

I know that I'm not breathing, that my stomach is knotted up, that something hurts, deep in my gut, but it's all behind mental plexiglass — distant and muffled.

Three to six months.

My eyes burn. Hot tears that are stuck, that just stay there, burning. "You're dying?"

She pats my hand and takes a deep breath, then raises her fingers in the air, showing off that oddly shaped tan. "It's something called Addison's disease, and if I'd gone to a doctor for it years ago, they maybe coulda done something. But I didn't, and that's that." She drops her hand, lifts her chin in the air, and casts a stare full of *don't be mad.*

"There's nothing they can do?" My palm has gone slick, the lifeline glittering.

She shakes her head. "Caught it too late, but from what I understand, it's a hard thing to catch to begin with. Got a drawer full of drugs to," she throws up thin fingers in feeble air quotes, "make me comfortable. And I don't plan on using 'em, *mmhmm*." There goes her chin again, daring me to defy her. But then, her posture shifts, softens somehow, and she turns her knees toward me. She grips my hand again. "Do you forgive me?" she whispers, and a tear forms at the corner of her eye.

I look at her hands, unfamiliar to me, her frail body, skin hanging loose along her arms, and I press close to her. "Nothing to forgive."

She sniffles. "I shoulda gone to the doctor the first time I fell, *mmhmm*. I shoulda—"

I wrap an arm around her and repeat her practical words. "But you didn't, so that's that. Let's deal with what we've got now, okay? How have you been paying for all this?"

She shrugs. "Medicaid plus the nurse down the way volunteers her free time. Over off Old Reed Lane."

"Someone lives off Old Reed Lane?" That road isn't even paved. Just some offshoot into the woods. "I thought it was a hunting road."

Mom shakes her head. "She and her daughter moved out there a few years ago. I fell in front of her house on my mail route one day, couldn't get up, and she's been checking on me ever since. Helped get me signed up for care through Medicaid. And Trina stops by with food and my medicine."

"How about everything else? How are you paying the bills?"

"Trina. Talked to the utilities for me. Some program for the disabled she got me in." Mom waves away my worries. "But you, we need to get you checked out. See if you have any symptoms. Sometimes this is hereditary, and I can't let you . . . I can't . . . I'm so sorry." She folds inward, arms wrapped tight around her ribs, as if holding herself together might keep the disease contained within, might somehow keep me safe.

I wrap an arm around her, rub her bony back, and she soon relaxes against my side, falling asleep once again. I gently lay her down on the couch, cover her up, and continue my ritual of cleaning, of getting to know this house again.

It's falling apart.

Mom moans in her sleep. She's so small now, so unlike the force she once was. I'm going to have to find a job. Take care of her, fix up this house, be the daughter I never was and the adult I've been imitating.

And talk to that nurse. This disease makes no sense to me, and if I have it too, I want to understand how it shows up and how it's killing my mother.

CHAPTER SEVEN

I yank another weed by its roots out of the front flowerbed, digging my nails deep into the hard clay, ever watchful of a surprise fire ant bed. The late afternoon sun beats down on my neck and the backs of my arms, and sweat trails tickle my lower back. Before I can plant the African daisies, I have to get this flowerbed healthy again. It doesn't look like it's been tended in well over a year.

Which tells me more about what Mom has been going through than what she's admitted.

A car with squeaky brakes slows down, and by the sound of tires crunching dirt, they've turned into Mom's driveway.

"Helloooo," a woman calls from her rolled-down window, then puts her car into park with one last squeal.

I stand, brush off my hands on my shorts, and brace myself for what's sure to be one of our town's gossips. I put on my customer service smile and get ready for the needle-like questions that stitch a town like this together.

The elderly woman pulls herself out of her car with a groan, one hand on the Jesus-handle, the other on a covered glass dish — chicken spaghetti from the looks of the cheesy noodles. And the glass means she wants to come back to pick up the dish. I feel like blood bait in a tank of circling sharks. It didn't take long for her to smell the fresh meat.

"I'm Eloise, from the Church. Came by to check on Suzanne, poor baby. And you are?" She walks toward me as she talks, her yellow peasant blouse and crop jeans almost too stylish for a woman her age.

"Darla. Suzanne's daughter." Defensiveness creeps into my voice, and I brace myself for the gust of guilt she's sure to blow my way. This woman has me on edge. She may look innocent and helpful, but her kind have sharp teeth.

Her pink lips form a wrinkly O, and her eyes sparkle as if she's just discovered buried treasure. "Darla? Baby girl, I remember you. Used to run around with Pastor Abe's boy."

I nod and reach out for the food she's brought. "Mom's resting, but I'll let her know you dropped by."

She clings tighter to the dish. "Oh, Suzanne won't mind. I'll just drop this off in the icebox so you don't have to track dirt all over the place. Lord knows your poor momma's got enough on her plate as it is." She casts a glare over me, dousing me in the cool disappointment I've been expecting. It feels strangely satisfactory, like I'm finally being treated the way I deserve.

I turn on the hose and rinse off, so I can follow Ms. Eloise inside. Like hell I'm letting a no-good busybody snoop through my mom's house while she's resting.

To my surprise, Eloise meets me at the door. "She's sleeping still. Just throw that spaghetti in the oven at three-fifty for about half an hour. It's ready when it starts bubbling." She sidles past me, but instead of walking down the uneven front porch steps to her car, she plops into one of the two chairs my daddy made when I was little. "Sit with me a bit, girl."

The Southern politeness I was raised with doesn't let me refuse. "Wish I had some tea or lemonade to offer, but I haven't gotten to the store yet."

She waves me off. "We ain't porch sittin'." She nods at the stool between us, a stand-in table, where the twig dolls still sit. "I see our witch-child has rolled out the welcome mat."

My attention jerks to her, a fish taking the bait.

She smiles. She knows she has me.

"After your time. These little dolls started appearing to the youngsters who play down by the river. Sometimes they show up at the cemetery, on graves that have been forgotten."

"And no one knows who's making them?"

She shrugs. "Every town's gotta have a mystery. This is ours. Started about six years ago, about the time Trina and her so-called daughter moved back to town."

"Trina and her *so-called* daughter? Why so-called daughter?"

Eloise tosses me a look like I've overstepped, or haven't earned the right to her gossip just yet, but she flicks a gaze toward the front door and lets out a sigh. "A lady her age having a teenage daughter? It don't make no sense, but what do I know. I'm just an old woman with nothing better to do than volunteer and gossip." She laughs a little, but her fingers tighten on her knees. "Yup, Trina had a boy once. Born a mute, if you can believe that." She looks at me from under raised brows and waits for me to show the proper response.

"Oh yeah?" I say, as is proper.

She gives a slow nod, as if she's just delivered headline news. "We've kept an eye on them, and me and the girls are pretty certain they've got nothing to do with these dolls." She flicks a knobbly, blinged out finger at my twig doll, and I have the strange urge to protect it from her.

"Trina is the nurse who looks in on my mother."

Eloise nods in agreement.

"You said she moved back. Trina lived here before?"

Eloise stares at me, eyes wide. "Darlin', you know Trina. That dead girl's aunt? Moved away about the same time you left town. Came back with a surprise daughter, no word on who the father is. And after her son turned up dead when he was four." She clicks her tongue. "Me and the girls have 'bout given up trying to get answers."

I clear my throat, and sweat prickles at my neck. "Trina is Caitlin's aunt?"

35

She mhmms, the tone sassy. "That's why I keep such a close eye on your momma. Everything about that Trina woman gets my hackles up. Can't believe Suzanne lets her in this house, let alone lets her help her with her medical situation. Don't trust her, no, I don't. Neither do the girls."

I take a deep breath. "And who are the girls?"

"Bunco group, of course. Suzanne used to be one of our favorite subs, but she can't make it anymore." Eloise brightens and sits a little straighter. "You play bunco? We always need another sub."

"Not since my thirteenth birthday party." My response is automated, my brain whirling through everything Eloise just laid on me.

Trina is Caitlin's aunt. Trina, who left town around the same time I did, moved back with a surprise daughter. Trina is taking care of my mother.

"Ah well. You tell your momma I said to eat up. She's turning into a bag o' bones." Eloise pats my knees, pushes herself up from the chair, and stiffly makes her way to her car. "I'll be back later this week to pick up that dish. Nice to see you again, Darla. Bet your momma sure is glad you're back."

I wave goodbye as she squeaks down the worn driveway, and that faint cry, the ghost that haunts my every moment, reaches out to me again, begs me to turn back time and tell my secrets, begs me to stay.

36

CHAPTER EIGHT

The scratchy speakers of our ancient TV spit out the bright jingles and too-loud contestants of *The Price Is Right*, their cheer grating against the edges of my worry as I carry our breakfast plates to the sink.

Mom sleeps a lot, and when she's not sleeping, she's too tired to do much of anything. The little I could scrounge up on the internet about this disease emphasized fatigue — along with skin-color changes, weight loss, no appetite. All things I could have seen without the diagnosis of WebMD.

She's in her spot on the couch, a blanket tucked around her legs, scribbling in a journal that she seems to always have on her. I'm not sure what she's so frantically writing, but if she really does have less than a year to live, then I get it. She's running out of time to finish whatever she's working on.

"I'm headed out to the store. Will you be okay for an hour or so?" It's a silly question, but one I can't help but ask. Of course, she'll be fine. She's been fine. My arriving out of the blue doesn't suddenly make her an invalid.

She looks up from her journal, lips pressed so tightly together they've lost color. "Sure will, baby girl. Grab some bananas while you're out?"

I kiss the top of her head, and she half closes the journal as if she doesn't want me to see. I don't want to see. Private thoughts are just that — private. And Lord knows I've got my own share of secrets. I leave Mom on the couch with *The Price Is Right* droning in the background and beg the car to start. She does, lovely girl, and I drive into town with the goal of spending my last paycheck on groceries, nails, and lumber, and looking on the job board at the food mart. If I can avoid seeing anyone I know, even better. At least I don't have car hair this morning.

My stomach grumbles as I pass the coffee shop, but it's not open for another hour — damn small-town hours. I'm finally home, but this place fits about as well as a pair of skinny jeans after an ice cream binge. I pull into the food mart parking lot and snatch a front row spot.

The store is mostly empty, it being a work day for most people, and I head straight for the job board. A list of odd jobs like house cleaner, babysitter, and earn a grand a week scams litter the board, most outdated by six months. I'd be happy to do any of those jobs, except the scam one, but the job gods are against me. Besides, a low-paying hourly wage that guaranteed I'd never be home didn't help Mom much, nor did it leave room for solving the mystery message.

I check with the customer service desk about any floor or shift manager openings and end up with an application for a stocker. Pays better than a checker, at least.

I do last-week-of-the-month shopping and stock up on dried beans, rice, canned fruit and vegetables, and bread from the discount table, doing my best to stretch my last paycheck from the gardening center as far as it can go. Hopefully, Dad's backyard garden is still intact, so we can have some fresh veggies. Mom was always meticulous about keeping his garden weeded and healthy, but gardens often reflect the gardener's stage of life.

I make my way to the home improvement section and grab a box of nails. Lumber's in the back, and I balance a few sheets of treated plywood on top of the cart. Not the best for outdoor repairs — barely passable — but it'll last for a little bit until I can afford something better.

I've almost made it to the checkout aisle, my plywood balancing precariously on top of the grocery basket, when I crash into something.

The something yelps.

"Watch it!" a shrill voice shrieks. "Ugh, you gave me a splinter."

My ears perk at the familiar complaining.

I peek around the pile of wood, and there's a pile of blonde hair, all Dallased up. I can smell the hairspray from here, *over* the chemical scent of the treated wood.

"Oh. My. Lord. Darla?" Her lined lips drop open. I brace for what's coming. "Darla!" she squeals, dog-whistle high, and her feet dance up and down faster than a kid who has to pee. Then she leaps at me, that sticky sprayed hair crushing against my mouth, her arms squeezing tight around my neck.

"Hey, Emmie. Good to see you too." I squeeze back. At least someone besides my own mother is glad to see me again. Of course, I didn't lie to Emmie like I did to Shelly and Tristan.

She pulls away and hits my shoulder.

"Ow." I exaggerate. Emmie could hurt a fly. But that's about it.

She crosses her arms in front of her used to be flat chest. "You could have called."

A twinge of guilt pings my ribs. "I'm sorry." I wait for her to forgive me. She will; she's Emmie.

It takes two seconds longer than I thought it would. "Ugh, fine. Forgiven." She squeals again and throws her arms around my neck in another hug. "I'm so glad you're back."

"Yeah, me too." *Lie.* I pull away. "Did you get a boob job?" I flick her right boob.

"Ow, and duh." She grabs at her shirt, then looks down and adjusts her new equipment, a large diamond flashing

39

on her finger. "Henry likes them. A lot." She waggles her eyebrows.

"Funeral home Henry? You married funeral home Henry?"

"Yeah-huh. No judging. He's well endowed." A grin spreads across her face. Emmie always did have a high sex drive.

"Ew. TMI, Ems."

"I meant rich, duh." She winks, which tells me exactly what she meant. "I missed you, you know." She pouts, an expression that looks fake and well-practiced, but I know her. Know it's real.

"I missed you too." I look around the grocery store and pull my cart out of the middle of the aisle. Emmie follows. "I ran into Shelly and Tristan yesterday." I lower my voice, as if it's some secret or Emmie and I are discussing a boy I like. Which I don't — can't. Not anymore.

"Oh *gawd*." She makes a gagging noise. "They're too sweet. Makes me want to vom. Their girls are super cute, though."

My spine tenses, and a slight nausea curls around my stomach. Tristan's happy. With someone else. And has daughters. Beautiful, beautiful daughters.

I swallow a hard knot, blink quickly, look away.

"Oh, I'm sorry, honey." Ems's face twists into an expression of shared pain that only a best friend could manage. "I mean, they are totes uggs. Totes. Uggs."

I'm about two steps behind her vocabulary, and it's not due to my lack of a college degree. "Are you talking about footwear?"

"Sorry. Volunteering at the high school library has destroyed my vocabulary. Totally ugly."

I study her, the best friend I left behind, who has turned into this gorgeous woman who speaks like a teenager. "Only you could work in a library and have a worse vocabulary."

She buffs her shellacked nails on her shirt. "Super talent. Sorry to hear about your mom, by the way. Guess that's why you're back, huh?" She waits for me to nod. "I check in on her every once in a while. I saw her maybe a month ago, and

I didn't think she was doing this bad. Seems so sudden, you know?"

Guilt surges through me, leaving an afterburn of shame. "Thanks for checking on her." I grip Emmie's hand and squeeze. "I need to be getting back. *Price is Right* is about over, and I want to get these beans in the pot for dinner."

"Of course, but let's meet later, okay? Coffee? The antique shop opened a café."

"Yeah, I stopped by there on my way in yesterday. I'll text you." We exchange our new numbers and part ways, and with that reconnection of a friend I thought I'd lost, I feel one step closer to home.

I step outside, the late summer weather unbearably humid and hot. One nice thing about North Texas is the seasons. Down here, we have two. Wet, windy, cold or hot, humid, miserable. I cross the parking lot, and my spine tenses up, a ghost feeling of being watched filling the space between my shoulder blades. I check over my shoulder and outside the store, but no one's there. The wind whips, whistling, through the East Texas Piney Woods forest.

Sounds a little bit like a scream.

* * *

I meet Emmie at the café later that afternoon. I'm already seated with a cup of tea when she waltzes in, dinging the bell on the counter as she passes and waving to everyone in the antique store. She looks like she belongs here about as much as she'd look at home on a safari, which is not at all. Despite her flashiness at odds with the dull and dusty antiques, Emmie has carved out her space and made it fit her perfectly.

She purses her lips at my tea and orders two glasses of wine. "It's wine time, *daaaarhlaing*." She drawls the endearment like she used to, squeezing my name into the word. "And after dealing with work today, no way is tea going to be strong enough." The two glasses of wine arrive, along with the

41

rest of the bottle, and she slides the second over. "You didn't catch alcoholism while you were gone, did you?"

A feeling of homesickness pours over me like that hot shower I still haven't gotten. Her special blend of being generous and completely inappropriate makes me miss all the years I was gone. "You can't catch alcoholism, Ems."

"Then that," she circles a finger around my cup of tea, "is a sin. You know they didn't even offer wine on the menu until I bought the place?"

I slowly put down my wine glass, not even making it to my lips. "You *bought* the antique shop?" Shock seeps into my tone. "I cannot even believe I said those words out loud. The high school library, and now this? What happened to you leaving, getting out of here?"

She takes a sip of her wine, holding up a finger. "First, I most certainly did *not* buy the antique shop. I bought the café. Antiques are a dead-end business." She pauses for a second. "Get it. Dead end. Antiques outlast their owners. Owners are dead."

I groan and slow clap. "Wow. That's a bad one, even for you."

She rolls her eyes and shakes her Dallas hair. "Fine, fine. There's a reason my stand-up career didn't last. Second, I did get out of here. I moved to Livingston, daaaarhla-ing, to Henry's lakeside estate." She reports in a clipped, crisp voice, nose in the air, and a slight curve to her bright-pink lips.

"Livingston is hardly out of here." Not that where I ended up in middle of nowhere North Texas was better.

She shrugs. "Look, I get that you hate it here — Lord knows you've got every reason to — but don't go around being down on the place so much. We all work hard here and are proud of our little town."

I sit back, her words on a bullseye path that hits between my eyes. "Ouch. Truth bomb." We make the exploding bomb motion with our hands, then I raise my own in the Boy Scout oath pose. "I promise to give this little town another chance."

"Good girl. Now drink." She tips the end of my wine glass, making me take less of a sip and more of a chug.

I've heard that when you have a true friend, you can meet each other after years of being apart and pick right back up where you left. Emmie's mine.

"So . . . wedding gift from Henry?" I gesture at our surroundings.

She narrows her eyes. "I'm no kept woman, bi-atch. I developed an app that took off a few years ago. My app, my money, my bistro. Got it?"

Words fall from her overly lined lips that should not fall from those particular lips. I look around the restaurant and widen my eyes. "App? You? Technology? I'm in the twilight zone, aren't I?" I hum the famous theme tune with a chuckle.

"Shut it." She throws her napkin, hits me on the side of the head, and we double over with a belly laugh I haven't had since before I . . . since before.

It's an immediate reaction, how the laughter dries up inside, but I force happy sounds to keep on going. I've become an expert at not showing how empty I really am inside.

"It's an app that picks out your outfit according to your calendar," Em continues, not noticing my mood shift. "You put in your wardrobe — brand name, style, color — and the app pieces together an outfit based on the weather forecast and the type of events you have scheduled for the day."

"That . . . actually sounds incredibly cool."

"Damn right." She raises her wine glass in a toast to herself, and the question I've had rolling around the back of my mind makes it to the front.

"I have a weird question for you, seeing as how you're now Mrs. Money Bags." I pause and, despite the wine, my mouth is dry, but I've come this far, and Emmie's the safest person I've got besides Mom. "Did you hire a private investigator to hunt me down?"

"*Nooo*." She screws up her face. "Whoa, wait. *That's* how you knew to come back?"

43

I nod. "And Mom and I have no clue who hired the PI. He handed me this." I pull the flyer out of my back pocket.

"The COES Feast?" She asks, using the abbreviated name for the Church of Elevated Souls. "You can't possibly think I'm a member."

I lift my shoulders up. "You designed an app. Who knows what's happened in this alternate reality."

She hits me again. "First of all, I hired programmers to design my app. Second, no way would I join that place."

"Even being married to the town funeral director? COES is a vortex."

"Oh, they've been trying to get us to join for years. Henry uses the excuse that he needs to remain unbiased so that all his customers feel comfortable. The dead can be picky, you know."

I roll my eyes. "Emmie," I groan. She grins.

"Look at the back of the flyer." I tap the table to get her attention again and watch the small changes in her expression as she reads the message.

"'It's happening again. Come home before she dies, too?'" She reads the message aloud, each syllable stuffed with questions. "What the hell does that mean?"

I shrug and reach out for the flyer. "In the folder was this flyer, the invoice, and a picture, Ems. A picture of us."

She furrows her microbladed eyebrows as she hands the paper over. "What do you mean 'us?' You and me?"

"No." I shake my head. "*All* of us. At the river. Taken from my bedroom. It's why I had to come back." I fold the flyer and shove it back in my pocket, taking advantage of Em's shocked silence to gather a little bit of courage. "What if this has something to do with Caitlin?"

"Caitlin committed suicide."

"I never believed that, and you didn't use to either."

She presses her lips together, twists her fingers against the stem of her wine glass. "How could this have anything to do with Caitlin?"

44

"I don't know."

"And why find you? Why you?"

My mind flashes to Caitlin's note, that torn piece of paper filled with badly erased letters and nonsense scribbles. I blink it away, shaking my head. "I don't know."

She hasn't broken eye contact, her dark brown eyes intense, and I feel a little bit like I'm in an interrogation room, not a mostly empty café drinking wine.

"Why now?" She asks after a moment.

"The Feast." I drop my voice. "It has to do with the Feast. Otherwise, why include the flyer?"

She nods slowly, on the same page as me.

Kat shows up for work, wearing my shoes, and ties on her apron. Her smile brightens as she sees me, and she waves hello. I wave back, and Emmie looks between us.

"You two know each other?"

"Met yesterday. Seems sweet, if a little churchy."

Emmie rolls back one shoulder, shakes her head, and takes a sip of her wine. "If you say so." Her voice drops, taking on the tone of Emmie about to spill secrets.

"Not a sweet kid?" I press.

"I mean, she's not Unabomber not sweet, just . . . odd."

I wait for it.

Emmie checks over her shoulder, making sure Kat can't hear. "She gives me the heebies, okay?"

"How? She's perfectly normal." I glance over at Kat, trying to detect a heebies vibe, and come up short.

"Yeah, no. You should see her at school. Speaking of, you need a job, right?"

I yank my focus from Kat, lean back, and cross my arms. "How do you know that?"

"Honey, I've seen your mom's house. That poor woman can't take care of anything, and she won't take my money. She's got a few months left, right?"

I sink back against my chair, any energy I'd found in seeing Emmie deflating out of me in a hiss. "Says she plans

45

on beating that, but from what I can see I don't think she'll still be around by Christmas." It's my first time admitting out loud the possibility of Mom not being here anymore, and it feels as if someone's punched me in the stomach. I blink back a few tears, look away.

Emmie drags her chair over with a loud screech and drapes an arm around my shoulder. "Let me put in a good word at the school once the office reopens after summer break. It's not much, maybe an aide in the special education department, but it's better than working at the food mart." She gives me a squeeze and dips her head to mine. "It's going to be okay. Not fine, not great, but okay."

I sniff, swallow, nod.

Emmie picks up her glass and raises it in a toast. "To mysterious messages, best friends, and stubborn-ass mothers defying doctors."

And just like that, she has me snickering again. "Yeah, to that." I clink my glass against hers.

CHAPTER NINE

It's seven in the evening, but outside the small kitchen window, the sun is still high. We're entering mid-summer's annual debut, and the heat and humidity want to make sure we know it.

I put plastic wrap around Mom's dinner and place it in the refrigerator. She didn't touch it, too intent on writing in her journal or just not hungry, I'm not sure. It's one of her favorites, or it used to be — pinto beans from the store and fried okra from Dad's garden. I'd found a few vegetables among all the weeds and added weeding the garden to my growing list. I go back to washing up the dishes, my mind whirring through all the things I need to do, including filling out that job application Emmie mentioned, when a woman on a bicycle turns into our driveway, her basket holding a black bag.

I frown and rinse the suds off my hands. A minute later, there's a quick knock at the door.

I hurry into the living room before Mom can get off the couch. "I got it."

She's already struggling to pull herself to her walker and eases back to the couch with a long sigh.

I swing the door open, and my heart stops. Time fractures, leaps backward sixteen years to a dark and empty high school, a too-bright room. I forget how to breathe, and all that old pain whets against a sharpening stone.

"One more push, Darla. You can do it." My school nurse lifts the sheet covering my legs in the small nurse's office, as the school is closed for the weekend. No one to hear me scream. "The baby is crowning."

I blink, try to shake off the memory, but that's a battle I've never been able to win.

"Ms. Delaine?" I whisper, my mouth so dry it comes out as a rasp. A punch of anxiety hits my throat.

She gasps, covering her mouth. "Darla?" Then she gives me a hug, reaching up on her tiptoes to press her cheek to mine, an herbal scent rising around her. "I always knew you'd come back." She holds me at arm's length, as if she's assessing the difference in me now versus pregnant me then, while my heart crashes to the staccato beat of *why is she here, why is she here, why is she here*. Ms. Delaine's expression crinkles, maybe in reaction to the panic on mine. "She doesn't know. I never told her," she whispers hurriedly.

My shoulders relax, and some of the tension leaks out. "Thanks," I whisper back, then step aside so she can come in.

Ms. Delaine has aged, but more gracefully than my mother. Her hair is streaked with gray among the short brown strands, and she's put on a few pounds, but it looks good on her.

"Hey, Trina." My mom waves hello, and Ms. Delaine sits next to her on the couch, but I'm frozen, one hand on the open door, Eloise's words acting as cinematic background music to my this-can't-be-real reality show.

Darlin', you know Trina. That dead girl's aunt? Moved away about the same time you left town. Came back with a surprise daughter . . .

"Trina Delaine?" I blurt.

Both Mom and Ms. Delaine turn toward me with confused expressions.

48

Mom looks between me and Ms. Delaine . . . Trina, a frown crossing her face. "Do you two know—"

"Darla was one of my students when I worked at the high school," Trina jumps in. "She helped me as an aide from time to time, so we got to know each other." Trina takes my mom's hand and pats it, as if they're old friends.

I nod and finally shut the front door. Mom frowns again, but she leaves her hand in Trina's. She doesn't remember what Trina's talking about, because I would have told her something like that. Because Trina is lying through her teeth.

Trina continues, as if there's nothing to be concerned about. "Darla, I'm sure you have questions about what your mother's going through. How about I help her to bed, maybe take a bath first," she turns as if to check in with my mom, who gives a grateful nod, "and then you and I will have a chat."

She stands without waiting for a response, places a hand under Mom's elbow, and leaves another hand open for Mom to grab if she needs it. She does. Trina gets her standing, and the two hobble into Mom's bedroom, Trina acting like a stand-in cane. A few moments later, the water in the bathtub runs.

I finish up the dishes, then pour two glasses of the blush wine. Gotta be Trina's. I settle on the couch and make doodles around my to-do list. I've thought of enough things that I'll be busy, busy, busy for at least a month solid. Too busy to think. And when I get a job, even less time to think. Win-win.

Trina joins me half an hour later, that herbal scent layered on even stronger. "She's in bed, asleep."

I nod and sniff the air, trying to place her perfume, and it brings back the memory of Caitlin, so strong it's as if she's here. That was Caitlin's scent.

"I make my own soap." She lifts her hand for me to smell. "Lavender and a spice with a hint of orange in it. I use it on a lot of my patients — seems to calm them."

"Orange." I roll my neck and look up at the ceiling. "*That's* what I've been smelling."

Trina chuckles and picks up her glass of wine. "Hope you don't mind that I keep this here. Sometimes I stay late, keeping an eye on your mom if she's had a bad day. I don't like leaving her alone."

I nod and turn the page on my notepad, in case I need to take notes about Mom's care. But Trina raises her glass in the air and waits for me to join her.

"To your mother. And to daughters reunited." She smiles, but something about that particular smile doesn't reach the corners of her mouth.

I freeze as she clinks my glass. It's a sales smile, one we plaster on when we don't like our customer or know they aren't buying.

Then the fakeness is gone, and a real smile slides into place.

"Thanks for being here, for taking care of her. I know she can't pay, but I'm looking for a job and—"

Trina shakes her head. "Don't worry about it. Your mom's disability insurance would pay for my services if I submitted them and fought a long fight to get paid. We've become friends. I'd do this for any friend."

The *like I did for you* goes unsaid, but rings, faintly, through the falling-apart house all the same.

"With your mom, what we're waiting on is an adrenal crisis. The disease has stopped her adrenal glands from producing a hormone — cortisol — which her body needs to function. It's why she's lost so much weight, why her blood pressure is low, why she's tired all the time."

I nod to show I understand. "What does a crisis look like?" I imagine my mother passing out or having a heart attack.

"She might faint or vomit, run a fever, start slurring her speech or imagining things. Or her blood pressure might drop so low that she goes to sleep. That would be the best way, honestly." Trina sips at her wine and curls her legs up under her, her shoes on the couch.

50

I blink and bite my tongue. Who puts their shoes on someone else's couch? But she's here, helping, and I don't have it in me to insult someone who's nursing my mother.

"More than likely though, her kidneys will fail and that will be enough."

I take a deep breath and am surprised that it hurts, that I'm about to cry. This discussing my mother's body like she's not my mother . . . I don't like it. I turn away and blink back tears. Trina pats my knee, and I can't help it. I move away. The rhythm, the weight, it throws me back to her old office. That day. I dart a glance at her, and she doesn't look hurt but has *I get it* plastered all over her face.

Of course she does. She's a nurse.

"So, what do I need to do for her now? Any special diet or medicines or . . ." I trail off, not knowing how to begin this kind of list. Caregiver to my mother, whom I haven't seen in half my lifetime.

She finishes off her wine and sets her glass on the coffee table, next to the bowl of stale candy. "She signed a DNR — a do not resuscitate — back when she got her diagnosis."

The words take a second to sink in and find definition, and once they do, the few sips of wine I've taken burn worse than a shot of Everclear.

"We have medication to make her feel better, but she won't take it. Wants to keep a clear head. Besides, they won't fix anything. If she's feeling pain, try to talk her into some pain medication. If she wants to sleep, let her sleep. If she's hungry, feed her. If she's not, don't force her. End-of-life care is centered around helping the patient's body gently shut down. It's all we can do."

I let out that deep breath, blowing it out in a single huff, and put down my useless notepad.

Trina stands and hands me her card. "I'll stop by every few days to check on her, but if you need me, no matter the time of day, give me a call. Doesn't matter if it's a question or you want me to check on her breathing."

"Thank you." I stand so that I'm eye level with her, so she's not towering over me, but my feet stick to the floor.

Trina walks herself to the front door and swings it open, and I can tell she's been here a lot. She stops the swing before it catches.

She's almost out the door when the words fall out of my mouth. "Where did you bury her?"

I hold myself still, my breaths, my heart, my everything stops, waiting, hoping.

Trina comes to a standstill, her hands clench into fists, her shoulders rise to her ears, but she doesn't turn around. "I didn't," she says, so soft I almost miss it. "I took her to the hospital."

My heart squeezes tight. "What did they do with her?"

But Trina keeps walking, as if she didn't hear me, climbs onto her bike, and rides away.

And I, because once again I'm not brave enough to know, let her go.

CHAPTER TEN

I open the rusty door to the gardening shed with a loud creak. The moon is high, the mosquitoes are whining, and I know this is a dancing-naked-under-the-moon weird way of dealing with . . . everything.

But I don't care.

My earliest memories are working in this garden with my parents. For a long time, the neat rows of vegetables had little wooden signs I'd made when I was five. Misspelled words with barely recognizable drawings of carrots, green beans, and tomatoes. Of course, those are long rotted away, and I can barely tell what's a carrot and what's a weed now.

Doesn't help that I'm out here in the dark.

I've left a window open so I can hear Mom if she needs me, but I needed to get out of that small, boxy house after Trina left, after she arrived under the guise of help, but really all she'd done was deliver a truckload of mental chaos. Thoughts twist around my mind, like how Mom is going to die — so many options there — and how I still don't know what happened to my daughter's body.

I squint to see through the shadows in the shed. Everything is still neatly ordered with Dad's precision, and I go straight to the gardening spade he made himself. Dad could have been a wood craftsman in another age, another life, his Atakapa heritage lending him oft-forgotten skills. Dad wasn't a tribe member, but he had a great-uncle who was, who taught him a little.

Dad's spade is warm in my grip, and I attack the edges of the garden first, redefining the boundaries. With each shove of the spade, my mind shoves out another thought. What did the hospital do with her?

Shove, break through weeds, clear space.

Trina heard my question and didn't answer me, so it had to be bad. It had to be traumatic. That's Trina's gig. Taking care of people and protecting them, like she did for me so many years ago. But still, I wish she'd have let me see my daughter.

I wish I'd been strong enough to make her.

By the time I've cleared the edges and met where I started, the moon has started to sink, I have enough mosquito bites to be worried about West Nile, my muscles tremble, and my mind is quiet.

I clean off Dad's tools, place them back where they belong, and survey my work. Someone walking by would say the garden looks a wreck, but I can tell the difference. Slow progress is still progress.

The shower is warm, if not hot, and dirt falls away from my fingers and knuckles in a layer of gray water, then runs clear. I fall into bed minutes later with dirt stuck deep under my nails and my muscles blissfully sore, but once I get still, sleep becomes impossible. Like Dad's garden, my mind is too overgrown. No room for a thought to take root, let alone grow.

My old JanSport backpack — my go bag — is hanging off my desk chair, exactly where it used to hang, the faded blue jean fabric the only physical evidence of time passed. I still haven't unloaded it, except for my toothbrush and hairbrush. The clothes hanging in my closet still fit, though a little snug and a lot outdated, so I've been making do. But now . . .

I make myself get out of bed, the cool sheets rough against my bare legs, and cross the bedroom in three steps. In the outside pouch, behind the pen holders and tucked into the little zipper pocket, is Caitlin's note. It's not often that I take it out, look at it again, and try to figure out what I could have done differently, but Emmie's question is stuck in my mind.

Why you?

Why would anyone go through the trouble of tracking me down and bringing me home, unless I had some piece of the puzzle? Some knowledge or possession that I could use to stop someone else from dying.

Caitlin's note has become soft at the edges, but it's not that part of her final message that I reach for, but rather, the origami-folded square. I've never been able to make sense of it, and probably still won't be able to, but I carefully untuck the edge of the folder paper from its origami pocket and gently unfold the paper along the creases.

The original had to have been a piece of notebook paper, eight-and-a-half by eleven, three-hole punched, college-ruled. It's been scribbled on horizontally, the paper torn straight down the middle, starting at the middle hole. Not with scissors, because the tear isn't quite clean. More as if Caitlin folded it, licked the fold on both sides, then tore it on the edge of a desk.

Best I can tell, I have the bottom half. No large white space on the edge, and the holes are at the top. The letter *A* is just under the middle hole, and I assume that, like the rest of the paper, there's another letter on the missing side. From the *A*, a line is drawn diagonally up and to the left of the page, the pencil black and heavy, running into another pair of letters, *J.S.* The *J.S.* letters connect to more pairs of letters below, but these with a double line. And some of those are connected to another pair of letters with one vertical line, though it's hard to make out the final letters, written on top of other letters that have been erased, as if she did this all in a hurry.

It doesn't make sense.

I should have followed through on it back then. I owed it to Caitlin. But I was a teenager, ears-deep in my grief, my loss, and my desperate need to get out of this town and leave everything behind. Shoving the note into my backpack all those years ago, and taking it out now and then, felt like keeping a bit of Caitlin with me. Figuring out what it all meant, though . . . that was too much. Too much thinking about old hurts I couldn't change.

Yet I'm here now. And if I can face Momma dying, as much as I don't want to, I can face Caitlin's death. And maybe solve the mystery she gave me. My stomach feels acid-lined and fragile. What was Caitlin trying to tell me?

If these are initials, I need a town directory to cross-check possibilities. Or . . .

My high school yearbooks are still on my bookshelf. *If* these are initials, then maybe they're initials of people we knew, maybe went to school with.

It's well past midnight, but sleep's not happening, so I kneel in front of my dusty bookcase and pull out the most recent yearbook I own — junior year. Inside are notes from friends and acquaintances, messages of *best friends forever*, and *I was the first to sign your crack*, but I'm not here for the nostalgia trip.

I flip to the pages that include our class, grab a pencil from my desk, and put asterisks next to all the people who share initials with the coupled letters on Caitlin's paper. There are a few hits, mostly at the bottom of the page, me included, but I'm not confident I'm on the right track.

The brittle edge of the pencil's eraser finds its way to my lips, and my gaze strays back to Caitlin's note. It almost looks like half of a detective's suspect board.

She gave me a half-page clue.

I need that other half-page. Perhaps whatever secrets Caitlin shared with that person would give me some answers.

Suicide or murder. Someone has to know.

CHAPTER ELEVEN

Can you help me get the gang back together? My text to Emmie goes out with a soft whoosh.

By the time I've made coffee, checked on Mom, and started breakfast, her reply is waiting — faster than I expected, but not fast enough to feel hopeful.

Emmie: *Not sure they'll be up for it . . .*

It's important. I send back.

She doesn't respond. I tell myself not to overthink it — Emmie was always the girl in the group project who got things done before asking for help. She's probably checking in with everyone before she gets back to me.

I carry Mom's breakfast into her bedroom on a tray and gently shake her awake. "Hungry?"

She moves into a sitting position and rubs the sleep from her eyes. Her hand trembles as she picks up her fork and picks at her scrambled eggs. "Were you out gardening last night?" Her voice is gritty, but focused.

"Couldn't sleep. Still some good plants in Dad's garden."

She nods, her eyes bright. "You always did have his gift, *mmhmm*." Her gaze flicks to the journal on her nightstand.

"What are you writing about in that thing?" I nod in the direction of her journal.

She shrugs. "When you've got just a little life left, guess there's an urge to write down some of it, so somethin's left when you're gone."

I stare at her, once again wondering what it must feel like to see the end of your own life. Moving from philosophically knowing to tactically knowing that there is an actual end.

She lifts her chin as if she knows my exact thoughts. "Don't go startin' with pity, I won't have it. We all die, and that's that. Point of life is to make a point. And I'm makin' mine, *mmhmm*." She flicks her hand toward her journal with a defiant wave, and her expression dares me to argue.

I hold my hands in the air. "I've no doubt of that."

Her eyes hold me a second or two longer, then she relents. "Do me a favor, baby girl?"

I nod, committing without knowing. I'd do just about anything for her — owe her that at the very least.

"See to it that everything in there gets published after I'm gone. Trina said she'd help too, but it doesn't hurt to have back up."

"Published? Like a memoir?"

She flips her hands over and back. "Not quite sure I'm that interesting, but you'll see what I mean after you read it. *After*," she shakes a bossy finger in my face, "I'm gone."

My phone pings with a text message. I hook her finger with my pinkie. "Okay, Mom, I promise. Pinkie swear."

Her mouth relaxes into a smile, and she squeezes her finger around mine. "Now get on outta here and let me eat in peace."

I kiss her head, pick up my phone, and leave her be. The message from Ems reads, *Today, 5 p.m. Our spot*.

* * *

Bills are perhaps the furthest thing from a relaxing Sunday afternoon activity, but the pile of unopened envelopes promises hours of distraction before I need to meet up with Emmie and whoever else is showing up.

Mom's asleep on the couch, again, her journal tucked under her hip, and I'm sitting at the small kitchen table, the Formica chipped and dented from the years. I divide the envelopes into piles of appearance, most important looking to least. The first bill I open is from her previous employer.

Dear Mrs. Caraway . . .

I skim to the important piece.

Mom's first year of disability is coming to a close. Meaning she'll receive even less of her meager salary. A good forty percent less.

The next envelope is an overdue water bill. Then electricity. Then gas. Even with her disability plan, she's not making the small amounts due. Then, a credit card statement quoting the minimum payment as something Mom cannot afford.

I drop my head into my hand, rubbing between my eyebrows. I knew I'd have to get a job to make our ends meet, but I didn't realize the gap between our ends was so very far apart.

"Okay, Darla, you can do this," I tell myself. "Mom did it for years. You've done it for years. Take the next step."

I roll back my shoulders and start a balance sheet of Mom's bills versus her income. The gap in earnings versus expenses is large, especially when I calculate the overdue fees and interest rates on the credit card, but if I can land a job that pays a bit better than minimum wage, we should be able to stay on our feet.

The next envelope is from Mom's bank. I tear off the end of the envelope and slide out the letter. The paper unfolds, as if it is a dramatization of a scroll about to be read, and the numbers on the letter flash neon.

There's a second mortgage on the house — of course there is — and Mom's about to default on the loan.

A burning sensation threatens the corner of my eye. I want to cry, but it's been years since a tear has escaped.

The balance sheet I've created suddenly seems comical. There's no way I can get a job that will pay all these bills and keep the house. We're going to lose our house. And then what will we do? Where will we go?

Pastor Abe might finally get his wish.

My breath comes short, fast, and my head feels light.

I stand, pace the small kitchen, and rest my hands on my knees as the room goes unfocused.

Deep breaths, Darla.

I breathe in through my nose, hold the air in my chest, and slowly release it through my lips. I keep doing that until the room settles, until the worry tornado evaporates in my mind.

A squeak on the floor grabs my attention, and I straighten, looking behind me. Mom stands in the doorway, holding onto her walker, a sad and tired expression tilting her lips and dulling her eyes.

"It's been bad for a while, hasn't it?" I ask.

She lifts her hand in an apology. "System's not built to take care of those who can't take care of themselves. I did try, but . . ." She looks down at her betrayer's body.

"We'll figure it out," I reassure her — or try to — even though I have no clue how we'll dig out of this financial hole. "Like you've said before, we just gotta keep moving forward, right?"

"I'm so sorry, Darla. To leave you with all this." She gestures at the table, at the debt this handful of paper represents. I try to ignore the feeling that a deep sinkhole has opened beneath my feet, and I'm clinging to tree roots that *will* give . . . Not a matter of if, but when.

"Not your fault." I sit at the table, as if I hadn't just had a miniature panic attack. "Our new plan is to do whatever we can to keep the house. So that bill comes first." I make a note on my balance sheet and put the letter from the bank on top of the rest. "Emmie thinks she can get me a job at the school, and I bet I can grab a few hours at the café . . . since she owns that place. Did you know about that?" I'm babbling, but it's better than worrying, and since it's all up to me to bring in the bucks, I get to babble.

She doesn't interject, so I press on.

"Between tips and any income I can bring in, we should be able to at least make the mortgage payments, yeah?" I'm not really asking. I'm not even looking at her. I don't even know if she's still in the room. But this is what I need to do. Talk it out as if I'm throwing a ball at the wall and catching it when it bounces back. I need to hear the sound of my next steps in my own ears.

"And maybe plants," I say, and make notes on my balance sheet. "Once I get the garden in good shape again, we can do cut flowers and fresh tomatoes. The Juliets and the Early Girls will be good varieties to get in before winter. Maybe we can sell them at the—"

There's a clink on the table. I look up from my frantic note writing. It's Mom's wedding band. A delicate white gold band with a tiny, triangle-shaped diamond.

"Absolutely not." I interlock my fingers, making a fist.

"It's better than you working yourself into an early grave. The good Lord knows we've got enough of that at the present." She presses her lips together and flicks the ring across the table. It hits my hand.

"I am *not* pawning your wedding ring."

She rolls her eyes, her attempt at being flippant, but her irises shine with traitorous tears. "This is how I can help. Your dad would have rather me pawned this piece of metal than us lose the house."

My heart is thin glass, and each beat threatens to shatter it. I cover the ring with my hand and wait until she's looking at me.

"I am not going to pawn your wedding ring unless we absolutely have to, okay? Give me a chance."

She takes a shuddery breath and finally nods.

I scoop the ring into my palm and hold it out to her. "*If* I need it, I'll let you know."

The stubbornness rushes out of her, and she suddenly turns wobbly. I scoot out the other kitchen chair, and she sinks into it. Her position mimics mine from earlier. Slumped, head in hands, defeated.

"We're going to get through this," I say, as if we've always been a team. As if we have experience beating the odds together. But not since Dad have we done this, and it's a foreign language that we're both having to remember.

I send Emmie another text, this one about a job, and show Mom so she knows I'm on it. So she doesn't have to worry. This time, Emmie replies immediately with a start date of the next day at the café. The school will take longer to finagle, but she's confident she can get me in once the office reopens, as long as I pass the background check . . . which I will. Darla Caraway has been on ice for the past decade.

"Your disability and social security payments will help with the mortgage. The rest we'll attack as we must. Obviously, utilities need to be paid, but I'll call tomorrow and see if I can get an extension. I'll also go over to the food bank at Catholic Charities after my shift tomorrow, and see what I can get with my tips. But for now . . ." I stand and pull the pot of beans out of the fridge. "We're having leftovers for dinner. Sound good?"

Mom shakes her head, a sad smile swinging from her lips. "I musta done something right in my life to deserve you." She gets up and makes her way from the room, but I have no words. She thinks I'm a good thing in her life? The idea makes me snort.

Wonder if Addison's also affects the brain.

I add water to the pinto bean soup, heat it all up, and take it into the living room on a tray. She's watching a rerun of *Friends* while journaling, but looks up from her place on the couch and gives me that smile again. I leave her with her bowl of cheap protein and go back into the kitchen for mine.

When I come back, I sit beside her, and together we watch Ross and Rachel break up and get back together, and we sip our soup, and we push our worries to tomorrow.

CHAPTER TWELVE

It's almost five when I leave the house, the sun about as high as it was at midday, and the heat about the same, too. Ems didn't need to specify our meeting spot. It's a frequent visitor in my dreams. When I pull up to the side of the bridge, though, it's more crowded than I expected.

Emmie's Jaguar convertible is snuggled comfortably next to a pristine F350, along with a beater that's too rusted to see the make and model, but I recognize the dents and scrapes and sun worn stickers of one-hit wonders plastering the rear window.

I park and get out, and another car turns in behind me, blocking my exit. The tree-filtered light doesn't let me see the person's eyes, but if I'm reading the situation right, it has to be Ivan in the black Jeep.

The door opens, and long legs unfold themselves from the driver's seat. It is Ivan, though not the Ivan I remember. Gone is the gangly guy dressed in basketball shorts and stained t-shirts, and in his place is a business casual man who obviously spends a lot of time in meetings and the gym.

I whistle. "Look who grew up." And step forward for a hug.

He doesn't reciprocate, but looks me up and down, his brown eyes hard. "Wine coolers in the back. Grab 'em, will you?" He reaches back into the Jeep and grabs an eighteen-pack of Blue Ribbon.

"Right," I mutter. "I'm in trouble." I fumble trying to open his fancy car, and he rolls his eyes, clicking a button on his key fob. The back swings open, and I grab a cooler packed full of ice and wine coolers.

I make my way down the path to the riverside beach where a campfire is already blazing, despite the high temperatures, and the smoke helps keep the mosquitoes at bay. I thump the cooler down on the edge of the fire ring and stand there, silent, while the rest of them decide what to do with me.

A few days ago, I didn't linger here. It'd been too hard to stay and to take in all the details in the pre-dusk and early dawn. But now, with the sun high in the sky, I can see that logs have been added to the space, dragged in from the surrounding forest. Someone has dug a hole in the dirt, probably to help keep beer cold. Beer caps litter the soil, providing a packed floor and a tetanus hazard, all in one. Old bags of Taco Bell and Domino's pizza boxes are at the edges of the fire ring, ready to be used for fuel.

This was our spot. But it looks like it's been passed down to the next generation of bored-in-a-small-town. Today, for a brief moment, we've reclaimed it.

Karl and Emmie share a log. Karl looks the same, though with longer hair and a fuller beard. Emmie gives me a little wave and a look that says, *I'm here; I'm on your side*.

Shelly stands next to Tristan, hip pressed against him once again as if she needs to make sure I know that he's hers.

Ivan drops the pack of beer next to the cooler and steps away from me, joining the others on the other side of the fire, leaving me to sit by myself next to the cheap alcohol.

Last time we were all here, it was Tristan and me cuddled up next to the fire, Emmie dancing under the stars, Karl and Ivan threatening to throw Shelly into the river, Caitlin's ghost ever-present over the proceedings.

This feels like something she'd organize — a Come to Jesus talk to clear the air and establish a new baseline.

"You gonna pass those out, or did you forget how to be in polite society?" Karl says from his seat next to Emmie, his tone tough, but I can hear his old, couldn't-care-less undercurrent. He's here because someone — Ivan, likely — told him to be here, and there's free beer.

"Since when have you ever been in polite society?" Tristan ribs him, and it breaks the tension enough for everyone's shoulders to dip a level.

I tear open the soggy carton of Pabst Blue Ribbon. "I didn't know people in polite society drank this piss." And toss him one.

He cracks the smallest smirk as he catches it, pops the top, and sucks the foam out like an expert.

Next to him, Emmie rolls her eyes, walks over, and grabs wine coolers for herself and Shelly. I grab one as well, screw off the top, and take a chilled, slightly fruity sip that does absolutely nothing to break the heat, humidity, or tension.

"You going to tell us what this is about?" Tristan says, his hands linked together.

"Oh, she doesn't get off that easy." Ivan turns to me. He stands behind everyone, arms crossed. "You don't just get to show up, demand we all meet you, then control the conversation. You left."

His reaction surprises me the most. Ivan, at least the Ivan I knew, was the never-gets-bothered guy, the one who, no matter what, was never overly emotional, never got involved in drama. He was Switzerland in our friend group, never taking sides.

I take a deep breath, exhale slowly. "I did."

"Why?"

All the practiced lies I've told myself over the years circle around the tip of my tongue, lies grafted to partial truths to protect my secrets and, impossibly, naively, make everyone happy. Their bitter taste is at odds with the sweet simplicity of the wine cooler.

Here, now, facing them, I know that none of them will be believed.

They've all leaned forward, hands frozen around drinks, and they are going to hate me.

"I just . . . had to get out of here."

"Bullshit," Tristan says, his voice deep, his tone hurt. "Was it another guy?"

Shelly cuts her eyes at him, but he keeps his stare on me, seemingly oblivious to her insecurity. Or maybe doesn't care.

"You left, without saying a word. To any of us. So it was either another guy or drugs or a fight with your mom or . . ."

Shelly shifts, clearly uncomfortable with Tristan's intense focus on me. "We've come up with theories over the years." Her tone is less offended, more pissed-off. "Big unsolved mystery of the town. Why would Darla Caraway, primed to be prom queen, disappear?" She slides her hand into Tristan's like she's staking her territory. "At first, we thought you were dead. Like Caitlin."

They all nod, a display of worry I never imagined, never let myself consider. Old guilt sprouts up like a stubborn weed in the pit of my stomach. "I didn't think you guys would think—"

"How could we not?" This time it's Emmie, and somehow that hurts worse. "Caitlin had died the year before, then you disappeared, and . . ." A sob cuts her off, and Karl wraps an arm around her shoulders. She shakes her head, pressing her lips together.

Part of me longs to sprint across to her side, give her a big hug and a bigger apology. But some other part keeps me nailed to my seat, letting them act as my judge and jury.

"Your mom let us know you were okay," Ivan says, "after you sent her that postcard. You broke her heart. And she wouldn't let any of us pick up the pieces." His eyes shine, clueing me in that her heart wasn't the only one I broke.

That weed of guilt shoots a tap root straight through my stomach and into my gut. I'd thought that Tristan and my mom would be the only collateral damage, and that alone had almost been enough to stop me from leaving. Almost.

I spread out my hands. "I'm sorry guys. I didn't mean to hurt you. And I can't tell you all my reasons, but it wasn't because of you, and," I look at Tristan, "it wasn't because of another guy. I didn't want to leave." I meet all of their gazes this time. "Please trust me when I say I had to."

"That's the thing, Darla," Ivan says, his tone ice cold. "We can't trust you if you can't trust us."

"I can't trust you with this," I whisper, the words escaping before I have time to register them.

Their expressions freeze, and the silence that follows is stuffed with shock. Not trusting each other didn't exist in our world, way back when. It was all or nothing in every sense.

I take them in, one by one. Tristan — he was always first — someone I never should have been involved with, brought up by the Church to be the Church. Shelly, perfect cheerleader, perfect choir girl, perfect wife for a preacher's son. Ivan, whose dad was a deacon, whose mom lived for the charity work prescribed by the Church. Karl with his single mother who benefitted from that charity, who took it for granted, who couldn't survive without it. And Emmie . . . she'd broken from her grandmother's crucifix embrace, but got sucked back in for business reasons, needing to make nice with the town for her business and her husband's business.

I sigh. I can't give them everything, but I can give part of everything.

"The Church threatened me," I say, focusing on Tristan. "Or rather, Abe threatened me."

Tristan stands, his fists curled at his sides. "Threatened you how?" There isn't an ounce of disbelief in his voice. He knows his dad.

"Said if I didn't start Initiation by the end of the school year, he'd run Mom and me out of town." I half shrug, as if the memory doesn't hurt. And it doesn't . . . not compared to losing Caitlin. And then Tristan. And then all my friends.

But none of that compares to losing my daughter. "I left so she didn't have to."

"You hate COES that much." Karl's turn, his arms folded tightly in front of his chest.

"Look, I know you don't see it, what with your families indoctrinated for years, but COES is a cult."

Tristan's mouth turns to granite, and pink rises up Shelly's cheeks, but I can't stop, not now, now that the words are vomiting out.

"I convinced Caitlin to get out. And she wound up dead." My voice rises, bounces over the river, off Suicide Rock, and into the reservation.

Emmie stands and walks over. "Darla, the Church didn't kill Caitlin, honey . . . and neither did you." She rubs my arm. "Time to stop putting every bit of blame you can scratch up all on yourself."

Ignoring the others, I meet her gaze, understanding and concern flickering through every watery blink.

My next breath wobbles on the way out, but I have to push through and brush aside the comfort she's offering . . . otherwise, I'll never get through this. "A private investigator was hired to find me and delivered a note. It was written on the back of one of the Feast flyers."

Emmie keeps her arm around mine, supporting me against the firing squad.

Shelly and Tristan exchange glances, Karl's eyebrows push together under his red Ford hat, but Ivan hasn't moved. Has done nothing but stare and stay silent since the beginning.

"What did it say?" Shelly puts a little distance between herself and Tristan. Not much, but no longer connected.

Instead of answering, I pull the flyer out of my back pocket and hand it over to Shelly. "It's happening again? Come back before she dies, too?"

The group goes silent, still, mouths slightly parted, nothing but glances darting around.

"I think it has something to do with Caitlin. With her death. She left me a note and a piece of paper that had been torn in half the day she disappeared."

In the past, we'd argued about it. Murder versus suicide. None of us wanted to believe our friend was capable of suicide, but having an unidentified murderer walking through town was worse.

Now, there are no arguments.

"My theory is that Caitlin left one of you the other half of that paper. Maybe if we put them together, we can figure out what is going on. What happened to her." I look around the group, trying to read their faces, but it's like staring at a fortress wall.

Shelly licks her lips. "But why do you think it was someone in the Church? It could have been anyone, even . . ." She thumbs over her shoulder at the reservation. "You know they hate us." Her voice drops to a whisper.

"And you know that's a rumor the Church has worked hard to spread," I shoot back. It's not the first time she's said it, and it's not the first time I've had that word reflex. I'd fit in well enough in high school, but the town's prejudice toward the Atakapa wasn't lost on me. I'd seen how people treated my father, like he belonged up to a point, but could never fully be trusted.

"The Church's roots weave completely through this town." It's hard to look at Tristan, but he's always been a better man than his dad. I hope he still is. "Caitlin was afraid. Her note said that I was right. The only thing we'd been talking about had been her leaving the Church because it didn't seem healthy for her. And now, this message on the back of a Church flyer? The Church is involved, somehow."

Again, no one argues, but the mood has shifted.

"Not healthy?" Shelly mouths. Her back stiffens. "We're raising our children in that church. We wouldn't have gotten through those first few months of Madeline's life without them. And you want me to believe that somehow, this church that I've been a part of since I was a little girl, this church that I devote my time to and trust my family with, this church somehow, what? Killed Caitlin? That she's dead because of the Church?"

Tristan puts a hand on her back, maybe to calm her down, but it does the exact opposite.

"No!" Shelly elbows him off. "If you want to believe this," she daggers Tristan with her gaze, "go ahead, but Darla has never had my back or yours. And certainly not the Church's. I'm not listening to another word of this . . . this heresy."

She stomps by me without a word or a look, shoving the flyer against my hand as she passes, and it hurts more than it should. But she was my first friend. And it's hard to watch that walk away.

Karl stands, pours the rest of his beer into his mouth, then crunches the can and throws it into the fire. "Back in high school, I never understood these twos' fascination with you." He thumbs at Tristan and Ivan. "Always seemed to me you thought the sun shone out of your ass and the moon revolved around your head." He laughs. It's not nice. "And now you're back, thinking you can just say whatever you want, and we'll all fall in line." He laughs again, but this time it leans closer to a scoff. "Shelly's right. You ain't worth it."

He turns around, walks to his car, backs out with gravel spitting out from his tires, and speeds off with a screech.

"The Church has been good to us, Darla," Ivan says. "Takes care of Karl when Karl can't take care of himself. Supported me when I started my real estate business. Even set your mom up with hot meals from the ladies' group. You got a lot of nerve coming back here, making accusations, when the only thing you've done is be good at being gone."

He gets in his Jeep and follows Karl down the road, leaving my car free once again.

I don't move. Don't argue. Don't let myself feel. Because, maybe, I did have a lot of nerve coming back. Maybe because

I had a lot of nerve leaving in the first place . . . and I don't expect them to understand.

"Tell us why you really left, Darla," Tristan says, his voice low. "Please."

Us now consists of Tristan and Emmie, everyone else having said their piece and left.

I sink to one of the logs and drop my forehead into my hand. My chest squeezes, nearly crushing my lungs, but I take a deep breath and reset. "I . . . I can't. But Tris," I fall back onto my old pet name for him, "I'm not lying."

He doesn't answer, just gives me another long stare, then gets in his truck with his wife and drives back to town.

I watch him go, reality and too many years of could-have-beens knotting around each other in my throat.

Emmie huffs. "Well, that didn't go very well." She sits beside me and wraps an arm around my waist. "At least they left the wine coolers."

I toe at a stick, then pick it up and toss it into the dying fire. Embers pop into the air and float away like little fire spores.

"Why didn't you tell anyone Abe threatened you?"

I shrug. "I was seventeen. I didn't think anyone would believe me."

"I would have."

"I know that now."

Emmie's voice softens. "I also think I know why you left."

She doesn't reach for me, but her eyes don't waver — steady, searching.

I hold myself very still, but my heart is going a million miles a minute.

"Baggy clothes, nauseous at the scent of French fries, not drinking out here with us . . ." She ticks off the evidence one by one on her fingers.

My mouth has gone West Texas dry. "You knew?"

"Not then. Looking back, it makes sense."

I drop my head onto her shoulder. "She was Tristan's. Stillbirth."

71

"Jesus, Darla." Her words come out as a whisper but echo against my chest with a boom. The truth is out, and nothing will ever be the same.

I take a moment to find my breath, my center, some hint of courage. "I couldn't have told. Abe would have sucked me into the Church, Tristan would have been stuck here, and Mom always hated that Tristan and I were together. God if she knew he'd gotten me pregnant . . . I couldn't stay after the baby died. It hurt too much."

She strokes my hair. "I get it. They would have as well." There's more behind her words, but thankfully, she keeps her answers short. I couldn't handle much more.

"It would have destroyed Tristan," I murmur, partly to her, partly to myself. "And Shelly can't handle that truth." Shelly, Tristan's new-and-improved partner. Who likely never disappointed him like I did.

"You don't give her enough credit," she sighs. "Never did."

"Maybe not."

We're silent for a bit. The whine of the mosquitoes increases with the dying flames. "Ems, could you do me a favor?"

"Another one? So soon?" She gives me a look that says I shouldn't push my luck, but also that she'll help.

I summon my last bit of courage, all I have left, but need to use. "Can you ask Henry where the hospital plot is at the cemetery? Or if there's a place where baby Jane Does have been buried? Or a record of baby Jane Does from back then?" The flood of memories washes over me again, and all I want is for the closure that simply *knowing* could bring.

She cocks her head at me.

"I just need to say goodbye." And, I'm sorry.

She pats my knee. "I'll let you know what he says."

"Thank you." We're not looking at each other, instead staring into the fire, but I think she hears the tears in my voice.

She sighs, hands me another wine cooler, clinks hers against my bottle, and we sit there as the day fades into the forest and the fire dies.

CHAPTER THIRTEEN

Stepping out the front door, I feel as though I'm walking into a wet blanket. It's eight in the morning and already eighty-five degrees, the humidity high. My patients seem to like the thick, moist air, though. Even Percy perked up after his bout of pouting the first few days.

I rearrange the plants so they get their favorite patch of sunlight and give everyone a good spritz. The two twig figures seem at home on the windowsill. If I had my own nursery, I'd hunt down whoever was making these and convince them to sell them in my shop.

Dreams for later.

My shift doesn't start at the café until after lunch. Before the heat of the day truly hits, I walk around the house with a notepad, making a list of home repairs that, should we have any additional funds, we'll have to take care of. There's rotten wood about everywhere I look, and I'm surprised the roof isn't leaking, especially with how many shingles are missing. How expensive are shingles? And surely, with a ladder and some nails, I can fix it myself? There's gotta be a YouTube channel on home repair for broke homeowners.

I stop at the garden and survey the rest of the yard. Our land isn't much, but it offers a private backyard that's bordered by the forest. Town's close enough to hear the occasional semi drive through, so it's not like we've got prime property. But this part is nice.

Over the years, the forest has grown. Skinny pines that pop up like weeds have brought the shadows closer to home. Unlike the rest of the town, we're not afraid of their closeness, their dark inner parts — that comes from Daddy's side of the family. I wonder when's the last time Mom took a stroll through the woods. I wonder if she'd be able to now.

I set my notepad down in the garden shed, pull on my gloves, grab a worn knee cushion, and reach for the three-pronged cultivator that'll help me clean the area and get it ready for tomatoes.

My body reacts before I do, and I jerk my hand back.

A sculpted bit of wood has been positioned on the dusty shelf. Unlike everything else in here, it's clean. I scoop it into my hand and take it outside to look at it closer.

It's me.

From the other night.

Kneeling, with my hands outstretched, holding a small bunch of roots. Midnight gardening.

It falls from my palm and bounces once on the dirt.

My heart races, and a feeling of being watched claws at my spine, itching right between my shoulders, and I'm suddenly seeing the forest the way everyone else does around here.

Someone's been spying on me.

"Think, Darla." I clutch my hands into fists until my fingers go numb, then release the tension. My head clears the tiniest bit. I kneel beside the fallen doll and study it from a safe distance.

The work is intricate. The artist is a true craftsman. Rather than twigs fastened together to make a shape, this one's been carved from a bit of wood, and even the discoloration and the grains of the wood have been used in the design. I pick the doll back up, run my fingers over the smooth edges, and look for a hint, a clue. Why is someone watching me? And then telling me about it through dolls? I don't understand.

I'm no detective, but there's no motive I can see that makes any sense. However, someone *did* orchestrate things to get me back home. I can't help but wonder if the two are connected.

I stand back up, pocket the doll, prop my hands on my hips, and stare into the forest. My hands turn into fists at my side.

Right.

Before I know it, I'm marching toward the shadows. I reach the barrier of the forest, and the temperature drops a good six degrees. Up close, the shadows aren't black, but deep purples and welcoming grays. A bird twitters here and there, and high above, a squirrel leaps from one branch to another, sloppily spilling down old pine needles.

"I don't know who you are, but you're not scaring me," I shout into the trees. "I could use a friend. Someone who knows what's going on. So, if that's you, I'd appreciate you watching my back." Is this the right approach? I don't know. It feels safer to make this person my ally rather than assume they're my enemy. I cup my hands around my mouth so my next words will be heard, loud and clear. "Also, your dolls are truly beautiful."

Everyone likes a compliment.

* * *

I walk into town for my first shift at the café, a tiny bubble of First Day nervousness caught in my chest. Already, changes have been made to Main Street, likely from Shelly's or Tristan's mom's visions. A banner's been strung across the road, just before the intersection of Main and First. It just about blocks the view of the Second Saturday Flea Market sign, the tattered, faded, and yellowed one that's been there since before I can remember. Shelly's — I assume it's Shelly's

— new sign is bright white, with the Church's dove symbol displayed in gold on the top two corners.

*JOIN US FOR THE FEAST, A CELEBRATORY
TIME OF FAMILY AND FAITH*

The words are bold purple in a font that shouts, I'm sophisticated yet relatable and most definitely trustworthy. Below the words is the image of a cornucopia spilling out a roasted turkey and vegetables. Wholesome, family-oriented, and only one week away.

And the Church's biggest recruiting event.

Down the road, the gas station's awning and signs have been washed for the first time since who knows when. The resale shop's windows are being cleaned, and just past the reflection of the street, I can see the gentleman who has owned the place since before I was born and also hasn't changed one bit — he was old then, and he's old now — refreshing the window display. Even compared to two days ago, which was a market day, the town seems to vibrate as if it's an elderly woman who's just been granted her wish of youth.

All this for a church revival. I take a deep breath and let it out slowly. Of course, I was called back home in time for The Feast.

I shrug my shoulders and hurry under the shadow of the banner to Emmie's café. At the door, I'm greeted with the musty smell of mothballs, but, as Emmie said, one can't be choosy in a town this size.

"You Darla?" a woman calls out before my eyes have had a chance to adjust to the dim interior.

"Yes ma'am," I call back.

"Well, git on back 'ere. We got a few groups comin' in and ain't no time ta spare." Her accent is all gravy and fried okra and Texas Toast, and it immediately grounds me in home.

I meet the woman in the kitchen. My new boss is everything you'd want in the matron of a diner. Apron wrapped around her generous hips, flour on the side of her nose, curly, graying hair in a hair net.

"Emmalyn says you're a shit server, so you're on bar duty 'til I can figure out what to do with ya. Deliver drinks and such and don't go sellin' any of those fancy cocktails they sell up north or wherever you came from. Ain't no one got time for that."

I catch a snort at the back of my throat. "So, beer and wine?"

"And manage that dang espresso machine. If you can work that beast, you've got a permanent position here. Hate that thang. Name's Lola." She holds out a hand, grabs mine and shakes it, turns my hand over and looks at my dirt-stained nail beds. "You better scrub up first. Next time you enter my kitchen, those hands had better be clean."

I do as Lola says — Lord knows I don't want to be caught on her bad side — and am introduced to the rest of the small kitchen and waitstaff, none of whom I know from childhood. That, at least, is a relief. Kathy, Lola says, will be in for the later shift. Until then, she'll have to put up with my subpar serving skills.

The mid-afternoon crowd filters in as I familiarize myself with the bar. It's not my first time behind a bar, but it is my first time behind a bar that's this fancy. Emmie had fun with the design — from the mirrored countertops, which will be hell to keep clean, to the red leather barstools with the big gold buttons pinned in the middle, to the reflective black tile behind the bottles of liquor and wine, it all screams Emmie.

Despite Lola, or maybe to spite Lola, the only orders coming in are for Bloody Marys, sangrias, and white wine spritzers, but seeing as it's technically cocktail hour, I can't see how she'll complain.

A young woman in pink scrubs slides into one of the bar stools. She drops her head into her hand and her hospital badge — maternity ward — swings back and forth. Her expression is tight and withdrawn and exhausted, and I can practically smell the scent of baby wipes coming off her.

"Vodka tonic," she blurts out. "Make it a double. Actually . . . hold the tonic."

"Hard day?" I slide over her drink, complete with ice and lemon.

"One of the worst. A newborn baby was left in the Angel's Cradle." She meets my eyes then, her own suddenly glossy. "She didn't make it. Nothing we could've done. You tell yourself that over and over but . . ." She swipes under her makeup-free eyes, then covers her mouth with a sob. "I'm sorry. I shouldn't be talking like this." She drops her head into her hand again, digs her fingers into her scalp.

But me? I've frozen, gone cold, my hand looks like sculpted ice clinging to my side of the bar.

Trina did that with my girl. Someone had to grieve like this after.

"What, um—" I start, my voice dry, soft. "What happens to a baby like that . . . one that's . . . left?" I almost can't get the words out, am not even sure they're audible.

The nurse lifts her head and stares at me. "I really don't mean to upset you too. We just take care of things. It's what we do."

My lungs grip my next breath as if they'll never let go. But I need to know. "I'm just curious. You can tell me. I can handle it."

She takes a swig of her drink, sets it down carefully, then returns her gaze to me. "We record the time of death. If they're DOA, we just record their time of death as their arrival time."

I swallow. Nod.

She studies me, like she's checking my vitals to see if it's okay to keep going. "Afterwards, they're taken to the morgue and, eventually, buried in the hospital burial plot in the cemetery."

"And these records . . . are they public?"

She doesn't respond for a while, and I start to think she's not going to. She just plays with the edge of her glass, the condensation creating a puddle on the mirrored bar, then slams back the rest of her drink and reaches for her purse.

But instead of pulling out her wallet, she pulls out a small notepad and a pen and begins writing. "This is my friend in the medical records department. The records are available online, but not all Jane and John Does are transferred to the database."

My heart stutters. She knew I wasn't just curious. That it was personal. That I was asking for me.

She's still writing, not looking at me. "However, it'll be in Eileen's archives. She can pull the records from a particular time for you, but you'll have to do the searching yourself. Tell her Janie sent you." She hands over the note, along with a ten-dollar bill. "Good luck," she says, then slides out of the stool and walks out the door.

The note feels heavy in my hands, heavy with the weight of years of not-knowing and the hope that I really can get some answers.

Closure.

CHAPTER FOURTEEN

Kat walks in the front door as she ties a faded black serving apron around her small waist. A look of confusion sweeps over her face when she sees me behind the bar, and she beelines, her dark hair swinging behind her in a braided ponytail.

"You work here now?"

From her tone, I can't tell if she's happy about it or not.

I keep wiping down the counter with glass cleaner — damn Emmie and her mirrors. "For the moment. My mom's sick, and I need to stay in town for a while."

She blinks, then shrugs. "The tips suck. But the dinner rush isn't too bad. Couple of the regulars are nice. But you gotta watch out for Benny — he's always trying to sneak off with extra creamer in his pockets."

I keep my face serious, though I want to laugh. "Thanks for the advice. I'll keep my eye on him."

She nods, as though she's just given me the keys to the city. "He's the one with the ten-gallon Stetson and the starched Wranglers. Fancies himself out of a movie, I guess."

"So, easy to spot in a crowd?"

"Yup. Gotta clock in; otherwise, Lola'll be on my butt all shift." She rolls her eyes and walks off, radiating that teenage 'tude that believes everyone over the age of twenty-five is lame and out to judge them.

The bistro begins to fill with the dinner crowd. Kat rushes back in as a large group queues outside the front door, waiting to be seated. COES people, from the look of them. I don't consider myself a judgmental person, but the Church has a certain look, feel, scent — too polished, too smooth, not enough visible edges, though I know they're there, razor-sharp just below the surface.

Kat leads the group into the semi-private room at the back of the restaurant — about ten women plus Pastor Abe, Tristan's father, confirming my suspicion — and waits as they seat themselves around a large, round table. The room is outfitted with a whiteboard and a TV and can be closed off if necessary, so I assume it's a meeting about the Feast. The last one in has her back to me, but she leans in and gives Kat a half-hug and a kiss on the cheek, before turning, seating herself, and spreading out a stack of papers.

I do a double take. Trina?

Kat takes the table's drink orders, hurries over to me, flings me an order slip, and presents her cheek. "Did she leave a lipstick mark?"

"Yup. Here." I pass over a damp paper towel.

Kat groans. "Mothers." And ducks into the bathroom to scrub her cheek.

I go still, the restaurant seeming to move at an impossible pace around me. Trina is Kat's mother?

But . . .

A knot of unease settles into my stomach, and I can't help it, my gaze is a laser beam to Trina, who still hasn't noticed I'm here.

But Trina wasn't pregnant. Not back then.

My rational brain fights for space, but all I can hear in the noisy bistro, above the white noise of conversation and speakers leaking music meant to fill the room, is the distant cry of a baby.

Kat comes back then, and she's suddenly different, looks different, pockmarked with all the what ifs whirling around my mind. "Good Lord, Darla, you look like you're about to be sick."

"Cover for me for a minute," I yelp and rush to the bathroom.

I flip the lock, turn on the cold water, and splash my face, my neck, and stare into the mirror. In the dim light, my reflection is ghost-like, shadowy in all the unflattering spots. I grip the cold porcelain and stare into my reflection's eyes.

"She's dead, Darla," I tell myself, my voice hollow, a tree that's been eaten from the inside out. "She died." I know this. I know this. I know this.

And yet, a translucent spider thread of hope that has held on all these years, just waiting for the wind to blow the right way, tickles against my bones, and latches on.

I never saw her.

And what I think I heard, I'm not sure I heard. It could have been the wind, the creak of the building, my own grief screaming in my ears. It could have been anything. It didn't even occur to me until much later, after I'd done and run away, that it could have been a newborn's wail.

I double-check that the number of the woman in the hospital records department is tucked safely in my pocket, and address my reflection once again.

"The only way through is through," I tell myself, repeating another one of Mom's well-worn phrases.

I had every reason to trust Trina back then, and there are a million other explanations for Kat. But to quiet my own brain, I need to be absolutely sure. There would be an entry in the records about a newborn Jane Doe, DOA, on January 17, sixteen years ago. I need to see it with my own eyes, and then I can move on. Let these crazy thoughts go. Focus on figuring out who killed Caitlin and who is their next victim.

I leave the bathroom sanctuary to find Lola behind the bar.

"Ya cain't put a seventeen-year-old behind the bar — you want us shut down?" She slaps at me with a dirty dish towel, hitting nothing but air, then huffs her way back to the kitchen.

"Right," I mutter, feeling stupid. I should know better. Lola's already made half the drink orders for the COES table, so I finish up, load them on a tray, and walk them over, just as Shelly and Pastor Abe's wife, Karen, rush in through the front door, their arms full of rubber-banded folders, and they take the last two seats.

Shelly gives me a once-over, then pretends I don't exist, while Trina gives me a half-wave. Inside, the room is almost chilly with the air conditioning on full blast, and Pastor Abe lords over the table as if he's a king and the rest of the committee are his harem.

While I pass out drinks, whatever they were talking about is hushed. Trina goes as far as to flip over one of her papers to the blank side.

"Do my eyes deceive me or is that Darla Caraway, returned to us from her merrymaking in some distant country?" Pastor Abe's Southern gentleman voice booms through the small room, his orator's volume not needed, but always in use.

I know enough about the Bible to decipher the insult.

I place an already sweating glass of sweet tea in front of him. "Just back to take care of Mom. Can I get y'all anything else?"

He stretches back, his large form taking up even more room than it should. "Tell me, how's your Momma doing?"

I'd rather stick a fork in my eye than have a conversation with Tristan's father, but here we are. "Not great." I turn to Shelly and Karen. "Something to drink?"

Karen presses her lips together and tilts up her chin. "Just water." She reaches over and pats Shelly's hand.

"Me too," Shelly says.

Pastor Abe's laugh fills the room, the entire bistro. "That's right, darlin'. You take care of my new grandbaby growing in your belly. Just think, Darla" — he elbows me as if we're chums — "that coulda been you, had you not left my Tristan the way you did."

The room, which had been quiet before, goes before-the-storm still. Shelly's cheeks have turned an impressive shade of pink, and Trina looks between the three of us with her mouth in a perfect circle.

My ears feel on fire. "Then I guess everyone's grateful I left. Excuse me."

"Now hold on, hold on there," he says and grabs my wrist. He presses his thumb into the underside of my wrist, not hard, but firm enough to be effective. "You can't run away again. People will start thinking you've got a bad habit." He chuckles again, as if he's made a funny joke, but no one laughs.

"I'm not running, I'm working." My teeth are clenched, and no one is mistaking my words for a joke. I shake him loose.

"Well, have it your way. We've been prayin' for your momma, you know. Prayin' for our good Lord's healing touch. You should bring her over to the Feast next week. Miracles do be happenin' in that revival tent."

I don't answer. Trina, at the very least, has the sympathy to look embarrassed — either for me or for Pastor Abe's behavior, I'm not sure. I let out a deep breath as I walk out of the room and head back to the bar to bury myself in the dinner rush. Kat will have to deliver that table's drinks the rest of this evening 'cause I'm not stepping a toe back inside that room.

Pastor Abe never was good at letting people leave the Church, and as his son's high school sweetheart, he'd seen me as one of his own. Sure, I'd gone to a few services, but once they began talking about Initiation, I stopped going, started making excuses. Cramps, a headache, too much home-work, Mom needed me. It wasn't too much later that Caitlin died, and I got pregnant, then left for good — Abe's threat the final push I needed to leave.

Never truly thought I could escape his reach. Once the Church decides you belong to them, they don't let go.

CHAPTER FIFTEEN

The blare of my phone's ring tone startles me awake, and I jump for it. It's louder than it's supposed to be, and I don't want to wake Mom.

"Need you for both shifts today. Can I count on you?"

It takes me a moment to place the voice and make sense of this new reality in which I work shifts. "Sure, Lola," I yawn. "Where's Kat?"

"Sick. That child catches everything that comes her way."

We end the call, and I check the clock. I have just enough time to visit the hospital's records department and come back to check on Mom before my shift starts. Should probably call ahead to the hospital first, but I don't have it in me. The more thought I put into it, the more likely I am to chicken out.

Mom's still asleep. I leave her a note by her bed, along with a fresh glass of water, a banana, and her phone so she can text me if she needs me, and head for the car. I grab Percy as I leave and buckle him into the front seat. I need all the emotional support I can get.

For the first time, I'm playing with fire. If there's a record of my daughter's death, that whisper of hope will be gone. If there's not, I'll be worse off than I am now.

The car starts without a hitch, and I take that as a good sign. The drive to the hospital is less than fifteen minutes at a normal speed, but I go slow and gentle, question myself with every lane change, and each click of the signal.

I pull into a spot in the visitor parking lot and waste a few more minutes I don't have to spare.

"Whatchya think, Percy? Am I opening an emotional can of worms here?"

He's a quiet companion, which I'm grateful for most of the time, but I could use a companion with an actual voice box at the moment. I could call Emmie — probably should — but I'm not ready. I started this alone. It feels right to continue it alone.

"Right. Only way through is through, right?" I roll the windows down a crack to give him a breeze . . . not that it'll help with the heat much. "Thank goodness you're a tropical plant, huh." I pat one of his wide, firm leaves and leave him to his car sauna.

The hospital isn't big, not like one of those almost-city-sized ones in Houston or Dallas, but it's big enough for our county's needs. A small maternity ward is on one end, and the emergency room is on the other. In the middle are specialist offices, and somewhere between the department that gives life and the department where some go to die is a woman named Eileen.

I march through the center sliding doors and find the information desk. A young security guard points the way to the elevator bank, and I take it to the third floor. Not sure why, but I expected the records department to be in a basement, not an office with a view.

The room is white, with bright lights and big windows, and clear glass separating the small lobby from the rest of the department. A bell sits on the desk with a note to ring for service.

My palms are sweaty, but inside I've reached a calm sort of resignation. I ding the bell, and a voice from the back calls, "Coming!"

A woman hustles in, brushing off her slacks, reading glasses bouncing from a long chain against her blouse. "Can I help you?"

"I hope so. Is there a woman named Eileen who works here?"

She folds her arms across her chest. "Depends. You a lawyer?"

I shake my head no.

"Work for a lawyer?"

No, again.

"Hired by a lawyer to deliver documents?"

"No, I'm here purely on a personal basis. Janie sent me."

She relaxes her shoulders and holds out a hand. "Whew. You never know when these legals will come around, asking a bunch of annoying questions. I try to not be here. I'm Eileen."

I shake her hand. It's refrigerator-cold. "Darla. Janie said you'd be able to help me research some old records?"

She shakes one finger at me. "Can't do your work, but I can pull anything older than ten years without a formal request. One month at a time."

"The record I'm looking for is January, sixteen years ago."

She makes a note on a small notepad. "Department?"

I clear my throat. "Maternity or morgue. I'm not sure which one."

Her expression changes, a slight raise of her brows, a slight thinning of her lips, a slight prejudgment I'd hoped I could avoid. She hmms, taps her lip. "Be right back."

I pace while I wait. No one else is here, and from the looks of the small lobby, it doesn't appear that this department gets many visitors. It has library vibes, and even though everything about the room screams I'm-an-open-book, I want to keep my voice quiet and make sure my steps aren't heard.

When I was little, Dad used to tell me stories about his Atakapa heritage. His blood was diluted enough that he couldn't legally claim that heritage, but his great-uncle had been half Atakapa. We used to practice walking through the forest silently, a rolling step from heel to toe, each new step tested softly before commitment, the simple act of walking a communion with the wild in which we lived. I do that now, rolling my sneakers from heel to toe, pacing silently as one of my ancestors, both from a respect for the room and from a need not to be discovered.

Eileen has no such reverence.

"I'm back," she singsongs and slaps two dusty binders on the counter. One is black, the other is baby blue. "These be the bibles from that January. More accurate and more detailed than anything you'll find online, but that's just 'cause I wasn't working here then. I've been here about five years and am working my way backward, getting everything in these books up on the DSHS site." She grins. "Once I get all these records online, there'll be no excuse for anyone to come in here and bother me."

"I—"

"Oh, don't apologize. Next time, bring coffee. You can use that table over there."

And with that, she disappears back into her stacks.

"Alrighty then," I breathe, heft the two binders into my arms, and carry them over to the small, square table in the corner.

I start with the baby blue binder first, assuming it holds the maternity records. I flip to January 17 and trace the entries with my finger. Seven babies were born on January 17 in Polk County. Three boys, four girls. One to a single mom. All healthy.

I scan through the rest of the maternity ward records — maybe there's an extra section for the Angel's Cradle babies.

January 20, a baby girl was found in the Angel's Cradle at 6:15 in the morning. The notes state that she was immediately taken to the NICU and treated for opioid withdrawal symptoms.

I exhale and glance away, my relief quick and quiet — with a stowaway of something heavier. Not my baby.

I'm tempted to follow the notes on this baby Jane, but I'm limited on time and there's no way this could be my girl. I close the book and push it to the side.

Choosing a black binder for death records seems a little cliché, but I'm not sure what other color would be appropriate.

I hold my breath, flip to the middle of the book, and start working my way to January 17.

At the top of each page, scrawled in barely legible writing, are column titles. Name, time of death, notes, and the signature of the attending physician. Some days are blank. Others have a few entries. In a county this small, the cycle of life and death can't be too overwhelming.

January 17

The page is blank.

I hear my breaths, fast and short, and my body feels heavy and sticky and not-quite-mine, as if I'm wearing a rented diving suit. I flip the page, scan the next, the next, the next, the next.

No Jane Does. No John Does. No babies. Nothing but normal deaths for the rest of the month.

The room tilts. Trina said . . . she said . . . she definitely said . . .

"Eileen?" My voice comes out shrill, startles me. I spin around, leap for the bell on the counter. "Eileen?" I call again.

She rushes from the back, her glasses hanging on the end of her nose.

"Is there another book somewhere? For Angel's Cradle babies? Or another book that lists Jane Doe babies? Or . . ."

She's shaking her head, slowly, her lips pressed together in a line perfect for a funeral.

"Please." I need her to have a different answer, any answer. Some evidence that my little girl existed, even for the briefest of moments.

"Everything that was recorded is in those books. If it's not in there, it wasn't recorded." Her voice still has that tone of these-are-the-facts, but softer, more cautious. She's walking through the forest, taking each step as gently as she can, so as not to disturb my wild.

"But . . . if she's not in there . . ." My hand slaps over my mouth, barely blocking a gasp's escape. I grab my bag, sling it over my shoulder, and hand Eileen the two binders. "Thank you for your help."

I hurry out of the department, take the steps, not the elevator, and head down, half-run to my car. The door swings open with a gush of hot air, and the vinyl seat burns the undersides of my legs, and the steering wheel is hot enough to melt flesh, and I don't care. Trina said she took her to the hospital, but she never made it.

Trina lied.

CHAPTER SIXTEEN

Lola gives me hell for being ten minutes late. She stalks off into the kitchen after giving me a good ol' fashioned Come to Jesus talkin' to, and I'm reminded of my own grandmother, the one time she found me with stolen lip gloss from the corner store. I should feel ashamed and abashed, but it's just the right verbal assault I needed to feel seen.

Tuesday night at the bistro isn't too crazy, but Kat's absence is felt. Between manning the bar and delivering meals from the kitchen — room temperature when they're supposed to be hot — I'm fairly certain my days at the bistro are numbered. The growing weight of tips in my apron, even if a bit skimpy, keeps my feet hustling.

The place empties around nine, and I clean up the bar, the espresso machine, vacuum under the tables, and clock out.

Lola manages to spare me a sideways glare. "Not too shabby tonight. You'll do in a pinch."

"Really?" The question goes high-pitched.

She smirks — first time she's approached a smile since I met her. "Be on time tomorrow."

"Yes ma'am." I resist the urge to salute her and hurry out of the restaurant, thankful I still have my skin and my job.

The sunset bruises the sky; all the pinks have sunk below the horizon, and all that's left are dark purples fading into blue and dusk.

My feet turn toward home, but there's a tickle at the back of my spine. The cemetery is at my back, down the road, about a ten-minute walk.

The hospital has no record of her, but could she still be there? In the hospital plot?

I've already turned around and started walking in that direction. The cemetery is on the outskirts, between the town and the forest. The iron gates at the entrance never used to be locked. I test them now with a rattle, but Henry has them bolted tight. Wonder if Emmie has a key . . .

I rest my elbows on the stone wall, heat from the day radiating through my skin. The wall is short enough that I could climb over, but the last thing I need is a trespassing fine on top of everything else. I walk the perimeter, trailing my fingers against the rough stone to guide my way, turn the first corner, and then the second. The moon peeks above the trees, a fingernail moon, as Mom called it when I was little. Not much light on it, but it makes me feel I'm not so alone.

The woods are close now, close enough that I see why the original settlers to the town built the cemetery here — almost as a defensive wall between them and the trees. The tribe.

The reservation's on the other side of the river, which runs right through the trees. I can't hear it from here — it's still a couple of miles off — but in the dark, by myself, I can almost put myself in the townspeople's shoes from two hundred years ago.

My fingers graze against rough wood, not stone, and I jerk back. An old gate is set into the stone. I dig out my phone and turn on the flashlight.

Honeysuckle, jasmine, and spiderwebs cover the door and wrap around its old latch, rusty and covered in dust and dirt. I clear a space, disturbing sleeping spiders from their webs, and press my thumb down on the heavy iron lever. The door unlatches and falls a few inches inward with a grating groan. I pull away the rest of the vines and push on the door until I gain enough space to squeeze through.

I'm in the oldest section of the cemetery — back in the original tombstones. The earliest grave I ever found was from 1818, a Mr. Thomas Kaminski, back before even the Church was founded. Caitlin and I had organized a town-wide scavenger hunt in high school to raise funds for homecoming, and a picture of giving Kaminski's grave a thumbs-up was the final item.

Here, many of the stones are worn smooth with nothing but a letter or a half-gone date to mark a final resting site. The light from my phone casts weird shadows over the graveyard, and it's obvious why so many horror movies either start or end in a cemetery.

I pick my way over headstones — some nothing more than an iron cross stuck in the ground or a pile of rocks — and try to stick to a path so I don't walk over any bodies, but it's an impossible task. The layout is irregular and, even when the headstones start getting younger, it's still a grisly maze. Family plots are clustered together, along with benches and sculptures donated in someone or other's memory. But where would those without families, without names, be?

The cemetery isn't big, but it's big enough and daunting to search every headstone with nothing but a flashlight. The moon falls further away in the sky, and the stars start to freckle the night. It's time for me to give up. Go home. Check on Mom. Either the hospital's plot isn't here, or it isn't marked.

I retrace my steps to the old gate, hidden beneath the honeysuckle unless you know what you're looking for, and gently lift the latch into place. The walk home is quiet, and Main Street is pretty much asleep. No streetlights in a town this size, just a few decorative black iron lampposts on the street corners, with a tiny flame flickering like an oil candle.

I'm not sure what I expected to find at the cemetery . . . not evidence of her but a feeling that she was somewhere near . . . that she had been resting, safe and snug, exactly where I thought she'd been and where Trina had said she was all this time. But this not knowing . . . it's like I can't see the ground or my shoes are too big for my feet. I've been clumsy with my life, more willing to run than to sit and think.

What does it mean that there's no record of her?

Any number of answers could suit, but I need the truth. I want it now, but my wants have to wait. If Trina is lying, she's been lying for a decade and a half, and there's no reason for her to start confessing. If she's not, I risk a relationship with the only nurse Mom can afford.

I should have asked Trina more questions. I should have demanded to see my daughter. I should have stayed and figured out how to own my life, rather than it owning me.

The porch light is on when I get home, and sitting on the doormat is an unmarked envelope. I look around, but no one is there, and I gently open the unsealed flap.

Inside is the other half of Caitlin's paper. My stomach clenches. I was right. Caitlin gave one of our friends the other half of her last message, and for some reason, they want to remain anonymous.

* * *

I unlock the door and walk inside, and the first thing I notice is the scent.

Not musty, barely covered up with Lysol, but something more. Something . . . citrus. Trina's been here today to check on Mom. I drop my bag by the front door and make my way to Mom's room — a shadowy sense of concern that Trina's been here hastens my steps.

Mom's room is dark, the curtains pulled closed. Not how I left them this morning, with a crack of morning light shining in should she wake. The banana and water are untouched, and not a wrinkle on the sheets suggests movement. Trina's orange and lavender soap is stronger in here, as if I missed her by mere minutes.

I creep closer. Mom looks as if she hasn't moved since I checked on her this morning, and my heart freezes for a microsecond, then rushes to catch itself back up.

"Mom?" I whisper and brush her cheek. Her skin is warm, but not feverish. However, she doesn't so much as flinch or flutter her eyelids at my touch.

I send Trina a quick text to see if she noticed anything out of the ordinary, or gave her any medicine to help her sleep. I'm not loving that the one person I have to depend on to take care of my mother is a person I'm not sure I can trust.

She doesn't text back — she calls. I duck out of Mom's room and answer.

"Hey, hun," she begins. "I was just there. She woke for a few minutes, but seemed in pain, so I gave her a little shot of morphine to keep her comfortable."

Morphine? My blood pressure shoots into the unhealthy range. "She said she didn't want to take any of that stuff."

"I know, I know, but we need to do what's best for Suzanne."

Her tone is so placating that I want to reach through the phone and grab her by the neck.

"I must insist that we respect Mom's wishes." I force my own tone to remain smooth, no hills, valleys, or potholes. "And now that I'm here, any medical decisions need to be approved by me."

Trina's pause is thick. "Darla . . . Suzanne signed a lasting power of attorney that allows me to make all medical decisions for her should she become incapacitated. I'm so sorry."

Each of her words is a heavy drop. A bag of marbles from somewhere high, or melted steel, or mercury. They hit with the same destructive impact.

"What?"

"Well, at the time, we didn't know if you'd ever show back up and . . ."

She lets the rest of that sentence trail off. There's no need to finish it.

"I'm happy to ask for your input from now on but, ultimately, I'll do what's in Suzanne's best interests."

I sink into the couch.

"I know this is hard for you," she continues, but all I can hear is a bunch of blahs.

I pull the phone away from my ear, wait for a break in her words. "I have to go. We'll talk later."

And I don't care if I am screwing up a relationship. I end the call and immediately start searching Google for how long morphine stays in the system. Four to six hours until the effects wear off. Which means I'm sleeping in Mom's room. I do not want her waking up alone after being drugged against her wishes.

I check her over, her breathing, her color. I don't know what I'm looking for, but I feel I have to do something.

A spot of red on her throat catches my attention. I turn on the overhead light and gently put pressure on her chin to get her to turn her head.

She's got a rash on her throat. It's slightly raised, red, and covers half her neck. From the image searches, it looks like a contact dermatitis, but I'm no expert. I take a picture and send it to Trina, with a question mark following the image. She doesn't respond immediately, but I can tell she's seen the message. A few minutes later, she responds with, *Nothing to worry about. Put some cortisone cream on it and let me know if it changes or spreads.*

"Helpful," I mutter, but do what she asks before I make a pallet on the floor with my old sleeping bag, cushioned by a few blankets and the quilt from my bed, and then get out the two halves of Caitlin's paper. Mine has a thousand crease lines. Whoever had the other half only has three simple folds. I match the torn edges, and a small thrill tickles at my chest as the lines and letters meet. I tape it together and stand back to look at my handiwork.

There is indeed a set of letters that becomes the focus — A.S. But connected to those via a single, horizontal line are another pair of letters — K.S. A little drawing of a bird, wings outstretched, rests above each set.

My heart beats at the back of my throat. Hard thumps that make it hard to swallow and impossible to breathe.

These are indeed initials — of Abe Smith and Karen Smith, COES pastor and pastor's wife, otherwise known as Tristan's parents.

Mom's still sound asleep, so I dart to my room to grab my yearbook, and come right back. An hour or two later, I have multiple matches for multiple initials, but only a few that make sense.

Abe and Karen are obvious, and the line going above Abe to the J.S. initials might be Abe's father or grandfather . . . both named John Smith. Abe and Karen are connected to T.S. below, Tristan, but Karen's line is connected to him with dots, rather than a solid line like Abe's. Other dotted lines connect to Abe's, but the initials either have multiple matches . . . or none.

But Abe's father, or grandfather, is connected by solid, double lines to almost every initial that's on Abe and Karen's level. And some offshoots below.

Is this a family tree of Tristan's relatives? But why? Why would Caitlin do this, then tear it in half . . . and then disappear?

What did she discover?

I trace the lines around the page, but I'm no closer to identifying any names other than Tristan's immediate family.

I need a town register. Or better yet, a history of the Smith family and a registry of Church members — current and, more importantly, past. I need to find the connections, what the connections mean. And how any of this is related to Caitlin's death and the threat of another.

I need to brainstorm with whoever dropped this off. I have half of the secret. They must have the other half.

"Darla?"

Mom's voice is groggy and hoarse, but at least she's awake.

I drop what I'm doing and go to her side, brushing a bit of her bangs away from her forehead.

"How are you feeling?"

She opens and closes her mouth. "Thirsty."

I hand her the water glass from beside her bed, and she sips it gratefully.

"Tell me what happened." It's a command, because I'm not asking. I'm demanding to know how I need to move forward with Trina.

She glances at the clock — how is it already two in the morning? — and her eyebrows furrow.

"Trina came by," she starts, but sounds confused. "Made me some tea . . ." She rubs at her throat as if it hurts.

I pull her hand away from her neck and check her rash. It's mostly gone. "And then?"

She raises both hands in an I-don't-know. "And then I woke up."

I give her a minute to wake up a little more. "I called Trina. She said she gave you some morphine. Were you having pain?"

Mom's eyes go wide. "No more than usual. She did what?"

"Morphine, Mom. She also said you'd given her power of attorney."

Mom shakes her head slowly, back and forth. "I said I was thinking about it, but wanted to wait until things got worse. I'm fully capable to make my own decisions, and I wanna keep making 'em as long as I'm able."

I yawn. "That sounds more like you. What do you want me to do?"

She pats my hand. "Nothin', baby girl. I'll talk to Trina. Nothing but a misunderstanding. She means well, she surely does."

"You sure about that?" I ask her, and keep eye contact.

"I've known Trina since we were teenagers. We've been through a lot together over the years. You don't go through life like we have and not learn to trust each other. Sometimes, it's all we've got."

My mind reels, thoughts digging like roots through dry dirt, finally catching on something that holds. So Trina was around when Mom was in high school; they were teenagers together. But were they friends? "What did you go through together?" I finally voice the lingering question.

But Mom's closed her eyes, and her breathing's slowed. I cover her up, turn off the light, and drag my pillows and quilt back into my bedroom, along with my research and Caitlin's notes. There's only a few hours left until morning, but I'm not sure I'll be able to sleep.

One of my friends is lying to me. The rest can't stand me. My mother is dying, and her one lifeline drugged her against her wishes. Caitlin was likely murdered, and someone else in town has a target on their back.

CHAPTER SEVENTEEN

My shift doesn't start until eleven, and even though I barely got any sleep, I'm wide awake, energy buzzing through my veins like a shot of caffeine. I get Mom settled on the couch, kiss her cheek, and promise to check in before my shift starts.

The garage that Karl still works at is on the edge of town. It looks as if it's sprouted from a scrapyard, and a jungle of metal, car parts, and vines weaves through the side yard. The garage itself is a sturdy, corrugated metal shed with a rusting roof. A Shania Twain song pours through the open, sliding doors, and inside, there's a truck raised on some stands and a pair of legs sticking out from underneath, toes tapping in the air to the beat.

I wait for the end of "Man, I Feel Like a Woman," let Shania give me one last boost of fake courage, then walk toward the man under the car. "Karl?"

His toes stop tapping, and his legs tense. There's no answer, but then he crooks his knees and slides out from under the car.

Grease smudges his cheek, just above the line of his beard, and his ball cap is turned around backward. It doesn't distract from his bloodshot eyes, though, or the frown half-hidden under his overgrown beard.

"Busy," he says when he sees it's me, and slides back under the truck.

"It's about my car," I say, not truly lying. He could find plenty wrong with my car.

"Bessie?" He pulls himself back out from the underbelly of the Ford he's working on.

My stomach warms a bit. "You remember?"

He shrugs as he hoists himself up, resting his arms on his knees. "Ridiculous name for a car."

"You named yours Bruce."

His eyebrows raise, and his frown lessens by a fraction. "Springsteen. Bruce Springsteen."

I allow a smile to spread across my face. He knows I'm teasing, but it's been a while.

"What's wrong with her?" He nods toward the outside, where I've left Mom's car.

"What's not wrong with her?" I mutter, but he hears. "She's clunky, and makes this whining, rattling noise whenever I start her from cold."

"Of course she's clunky. She's almost as old as we are." He stands and brushes his hands off on his jeans. "When's the last time you had her looked at?"

I feel like a parent admitting they skipped their kid's annual check-up.

"Few years ago . . ."

Karl doesn't waste a second before he's heading toward my car, muttering under his breath.

He doesn't ask before he pops Bessie's hood. Doesn't need to. He's my car guy, and I've never had another. It's odd how some things can seem so foreign, so difficult, and others are like a key fitting into a greased lock.

I stand next to him for a few minutes, listening as he explains this and that, both of us knowing I'm not going to retain any of the information. This is mine and Karl's foreplay. He's always been the quiet one, and it takes a while to warm up, but give him a car engine and vague descriptions of car noises, and he'll talk your ear off.

"Need a new gearbox," Karl finally says, taking off his hat and scratching at his receding hairline. "Timing belt, tires, head gasket . . . Damn, Darla, might as well sell her to me for parts."

I hold out my hands, palms up. "Can't afford another one. What will it take to get it running a bit longer? Worried she's going to give out on me at any second."

He scratches at his head with his hat, then puts it back on, bill forward so his eyes are shadowed. "Why? You leavin' again?"

I shake my head slowly. "No. Not for a while. But I need to get a job so I can pay off some of our bills, and I'm gonna need my car to get me there."

He nods, evaluating my reasoning. "I'll do labor for a couple of six-packs. Parts will cost you, but I'll see if I can find used that'll work." He looks around the yard, as if deciding which of his metal treasure boxes will best suit.

"I'll owe you more than a couple of six-packs," I say, trying not to let my emotions come through. If Karl is scared of anything, it's emotions.

He just nods and adjusts his belt. "You gonna tell me why you're really here?" His voice is molasses, slow, sticky, and bitter.

I press my lips together, not wanting a repeat of the other day, and take a deep breath. "Someone dropped this on my front porch last night." I pull Stone Adams's folder out of my bag, open it up, and hand Caitlin's taped notebook paper to Karl. "You guys are the only ones I told about it, so she had to have given one of you this half." I tap the paper.

He frowns and brings it closer to his face, and I bite my tongue as he leaves greased fingerprints on the sides. He's careful not to cover any of the initials, so no harm done.

"Any thoughts?" I prompt.

"What am I looking at?"

102

"My theory is that Caitlin found connections to the Church." I point to the birds above the J.S. and K.S. initials. "Connections maybe no one wanted out in the open."

I feel, more than see, his gaze flick to mine, and my insides flinch. I don't want to upset him again, but I need to know. "Did Caitlin give this to you?"

He's gone quiet, and his grip tightens on the paper. I place my hand on his wrist, and he doesn't move away.

"I need to know," I say, my voice sleeping-baby-quiet. "Caitlin gave two of us one-half of a secret. And then she disappeared. We owe it to her to figure out why."

Karl's tense under my hand, but he finally lets out his breath and hands the paper back to me. "She didn't trust me with this secret. But . . ."

He pauses, and I know he's not doing it to force me to hang on his words, but I still do.

". . . these initials, here?" He points at the M.W. on the lower right side of the sheet. "That's my mom. Marlene Waters." His finger follows the vertical line down. "And that's me."

My brain's buzzing, and I grab the sheet from him and look at what he's talking about. "You sure?"

"M and W with an offspring of a K ain't all that common. Sure, I might be wrong, but I doubt it. I was one of only about five last names starting with a W at graduation, and two of 'em were my cousins."

I breathe in through my nose. "Thanks, Karl. I definitely owe you more than a couple of six-packs."

He waves me away. "Just . . . keep me updated. I wanna know why we're on that sheet."

I clap him on the shoulder, giving him a small squeeze. "Of course." And walk back around Bessie to the driver's side.

Karl lets the hood fall with a thump, listens closely as I start her up, and nods at himself. "Definitely the gear box. Oh, and Darla?"

I hang my head out the window and raise my eyebrows at him.

"About the other day . . ."

It's my turn to wave him away. "We're good. I had it coming."

He gives me a single nod and shuffles back into the garage without another glance.

I back out of the drive, check my directions to Ivan's real estate office, and head that way. I'm all guesses at this point, but by my reasoning, it had to be either Karl or Ivan who had the other half of Caitlin's message. Emmie would have told me, and Shelly and Tristan are too close to the Church.

Ivan's office is a standalone, one-story brick building, about the size of a large house, and it couldn't be further opposite to Karl's garage. *Trinity Falls Real Estate* is engraved into a white marble sign, tastefully bordered by low-growing wax myrtles and landscape lights. Ivan's Jeep is parked out front, in a spot with a sign that says *Reserved*, and I let out a sigh of relief. I'd hoped that he wasn't out with clients, not this early in the day.

A wave of cold, air-conditioned air breezes out as I walk through the glass doors. A welcoming lounge is set up, all whites and creams and healthy potted plants, and a secretary mans a curved desk blocking the way to the rest of the office. He's a young guy, maybe around nineteen, dressed in a business shirt and tie.

"Welcome to Trinity Falls Real Estate. Do you have an appointment?"

"No, I—"

"Great, I can hook you up with one of our available agents." He reaches for the phone.

"Actually, I'm here to see Ivan."

His entire demeanor shifts, moving from friendly agent to curious gossip. He looks me up and down, eyebrows raising slightly. "And who may I say is visiting?"

"A friend." I have no idea if Ivan will want to see me, or if he'll have his skinny bodyguard turn me away if he knows it's me.

The young man gets on the phone and relays the message, and a few moments later, Ivan comes down the hallway, his steps brisk until he sees me. He doesn't even make it into the reception area. Just lets out a big huff and gestures me forward with a "shoulda known," under his breath.

I follow him down the hallway, and can feel his secretary's eyes drilling holes into my spine the entire way. Ivan leads us into a large office, complete with corner windows stuffed full of potted plants. He sits behind his desk, leans back, and steeples his fingers.

I turn my back to him and focus on the plants instead. "This mother-in-law's tongue is getting too much light." I lift a leaf that is starting to yellow. "She might be happier in the corner behind your desk." I turn to face him and nod at the corner currently occupied by a set of golf clubs.

"I'll take it under consideration. Wouldn't want her to be unhappy."

I nod, press my lips together, and take a seat in front of his desk, even though he hasn't asked me to sit. He's got a cross between a smirk and a grimace pasted to his lips, and I'm not sure which is going to win out.

"Nice office." I look around. "Who woulda thought—"

"Cut the crap, Darla." Ivan leans forward, props his elbows on his everything-in-its-place desk.

It's my turn to huff. Ivan may have been calm waters back in high school, but stir up those waters, and it takes a long time for them to find their balance again. I stirred up those waters a long time ago, and it doesn't look like I've made things better by coming back. "Fine. Did you drop this off at my house last night?" I pull the paper out of its folder in my bag and hand it to him.

He doesn't take it from my hand, doesn't even look at it. "Why are you so interested in this? Caitlin's dead."

"You are not this callous, Ivan." I let the paper fall to his desk, my fingers lingering a second too long before pulling back. My jaw tightens. "I know you're pissed at me, but let's be grown-ups for a second."

He clears his throat and shoots me a glare full of ice and thorns, but he holds out a hand, gesturing for me to continue.

"Someone hired a private investigator to track me down. Someone who knew I had information that no one else did, and someone who also sees a connection between what happened with Caitlin, and what's coming now."

His expression is entirely unreadable, but even that gives me encouragement. He's not disbelieving me. He's listening.

I take a deep breath. "Was it you?"

His expression doesn't change. He doesn't answer.

"Please, tell me." My voice goes quiet, but not to beg. I reach back in time, trying to touch the Ivan I used to know. "Don't make someone else suffer because you're mad at me."

"I'm not mad at you, Darla." His expression finally breaks, softens. "Disappointed, sad, shocked, yeah? After you left and we got news you were alive, it took a hot minute. Knowing I'd never see you again? Knowing you left because of something you couldn't share with us? Knowing you were alone, wondering if you were safe?"

I'm not expecting Ivan's eyes to glisten, and when they do, I reach out my hand to him, but he doesn't take it. He straightens, puts the wall back up.

"I'm not sure I'm glad you're back, yet. And until you figure out what you're doing here, the real reason you came back, I'm not interested in getting to know you again." He pushes the paper back at me and stands. "I can't be a part of this."

I press my lips together and nod. "I understand," I whisper, shove Caitlin's code back into its folder, back into my bag, and leave Ivan's office without a backward glance, not even at his paid gossip behind the counter.

It's not until I'm back in my car that I realize Ivan didn't answer my question.

106

CHAPTER EIGHTEEN

Kat shows up to work with dark circles under her eyes, rubbing her temple as if she has a headache. I fill a glass with orange juice and gesture her over to the bar.

"Looks like you need some vitamin C." I push it toward her and watch her teenage jadedness fade and exhaustion take over her hard gaze. She empties the glass and hands it back.

"Thanks. Probably allergies." She rubs at her temple again, and I catch a red mark on the underside of her wrist.

"Rash?" I point at her wrist, which she flips over and rolls her eyes at, but the hairs on my arm have gone alarm straight.

"Recurring. Honestly getting sick of getting sick. Maybe I need one of those tribe guys to come over and smudge my house."

"Your mom wouldn't like that." I do my best to keep my voice even, but her rash is a twin to Mom's. Different location, but same color and texture. My thoughts spin around like muddy water. What are the odds that she and Mom have the same rash?

"Hah." Kat flashes a mischievous grin. "You've met my mom, huh? She's like, head cheerleader for the Church. Busy shift?"

The abrupt topic change takes me a second. "Three tables for lunch."

"Cool. Wednesdays are slow. Going to clock in and do my Bible study."

I watch her leave, her hair tied back in a no-nonsense braid today, with her green eyes and her dark hair and her height and her shoe size the same as mine. That spider is back in my brain, tickling ideas into formation, ideas there is no running from.

"Hey Kat. How old are you?" I call out across the restaurant, heart thudding against my breastbone as if I've just seen a curled-up rattler about to strike.

"What?"

"How old are you? When's your birthday?"

"Turned seventeen over the summer. Why?"

"I'm nosy," I say coolly, but my ribs shrink two sizes.

She scrunches her nose up at me, then decides I'm just another awkward adult, and marches into the kitchen.

I grab a rag and scrub at this one stubborn spot on Emmie's mirrored bar top. A distant ring at the front door announces a new customer, but it's too far away to matter.

The timing doesn't work, but people lie. Trina could have lied — made up a birthdate. Kat doesn't look seventeen. She looks fifteen, going on sixteen. The set of her mouth. The way her shoulders stay tight, like she's ready to bolt. Her clumsiness — awkward and careful all at once, as if she's afraid of being seen. That glance — restless, guarded.

My stomach flips. She looks like me.

"I think it's clean," a deep voice says out of nowhere, and I drop the rag, let out a yelp, and bite my tongue, all in one point five seconds. "Shit. Ow."

"God, you really haven't changed, have you?"

An arm reaches over the bar, fills a glass with water from the beer station, and hands it over.

He's still wearing his high school class ring. And that same dark and spicy cologne that used to send me into a spin.

I take the glass from his hand, careful not to touch him, and sip at it until my nerves calm. "And you still haven't learned to wear a bell around your neck," I finally say. "What are you doing here?"

He looks around the bistro as if he's seeing it for the first time. "Well, this is an eatery, is it not?"

"Kitchen's closed."

"Bar's not." He plops into one of the barstools.

"Shelly know you're here?"

He does a slow nod, and it gives me a chance to study the changes in his features. Shallow wrinkles at his eyes, gray in his stubble. It's a little like seeing a ghost — familiar, but also not.

"She says Dad gave you a hard time the other day." He stares a little too intensely, like he's trying to see if Abe left some emotional bruise.

I shrug. "I was asking for it, turning up back here. She really doesn't mind that you're here?"

"She'll be fine."

"Great. She doesn't know. You are going to get me run out of town. Shelly will be the one with the pitchfork."

He waves his hand at this. "She cares about you. Despite what she said the other day. Now pass me a cold one."

I give him a dead stare, ignore the part about Shelly. "You are not still drinking Pabst."

"When you find the right one, you don't let go." His eyes linger too long on mine, and in them, what I did to him by leaving shines strong.

It's only a few seconds that we're silent, that this huge cord of tension tightens between us, that everything that should have been said, could have been said, is somehow transmitted, words that need to be said . . . and can't.

I break the cord, turn around, and grab a can of Blue Ribbon from the small mini-fridge under the bar and a frosted glass from the freezer. When I face Tristan again, he's not looking at me but across the room, at Kat, curled up at a back table, studying a book.

"She reminds me of her."

"Who?" He can't mean me. I plop his can and glass on the counter.

"Kat. Reminds me of Caitlin. Remember how she used to study her Initiation book as if her life depended on it?"

"You can tell what she's studying from over here?"

He turns back to me and wraps his hands around the cold can without popping the tab. "She's at the Church a lot. Dad's promoted her from the Cherished class to the Chosen class. Thinks she shows promise."

"You guys are still doing that? I always thought grouping the youth group into different classes, playing favorites, created cliques. Toxic ones."

Tristan lifts a shoulder. "It does a bit. When Dad retires and I take over, I'll change things up. But for now, he believes competition is healthy and it spurs the other kids to keep growing spiritually."

"That's still the plan?" I lean forward on the bar and find myself exactly where I don't want to be — in a conversation with Tristan.

"Taking over? Yeah. Family legacy and all that."

I hmm noncommittally at him.

"What?"

"Nothing, just . . . I always thought you could get out of here. Do more."

He lets out a breath that's half scoff, half laugh, and slowly shakes his head. "You're still on that, after all these years?"

"You made good grades, star quarterback. You could have gotten a scholarship to a state school, easy. Done something different."

He covers my hand with his until I meet his eyes. "I'm happy, Darla."

It's a sharp sting in the middle of my chest when it should be a dull thud. I gently pull my hand from his, turn to the sink, and pull out a wine glass to hand dry away the spots. His

110

eyes are still on me, though, and thanks to the mirrored wall behind the liquor glasses, mine are still on him.

"You could have told me, you know," Tristan says.

I freeze, polishing cloth still stuffed inside the wine glass. "Told you what?"

"That you were pregnant."

I whip around, faster than my thoughts, but inside, everything is frozen solid. Words, so many words, are stuck in a ball at the back of my throat.

"I was waiting for you to tell me. I thought you would when you were ready. I would have stood by you, Darla."

Blood drains from my face, my fingertips. "How did you—"

"I knew you. Knew every inch of you. That's kind of a hard thing to hide."

"But—"

"I never told anyone else," he interrupts, "Not even Shelly. But tell me . . . please . . . what happened to it?" There's a hesitation in his question, as if he's not sure why he's asking, or maybe knows he shouldn't.

I take a deep, shuddery breath and place the glass on the counter. "Stillborn. It was a girl." I don't recognize my own voice, or how it is that this secret, this strangling vine, has suddenly been loosened. Let go.

Tristan's eyes shine. "That's why you left."

I don't say a word. How can I? I didn't come back for him. He's married. Happy, in his own words.

"I'm sorry you felt you had to handle that on your own. I was always there for you. I would have been there for you . . . no matter what." His hands have somehow found their way to mine again, and it should feel wrong, but it doesn't. Not in this moment. Not with what we shared. Lost.

"And I'm sorry I left," I whisper.

He squeezes my hand, then lets me go, and a big portion of the guilt I've been carrying around dissolves away. After pulling a fiver out of his pocket and placing it next to his unopened beer, he stands to leave.

"Hey, Tris?"

His eyes meet mine.

"You didn't happen to leave an envelope on my front porch yesterday, did you?"

The confusion that crosses his expression is real. I used to know every inch of him as well. "Wasn't me. I'll see you around, Darla. Give me a few weeks to get Shelly used to the idea of us all being friends again. I'll get her there."

In the background, Kat has a coughing fit, a dry, hacking cough that lasts from the second Tristan walks away to the second the door closes behind him with a faint ring of the bell.

CHAPTER NINETEEN

Kat left work early, still feeling ill. And, thanks to town gossip, I know exactly where she and Trina live. I cut wildflowers from the overgrown meadow, tie them with a strand of ribbon, and walk the fifteen minutes to their house under the pretense of delivering a thank you bouquet to Trina.

The conversation with Tristan remains lodged in my head, like a song stuck on repeat. I thought my secret was safe. Turns out, it never was a secret. Trina, Emmie, Tristan . . . who else knew?

And what did Trina do with our baby?

But something else keeps picking at my mind. Tristan said Kat reminded him of Caitlin. And her symptoms are fresh in my brain. Rash, headache, nausea. It's familiar — Caitlin familiar. And now, Mom familiar.

One thing, at least, has become clear. I need to know more about Trina.

Trina and Kat's gravel drive crunches under my feet. The garden around the house is pristine but surrounded by forest on all sides. A tall fence with warped boards holds back the ivy and the trees, and the whole thing looks like parsley stuck in crooked teeth. Effective, but just barely.

There's no car in the drive, meaning that Trina might be out, doing nurse, Church, or charity business. All things considered, not seeing her is likely better. Kat should be home, resting. She's bound to know things that could help me figure out what happened all that time ago, and what Trina and the Church are up to now.

They don't have a front porch. It's a simple concrete path lined with pots of fake flowers, up to a solid front door with a small window at the top. A patch of concrete at the base is almost completely covered with a welcome mat that reads *Blessings*. A navy-blue flowerpot that matches the front door sits to the right of the welcome mat and it, too, is full of fake, white daisies.

Everything looks new compared to Mom's house, but not well constructed. I knock on the front door, and the sound is hollow, like the door is constructed of cardboard rather than solid wood.

Horizontal blinds rattle at the window next to the door, and a Kat-sized shadow figure appears on the other side. The blinds part between two fingers, and a second later, the door unlocks and swings open.

"What are you doing here?" She looks past my shoulder as if I've brought someone with me.

Inside, the house is dark, and Kat's face is obscured.

"Came by to tell your mom thanks for taking care of mine." I hold out the bouquet. "And to check on you."

She crosses her arms, spreads her feet apart. "I don't need checking on." But she sways a little bit, catches herself on the door frame.

I lay my wrist against her forehead. "You're burning up. C'mon. Let's get you inside."

I don't wait for her to invite me, but guide her inside. It's a simple ranch-style house, with the front door in the middle, the living room and kitchen to the left, and, I assume, the bedrooms to the right. I lead her to the couch, a stiff, modern looking thing that's definitely designed for style and not comfort. The scent of Trina's soap takes over my senses, as if she's diffused it or turned the scent into incense.

Kat plops onto the couch and presses her hand against her forehead. She's shivering, and I fall back into my old take-care-of-Caitlin routines. I fluff her pillow, give her a gentle shove so she lies down, and place a pillow under her knees. On a wingback chair is a stylish throw, and I grab it, shake it out, and drape it over her. It still has the new store smell on it, as if it's never been used.

The kitchen is laid out in a fairly common-sense way — plates and glasses next to the sink, silverware in a wide drawer opposite the oven — so I'm back within a minute with a glass of ice water and a damp kitchen towel for her head.

She's already asleep. So much for wiggling information out of Kat.

I check her breathing, and it's steady, but her fever worries me. The towel I've dampened was cool when I brought it from the kitchen, but on Kat's head, it warms quickly.

Trina's a nurse, so there has to be a supply of ibuprofen or aspirin around here somewhere. I check the rest of the cabinets in the kitchen first, then move on to the bathroom cabinets. I'm all too aware that Trina could walk through the front door at any second. How would she feel about me digging through her cabinets? Though she certainly made herself comfortable in my home.

I hit the jackpot on the cabinet above the toilet. It's stuffed full of drugs — some prescription, most over-the-counter. If I were a pharmacist, I could probably tell exactly what each drug was for. Or if my phone had a data plan.

I find a bottle of ibuprofen, check the dosage, and confirm the pills inside the bottle match the description on the label. On the way back to the living room, I pass a partially closed door. I look from the bottle in my hand to the allure of the slight opening.

Kat can wait a few more minutes.

I toe open the door. It's dark, with any light that would have made it through the outside trees obscured by a closed curtain. I feel around for a light switch and blink once I flip it on to adjust to the brightness.

115

It's a little girl's room, or an old nursery.

There's a small, twin-sized bed in the far corner, next to a nightstand and a lamp with a pastel pink shade. The window hangs in the middle of the wall that the bed is nestled into. A plastic dollhouse stands on the floor in the corner opposite the door. I turn in a small circle, unable to make this room make sense. In the remaining corner of the room is an old-fashioned baby crib.

I creep to the edge. In it lies a ratty teddy bear, a blanket spread smooth, and a yellowed pacifier. It's not a big house, but could it be some sort of guest room? Kat's old bedroom? Why would it be left like this, like it's frozen in time?

And if Trina moved here six years ago, why does she still have a crib?

The crib could be a family heirloom. They could just not have the money to redecorate. Maybe Kat's hanging on to her old toys. But the pacifier . . . It's small. Harmless. Almost nothing.

But my eyes keep drifting back to it—worn rubber, yellowed plastic. A relic that doesn't belong here. Too old. Too quiet. Like it's been waiting. The whole room gives me heebies, and I'm about to leave to give Kat her medicine when I notice the book on the bed.

It's Kat's Initiation book, the corners worn, the white cover tinged yellow. I press my lips together, step further into the room, and pick the book up.

On the inside of the cover are two names, one written in black pen, the other in a fading pencil.

Kat.

And Caitlin.

I force myself to not drop the damn thing, and instead flip through the pages. The spine is broken, and a few of the pages are starting to come loose — looks like some water damage on the edges and on the back cover. On the top crushed corner, where the cover has worn away, is a spot of something that has stained the exposed cardboard brown.

I've never seen the contents of an Initiation book. Sworn to secrecy about the process, only initiates were allowed the information.

That alone had convinced me that Caitlin needed to part ways with the Church. But now, skimming through it, I feel ill. The Church of Elevated Souls runs on membership dues and fear. It teaches a message of exclusivity, an ownership of the secrets to salvation, to be shared only with the deserving. Dedication to the Church is the most frequent teaching — once you're in, you're in for life.

A small envelope falls out of the back of the book. The yellowed paper indicates it's from Caitlin's era, so I feel no shame in opening it and examining the contents.

It's an invitation. Exclusive, only extended to a chosen few, to receive the Blessing of the Chosen. A blessing that will make a girl's innocence holy and solidify her dedication to the Church.

I remember this — Caitlin talking about it. She was excited to be chosen, and nervous, and didn't know all the details. After, she didn't talk about it, wasn't allowed, and when I'd asked her, she'd simply walked away.

The day she left me that note is the day she decided to walk away from the Church. I'm sure of it. I'd gone to the forest to meet her, but she wasn't there. Not that day, or the day after, or the day after that. Or any of the days ever again.

CHAPTER TWENTY

I gently shake Kat awake so she can take the two ibuprofen tablets. She swallows them without question, takes a small sip of her water, then covers herself back up and turns over. I brush aside a strand of hair that's attached itself to her sweaty forehead. She shivers, the chill wracking her entire body, and I tuck her in a bit better.

"Okay, now what?" I whisper and scan the room. It's pristine with everything in its spot. The room, the whole house, looks like a showroom for a generic furniture store. Except Kat's room . . .

If Kat's room is in that state, what is Trina's like?

I hold my breath as I pass Kat's room. There's more to explore in there, but my time is limited, and I need to do what I came here for — to figure out if Trina is who she says she is.

There's only two more doors in the short hallway. One is the bathroom. The other has to be Trina's.

The door is shut. I try the handle, but it doesn't turn. Locked.

Who locks their bedroom in their own home?

The watery, anxious feeling that's been in my gut since the private investigator found me turns more solid. I stretch up on my tiptoes and feel at the top of the door frame, hunting for a key. Nothing but dust. The lock looks like one of those cheap, push-in ones, with a small hole to one side. If I can find a straight, thin piece of metal, like a nail or a knitting needle, I can unlock the door from this side.

I tiptoe back through the house to the kitchen, looking for anything that will work to push open the lock. The counters are mostly clean, except for Trina's soap making paraphernalia. In a drawer, I find an ice pick. Kat sighs on the couch and rolls over. I hold myself quiet until I'm sure she's still asleep, before hurrying back down the hall to Trina's room. The ice pick slides in, and a small pop indicates the lock's been released.

I open the door, and a scent I associate with old lady perfume escapes. You'd think Trina's soap scent would be stronger in here, but it's almost completely absent. The room is dark, curtains closed, just as in Kat's room, as if they don't even want the sun to spy. I find the light switch, and a lamp next to Trina's bed turns on.

It's a twin-sized bed, like Kat's.

And like Kat's, the bedspread — dusty pink with white lace around the edges — screams little girl.

Unlike Kat's room, though, Trina's is cluttered. Stacked flyers for the Church obscure a small writing desk by the door. There's a crucifix on every wall, as if she believes she needs protecting on all sides. An old-fashioned wall clock ticks by the door. And above the small bed, a suffering Jesus looks upon her pillow, but something about this Jesus looks different. I get as close as I can without kneeling on her bed, and in the dim light, it looks like someone, probably her, drew on curly eyelashes in Sharpie.

"Creepy," I mutter, then push aside my feelings and focus. If her Jesus is a girl, good for her. But Trina has deeper secrets, and I'm going to find them.

The nightstand is the most obvious place to start. I set the ice pick down on top of one of the stacks of flyers on the desk and pull out a skinny drawer. Inside is a COES branded Bible next to a purple vibrator. I pick up the Bible without touching Trina's toy and shake it, in case she's hidden any notes or information inside. A small piece of paper flutters out, but it's only information about the Feast. Trina's written a note on the back, a time of 10:14 p.m., and a room number I can only assume is in the Church's building somewhere. B101.

I pull out my phone, snap a photo, shove the flyer back inside the Bible, and shut the drawer.

Under the bed is next. I drop to my knees and lift the bedspread. Predictably, there's a small storage box nestled between the box spring and the floor. I check the open doorway behind me, then slide it out. There's no dust on top, which means it's been opened recently. I lift the lid, and I am met by the sight of countless dolls. Carved, wooden dolls. Twig dolls.

Exactly like the ones I've been left.

My heart squeezes as if there's a vine strangling it. There's no time to think through what this means. I take a picture, hear rustling from the couch, and quickly shove the box back into place.

From the living room, Kat groans. She's waking up. The medicine must have started working, which means I'm almost out of snooping time.

I thrust my hand under Trina's mattress. My knuckles brush against metal, and I yank out a spiral notebook. The first page has Trina's name and date, as if she were taking notes in a classroom. The date is a good forty years ago. Little scribbles and drawings decorate the page, and she's written the name of the class — *my Initiation* — in bubble letters.

I flip through the pages filled with Trina's cursive, perfect even back then. At the very back of the notebook is a rough sketch. Trina's no artist, but I can make out the outlines of a table draped in cloth with the COES logo on the side. Tall candles are on either side, and a starburst halo hovers above the table. Something lies on the table, along with faint words that may have been tried to be erased, but I can't quite make them out. I bring it closer to the lamp.

While the rest of the picture is done in blue pen, the shapes and the words on the table are in pencil. Under the dim light of the lamp, I can make out the letters *T-R* something, something *H*. Truth? I rotate it around, trying to get a different perspective of the shapes on the table. Long lines hanging off one end could be hair. There's a lump at the top of the table. A lump for . . . a face? Another bump at the chest . . . breasts? And then two rounded triangles at the end. Knees?

"Oh my God."

It's a drawing of a woman on an altar, knees spread.

"What the hell?" I slam the book closed as if it's Pandora's Box, and if I can keep the lid closed, I can keep the sickening truth inside. I don't want to keep this, but I have to. It's evidence . . . not of whether or not to trust Trina, but of how to protect Kat. I shove it into the front of my jean shorts, cover the bulk with my shirt, and stay there, on my knees, frozen for a few seconds.

Tears burn at the corners of my eyes, but there's no time to process. I need to get out of here before Kat wakes up, before Trina comes home, before I vomit. I get to my feet and adjust the bedspread so the wrinkles I've left fall out.

"Darla?" Kat calls from the couch.

I'm out of time, but this opportunity may not come again. I turn to the desk by the door and yank out the one and only drawer. A vase full of cuttings from a plant, maybe oleander, rattles back and forth on top, and I steady it before it can fall over, focusing on the contents of the drawer. Inside is a collection of pens and notepads, out of date announcements about Church activities. Not much of interest, but I snap a picture of the contents with my phone, just in case.

Only one thing sticks out to me — a hand labeled notebook titled *Her Savior*. Likely Trina's prayer journal or something like that. But the rest of this room is a creep-fest, and I don't want to leave anything unturned.

I take a quick peek, and Trina's room, Kat's voice, the too-quick scat of my heart . . . everything fades.

Taped onto the front page of the notebook is a picture of a girl, cut out from the yearbook. A picture from sixteen years ago, with a crown of thorns drawn in red ink across the girl's head. The picture doesn't show the bottom half of my outfit, but I wore a black-and-white striped skirt. Emmie was in line behind me, making funny faces to make me smile. The photographer didn't wait for me to be ready before he snapped the picture.

"Darla?" Kat's voice breaks through, and it sounds softer, as if she's off the couch, moving through the other side of the house.

I fumble the notebook, and it slides under the bed, out of sight, out of reach, no time to retrieve it before I'm caught. I slide the desk drawer closed, push in the lock on the inside handle, close it behind me, locked, just as I found it.

Kat's nowhere in sight.

I dart to the bathroom across the small hallway and turn on the faucet, so it sounds like I've washed my hands. My reflection shows a very pale version of myself. I pinch at my cheeks to bring the color back. "Coming," I hear myself call back, as if I'm somehow apart from my body, watching myself do normal things. Walk, talk, breathe.

By the time I get to the living room, Kat appears from the other side of the kitchen and the out-of-body experience is in full force. "How are you feeling?" My mouth moves, but inside I'm focused on *get out, get out, get out*. My other self is shouting at me, pushes my body, edges me to the door.

She shrugs. "Better, I guess. You didn't have to stay."

"Nothing better to do." I flash her a fake smile that physically hurts. It's strange, shock. Strange that everything can feel shut down, but the body continues to move. Do what's necessary to survive. "I gave you some ibuprofen to bring your fever down, but you really need to rest. Want me to call your mom?"

Does she notice how hollow I sound? How I am about to bolt?

Kat shakes her head. "She's busy organizing things for the Feast. I'll be fine, thanks. Just need to rest."

"Of course." I walk toward the door. *Not too fast, not too fast*. "Feel better."

I let myself out of the house. A few seconds later, I hear Kat's footsteps, then the deadbolt flip over.

Trina's notebook pokes at my belly, but I keep it hidden until I get home. I unlock the front door, and a sharp pang of dread pierces through the fog. The ice pick.

I left it on the nightstand in Trina's room.

I close the front door behind me and lean against it with my eyes closed, heart panic-racing. I left the ice pick. How could I be so stupid? Trina will know someone was in her room. She'll notice that her journal is missing. The creepy notebook is out of place. Kat will tell her I stopped by. She'll—

"Darla?"

In my panic, I didn't notice the scent of orange and lavender. My running-out-of-beats heart skids to a full stop, and I open my eyes.

"Trina!" I gasp, doing zilch to hide my surprise. Only this is more layered. This feels like I'm being hunted, like I'm staring down the crossbow. There's a more primal part of me that's starting to take over, to keep me safe. "You startled me." My voice sounds lower to me, does it to her? Where's Mom?

She cocks her head to the side. "I'm sorry, I thought you would have seen my bike parked outside."

Nope. Hadn't. Had been way too lost in my thoughts.

"Where's Mom?"

Trina's eyebrows raise, and my pulse spikes. "Resting. We had a nice talk, and she explained that she'd rather feel pain than be drugged out, for as long as she's able." Trina clasps her hands in front of her, looking for all the world like a nice, normal woman.

I move away from the front door, keeping my back to the wall, as if that will keep me safe. Because Trina is a threat; maybe she always has been. Is she sane? Is she dangerous?

"That's great. I'm glad you two talked." I move further from the door, edge toward the hallway where Mom supposedly is. "I'll check on her. You can show yourself out." I gesture at the door.

"Darla, is everything okay?" She takes a step closer, and I have to force myself to stand still.

"Fine. Great. Just busy, you know. As I'm sure you are. Bet you have lots to do for the Feast." Babbling. I'm babbling. She notices.

"Are you enjoying working at the bistro? I love what Emmie has done with the place, don't you?"

"Yup. The place has her signature all over it. Speaking of, I need to get ready for my shift. Thanks for dropping by." This time, I take the few steps to the front door and open it for her, not giving her a choice.

At least, not giving a sane person a choice.

I can hear my heart in my ears, like a drum, a loud beating coming from a dark wood, and she can hear it too. I know it.

She cocks her head at me again. "Are you sure you're all right?"

I nod, unable to speak, my mind shouting to be heard above the drumbeats. *Please leave, please leave, please leave.*

"I'll try to stop by later to check on Suzanne, but it may not be until tomorrow. Like you said, preparation for the Feast calls." She smiles an innocent smile, but I see her teeth. They're sharp as thorns.

She pats me on the arm as she passes, gets in her car, and drives away.

I close the door once I'm sure she's gone, lock it, and check it twice to make sure it's locked. Then run to the back door and check that one, too. The windows need to be checked. I need to make sure this house is locked down as much as possible, but first, Mom.

I still don't feel quite in my body, and the leftover adrenaline has me feeling nauseous. Mom's room is quiet and dark. Is she resting, as Trina said? Or something more?

I slink in, and she turns on her side and takes a deep breath. Sleeping. She's sleeping.

My legs go weak, as if the only thing that'd been holding me up for the past hour was pure nerves. I make it to the hallway before I sink to the ground, bury my face in my knees, let out the sob that'd been caught in my throat since Trina and Kat's, and it comes out as a muffled scream.

* * *

"I'm changing the locks."

It's a few hours later. Percy and I are tending to our patients on the front porch, and it just occurred to me that's one measure of control I can enforce. Keep Trina out, set boundaries, and protect us from the crazy nurse.

Percy looks like he agrees this is a good idea.

I finish trimming away the dead foliage from the hydrangea, who is doing much better in East Texas's tropical climate than she did in arid West Texas, go inside, and count the tips from my past few days at the bistro.

I'll need a lock for the front and back doors. Thankfully in our small house, the entrance points are few. A quick search on Walmart's site shows I have just enough saved in tips to buy the new deadbolt and lock-and-key set and still have enough to do a grocery run. I'll have to do the labor myself, but elbow grease has a good return on investment. I'll go later, after Mom wakes.

I check on Mom — still asleep — and head out to the gardening shed. All my work on the garden plot is starting to pay off. The weeds are gone, I've worked my blend of fertilizer into the clay-like soil, and I just need to put down the landscape fabric I found in the shed before I can start planting.

It's old, with bits of holes that moths or ants have eaten through. Not the most effective barrier against weeds, but it'll help, and I can't afford new. I roll out the fabric over the prepped soil, use Dad's scissors to trim the fabric to fit, and take time to pin it down with brittle, plastic stakes and sticks when I run out of those. Next up will be to plant cornflower seeds, leafy greens, and winter root vegetables. In a few weeks, I'll move the pansy seedlings I've started in the kitchen out here, and we'll have a nice array of flowers and organic vegetables to sell at the holiday and winter markets.

The timer on my watch buzzes my wrist, a reminder to check on Mom and get cleaned up for the Walmart run. I stretch back, popping my spine, and look toward the house.

Propped against the back door is a large piece of paper-like river birch bark. It looks placed rather than fallen, and even from my kneeling position in the garden, I can see the charcoal marks. I dust off my knees and tools, sit on the steps, take a big gulp of my used-to-be-iced tea, and only then examine the ashy-white bark.

I'd bet money that whoever drew this is the same one making the dolls. Did Trina make the dolls? Or had someone given her dolls, too? The sketch isn't nearly as impressive as the dolls, but drawing with charcoal on curly bark has to be difficult.

I hold the picture away from my eyes, then close up, and try to make out the swirls and lines. It looks like a picture of a neat row of stones, some rounded at the top. There's a fingernail moon in the sky and a figure.

What the *hell*?

I set my tea down with a clink, go into the house through the back door, and find Dad's old magnifying glass. The reading lamp next to Mom's place on the couch is the brightest spot in the room, so I set up there, flip on the light, and examine the bark. There is no doubt.

It's me.

This person saw me in the cemetery. Or followed me there.

The need for answers twists through me like a bramble vine — barbed, relentless, tearing as it grows. I turn off the lamp, stash the bark away in my nightstand drawer, and check on Mom.

She's still asleep.

"Mom?" I shake her to help rouse her. "I'm leaving the house. Do you need anything?"

No response.

"Mom?"

I check her breathing. It's steady. I check her pulse. It seems slow, but what do I know? I'm a plant doctor, not a people doctor.

"Mom, wake up."

She doesn't.

I turn around in a slow circle, looking for . . . what? Evidence that Trina drugged her again? Nothing in the bedside trash can to indicate used medicines, nothing written on the notepad Trina keeps in Mom's room to track her visits and observations. I check Mom's arms for any signs of injection marks, check her breath for odd odors, but again, nothing.

I text Trina. *What did you give Mom?*

Nothing.

No immediate reply. I stare at the screen, thumb twitching, willing it to buzz. Finally, it lights up.

Just a sleeping draught in her tea. Melatonin. All natural. She said she hasn't been sleeping well.

I check the kitchen and, sure enough, the water's still warm in the teapot, and there's an empty cup in the sink. The kitchen trash holds a lavender tea packet.

My phone pings again.

Trust me, Darla. I only want to help ease your mother through this difficult moment.

I don't answer. Instead, I call Emmie. "Can you come over and sit with Mom while I run some errands?"

"Everything okay?"

"It's better if I explain in person."

"Be there in twenty."

Emmie makes it in ten.

I barely wave hi to her before I'm out the door, begging the car to start, then hitting the highway for the short drive to Walmart. I need to get the locks changed before Trina can see what I'm doing.

Trina and I have different goals. I want Mom alive and lucid as long as possible. Trina seems to want her to sleep until she dies.

CHAPTER TWENTY-TWO

When I get back, Emmie is waiting for me on the front porch, arms crossed. "You wanna tell me what this is all about?" she shouts before I'm even out of the car.

I hoist my heavy Walmart sacks out of the front seat, lock the car, and prepare myself for Emmie's retribution for keeping her in the dark.

"How's Mom?" I pause on the first step. Ems towers above me, not something she's used to at five feet two, and I can tell she loves it.

"Sleeping. Spill."

I check the drive behind me, but it's empty. Clear of any listeners. I catch Emmie up on Trina drugging Mom against her wishes, how Trina claims she has power of attorney over Mom's medical decisions, but Mom says she doesn't, how I have zero trust in Trina's motives and, finally, how I plan to change the locks.

"Okay, but changing the locks? That seems over the top for something that just might be a communication issue." Emmie sits on the front porch step, and I plop beside her.

"It's complicated."

"Darla, when are you going to figure out that you can't keep doin' everything by yourself? You gotta let other people in."

"I'm not—"

"You are too," she snips, "and you've been doing it since you left town sixteen years ago. Maybe you were doing it before then, and the rest of us were too self-involved to notice. Bottom line? You need someone on your side." She spreads out her arms, as if to say, *Look, I'm right here.* "Despite what all the movies and stories tell us, it's not the strong who survive. It's the people who learn that we're stronger together who survive. Who thrive."

I blink, give her a look. "Did you just spout wisdom at me?"

"Shut it. I'm right. Now tell me what's really going on."

I huff. She's not wrong. And out of all the people in this town, besides Mom, I trust Emmie most. "This requires wine. C'mon."

Once we're settled inside, I've double-checked the deadbolts are locked and Emmie tosses me an are-you-sure-you're-okay look, I pull out my stack of evidence.

"Evidence of what?" Emmie asks, picking up the torn pages I've taped back together.

"Not sure. Definitely that Trina's not trustworthy. And something creepy is going on at COES." I pass Emmie Trina's journal, open to the back page sketch.

She studies it, then looks up at me with a frown. "Darla, what is this?"

"I found it at Trina's house."

She dips her chin to stare harder at me.

"Under Trina's mattress."

Her mouth opens slightly, as if she's surprised.

"Inside her locked bedroom," I mumble, suddenly very interested in the dirt under my fingernail.

She closes the journal and hands it back to me. "You're telling me that you broke into Trina's house and stole her diary?"

"I didn't break in. Kat let me in. But this is proof, Ems. Proof that COES is up to some bat-crazy shit."

She shakes her head. "No, this is proof that in Trina's *private* time, she likes to draw bat-crazy shit. In her *private diary*."

"In her *locked* bedroom!" My volume hits a level not good for Mom's sleep, and I settle back down to a whisper. "Who locks their bedroom in their own home?"

"She's probably just a very, again, *private* person. Whose privacy *you* violated, and for what? Because you don't agree with her medical treatment for your dying mother?"

Emmie moves to stand, pushing aside her wine.

I pull out my phone and open my photos. "Then explain all this — the dolls. The notebook called *Her Savior*. It had my picture inside it, Ems. My picture with a bloody crown of thorns drawn on it."

"Everyone in town has a collection of those dolls," she says, but her voice has lost its certainty. She takes my phone and zooms in on the pictures. "Though this is quite the collection. What's this red thing?" She points to part of the picture.

While all the dolls in the box are similar to the ones that have been left for me — natural, no color other than variations in the wood — there's one in the box with a splash of red. The photo is slightly out of focus, and the doll is partially covered by other figurines.

I shake my head. "I don't know. I didn't have time to look."

She thumbs over to the next picture, the one of the notebook. Tries to swipe to the next picture, but that's the last. "Where are the rest?"

"I didn't have time. Kat woke up."

"And you couldn't be caught breaking and entering in her mother's bedroom." The look Emmie gives me is Judgment Day stern, then she sighs and relaxes her face. "Why was your picture in this notebook?"

I shrug. "Again, no idea. I dropped it and got out of there as fast as I could."

"You dropped it. Back where you found it, yes?"

I shake my head slowly. "It slid under the bed."

She looks toward heaven and says a quiet prayer, something to the effect of *Lord, give me strength*.

"So not only did you do something totally shady, but you didn't cover up your shadiness?"

132

I nod. She rolls her eyes, then flips back to the first picture, the one of the flyer with the B one-hundred-and-one note. Before I can stop her, she shares it to her phone.

"What are you—"

She shoves my phone back at me, opens her message app, and attaches the picture to a text.

"—doing?" I blink, because apparently we're just hijacking each other's lives now.

"Texting Tristan. If this is a room at the Church, he'll know where it is. I'm telling him we want to see it."

"But—"

"Like I said," she interrupts, "you have to start trusting people. And you can't do this on your own. I have no clue whether you're paranoid or right, but something doesn't add up and we're gonna get to the bottom of this," she waves a noncommittal hand in the air, "whatever it is."

She clicks on her phone app and makes a call to *Hubby Bubby*.

Hubby Bubby? I mouth at her. She holds up a finger, but she can't hide her smirk.

It's a little mindboggling to see Emmie in this mode.

"Need you to install new deadbolts at Darla's, sweetcakes. Bring your toolbox. Can you be here in thirty?" She waits for him to confirm, makes kissing noises into the phone, and hangs up. "He'll be here in thirty minutes. Go check on your mom. When Henry gets here, we'll head over."

"Head over where? To Trina's?" I can't help it. My voice screeches.

"Yup. Sounds like we've got some crime scene covering-up to do."

* * *

Mom's condition hasn't changed. Whatever Trina gave her, it wasn't just tea and melatonin. I kiss her forehead and whisper my plans. She's a little clammy, so I cover her up with a light bedspread and open the windows. Trina's scent lingers, and it's not comforting — it's suffocating.

Should I stay? Going back to Trina's is crazy. But Emmie's right. I need to cover my tracks. I need to see what's inside that journal with my picture on it. I need to find out if Trina has anything to do with the private investigator and message I was sent. Because what if the message refers to Mom? Or to Kat? Or anyone else in Trina's reach?

I have to break into Trina's place to protect us.

I grab Dad's old toolbox from the utility closet, just in case Henry needs other tools while we're gone.

Emmie checks the stats from her app on the couch while we wait, and it's almost like we're in high school, just hanging out again.

I set the heavy wooden box on the coffee table, but when I let go, the handle breaks. The toolbox catches the edge of the coffee table, and screwdrivers and a crowbar and other I-have-no-idea-whats tumble to the floor. I barely miss having my toes flattened by an ancient hammer.

"Smooth, Darla," Emmie says without looking up, used to my clumsiness.

"Yeah, yeah," I say back, and kneel to clean up the mess.

Something wooden peeks out from under the lid. I pick up the box, and almost drop it all over again.

It's a half-finished doll.

I swat it away before I can stop myself. It rolls with a rattle under the couch and settles next to a dust bunny and a stale potato chip. I take a breath and reach for it.

"You okay?" This time, Emmie looks up from her phone, but I ignore her.

The figure warms in my hand. This one isn't as finely crafted, but the style is similar to the other dolls left for me to find. I walk into my room holding the doll and compare it to the others.

Emmie's footsteps follow.

About the same height, with the same blocked nose and square jaw. The doll from Dad's toolbox is uncarved from the waist down, but I flip it over, examine every inch. It's been sanded and prepared for carving, and at the bottom, right in the center of the wood, are four letters contained within a heart.

J.C.

D.C.

My initials. Dad's initials. I rub my thumb over the old chisel marks. Could this be a doll Dad had been making for me before he got sick?

I turn to Emmie to show her my find, and a faint memory trickles to me. Dad sitting by a campfire, whittling at a stick, telling me stories of his Atakapan family. Traditions and histories and old family tales. I don't remember much of what he said, but I remember the knife in his calloused hands, the glow of the flames dancing along his cheek, and the shine of the moonlight in his dark eyes.

"This was in Dad's toolbox." I state the obvious and let her examine it. "Could the dolls be coming from someone in the tribe?"

"Your dad was Atakapan, right?"

"Barely. Not enough to claim status."

Emmie's silent for a moment. "Why would someone from the tribe be leaving dolls around town for people to find?"

Hesitation bubbles within me. Should I tell her — that the dolls that have been left for me are messages? That someone, maybe Trina, maybe from the tribe, has been following me? I place the dolls back on the shelf in my bedroom and add Dad's to the collection.

"Maybe they're just messing with us." I shrug, the confession lodged in my throat. Emmie already thinks I'm paranoid. If I tell her I'm also being followed by a tribe member, she'll be convinced.

A knock at the front door announces Henry, who greets Emmie with a kiss and an enthusiastic ass-grab. We show him the locks to be installed, wave goodbye, and walk the fifteen minutes under the lowering sun in silence.

"So, what's the plan?" Emmie asks as we approach Trina and Kat's road.

"I'll just say I must have dropped my wallet somewhere in the house and ask to take a look. Think that'll work?"

Emmie shrugs. "You're the felon, not me."

"This isn't a felony."

"Fine then, misdemeanor. Felony sounds better. It's more dramatic."

I elbow her in the ribs.

"And what is my role in this escapade?"

"Distract Kat."

"Distract the disturbed, Church obsessed teen. Got it." She dramatizes a shiver and, this time, dodges my elbow.

I take a breath and knock on Trina and Kat's front door. Inside, the lights are off, and no footsteps approach. I knock again, but unless Kat's refusing to answer the door, no one's home.

"Hmm . . ." Emmie mutters and stalks off toward the side of the house. A few seconds later, she's pushing through the bushes at the side of the house and jiggling the window.

I shake my head and lift the flowerpot that matches the front door. Underneath is a key.

"Ahem." I clear my throat, loudly, and dangle the key in the air.

Emmie rolls her eyes. "Fine, if you want to do things the easy way."

I insert the key, turn it over, and open the door with another knock. "Kat? You home?" I call out. "It's Darla. We're just checking on you. Found your key by the front door."

No answer. I look back at Emmie, shrug, and we both enter the house, shut and lock the door behind us.

Unlike Emmie, I don't waste time gawking at the looks-staged living room. I go straight to Trina's bedroom, pull the Allen wrench I grabbed from Dad's toolbox out of my back pocket, and unlock the door.

Except there's no click of the door unlocking. I try the doorknob. It twists easily under my hand.

I was sure I locked the door when I left earlier.

A tremor climbs through me like a twisting vine, coiling around my heart, gripping tight and refusing to let go. I stumble back a step.

This isn't Trina's room.

I let the door open the rest of the way on its own.

"Did you get it unlocked?" Emmie joins me at my shoulder. "Is this Trina's room?"

My lungs are tangled up in the vine's grasp. "It was," I rasp. And step inside.

Gone is the sad eyelash-Jesus above her bed. Only the clock and one crucifix remains.

"What do you mean?"

The desk has been organized into neat piles. The curtains have been pulled back, and the blinds have been opened to let in the dying sun.

And the ice pick is no longer on the nightstand.

I drop to my knees beside the bed and toss the bedspread out of the way.

"The box is gone. And—" I turn the flashlight on my phone and shine it in all corners under the bed. "So's the notebook."

I turn back and look at Emmie. There's a look on her face that I'm not sure how to read.

"Are you sure you were in here earlier, Darla?"

"I took pictures. I showed you pictures. I have Trina's diary."

"But no pictures of this room. Just pieces of paper. A notebook. And nothing in that diary identifies Trina."

"You read through it already?"

"Disturbing shit in there, but anyone could have written it."

I shake my head, trying to get rid of the buzzing sound that's growing louder and louder.

"Look. There was a crucifix hanging right here. There's still a nail . . ." The wall is smooth. No sign that anything ever hung there. I whip around to the bed and, this time, don't bother with not kneeling on Trina's pillows. "There was a Jesus on a cross right . . ."

Smooth wall. No nail. No hole.

Emmie gives me another look, and this one, I can read. It's full of doubt, concern, and maybe a touch of fear.

She opens the desk drawer and lifts a paper or two. "There's nothing here, hun."

"They can't have gotten rid of everything in there—" I shove past Emmie and dart across the hall to the other bedroom.

Like Trina's, the curtains in Kat's room have been opened and dusk spills through the blinds.

"Where did the crib go? The old pacifier? There was a plastic doll house right there." I point to the corner, turn in a circle, and see Emmie watching me by the door.

"We need to leave. There's nothing here. C'mon." She holds out her arm, encouraging me away from the center of Kat's room.

Instead, I drop to the floor, feel around the carpet. "See, right here. Four indentations. This is where the crib was."

Emmie looks down at me, her expression full of pity. "Darla, we need to go."

"But look. See?" I run my hands over the round indentations. "Please, just look. I'm not making this up."

Ems lets out a loud huff, kneels next to me, and feels the carpet. "Satisfied?"

"So, you believe me?"

She lifts her shoulders. "I believe something was here not that long ago, but why would they clean out their rooms? They didn't even know you were in them."

"They must have." I state the obvious, but Emmie isn't buying it.

"I'm getting out of here. We did what we came to do — cover your tracks — only there aren't any tracks to cover. Let's go." She stands and reaches out a hand.

Outside, a car crunches down the gravel road.

Emmie's eyes go wide. "Back door," she whispers, grabs my arm, and hauls me to my feet.

Two car doors slam shut as we run past the couch to the breakfast nook. A sliding glass door leads to the backyard. Emmie reaches for the slide lock, punches it down, and tries to open the door. It doesn't budge.

Her panicked gaze whips to me.

I sidle past her, pull aside the horizontal blinds, and there, wedged between the wall and the sliding door, is a security pole. I yank it out of the way just as the front door unlocks, push Emmie outside, and—

"Darla? What are you doing?"

I turn around slowly, still holding the wooden security pole, silently begging the universe to keep Emmie out of sight.

Trina and Kat stand by the couch, Kat with her arms crossed, Trina dangling her purse from limp fingers, shock etched onto both of their faces.

CHAPTER TWENTY-THREE

"I can explain."

"I think you better." Trina calmly puts her purse on the coffee table.

Kat just stares between us, mouth open, looking more entertained than worried.

"I was here earlier to check on Kat. She didn't look good when I left, so I came back . . ."

"And broke into our house?"

I shake my head. "No, no. I found your hide-a-key. Under the flowerpot. I just wanted to make sure Kat was okay."

Trina's gaze flits from my face to the wooden pole in my hand.

Right.

"Knee-jerk reaction. I panicked once I realized no one was home and I heard someone coming."

Trina folds her arms, and her lips spread into a hard line that screams, *not buying it.*

Outside, a horn honks. Trina furrows her eyebrows, then turns toward the door, but not before the doorbell rings and someone knocks. "Darla? You ready to go? How's Kat?"

Emmie. I don't know how she did it, but she's back, covering my ass.

"That's Emmie — I asked her to pick me up here, after I checked on Kat." See, story solid as a porous rock.

Trina goes to the front door and opens it wide.

Emmie is a shadow surrounded by headlights.

"Hey Trina. Darla asked me to meet her here." Emmie's shadow moves, and she peeks her head inside the doorway. "Darla, we're late, let's go."

I hand Trina the security pole, give Kat a little wave. "Glad you're feeling better. See you at work tomorrow?"

Kat, mouth still wide open, nods.

"Bye, Trina. Sorry about—" I gesture at the house.

She tightens her hands around the pole as I hurry past her, past Emmie, and into Emmie's car. Or rather, Henry's truck. Henry's in the driver's seat, and his glare is fixed on me with sharpshooter accuracy. I slide over to the middle, and Emmie slides in after me. Now that she's near, I can hear her fast breaths, as if she's been running, and feel the heat radiating from her.

"How?"

"Called Henry as soon as I got clear of the house." Her voice isn't full of we got away with it exhilaration. Instead, she's calm, her energy level lower than I'd felt from her before.

Without a word, Henry turns out of Trina's drive and heads back to my house. We pass through the center of town, where the Feast banner hangs prominently across Main Street. Two more days.

Emmie hops out, lets me slide out of the truck, then shuts the door behind me. In her hands are her car keys.

"Darla, I don't know what's going on, but it's obvious you need some help. I'll text you my therapist's contact info."

"Wait — Ems. What?"

"Tristan texted me back. Said there's no room B101 at the Church. Their rooms aren't even numbered. They're named."

141

"Maybe it's not a room, maybe—"

She holds her hand in the air.

"Look, I don't know where you've been or what you've been up to for all these years. I don't know if you're back to run a con or stir up drama or get revenge for something, or ... I. Don't. Know." Emmie throws her hands up, then drops them to her sides with a sharp exhale. "All I *do* know, Darla, is that nothing you've claimed so far appears to be true in anyone's mind but your own."

She takes a step back. "Take some time off work from the café. Get your head on straight. Until you do, please give us some space."

Henry waits in his truck until Emmie gets into her car. With Emmie securely in place he starts the truck and drives off, following her out onto the main road and out of sight.

For a moment, I can't move. And when I can, I don't want to. The firefly light slowly fades, and the stars become visible. Looking into the vast swatches of dark sky, I've never felt so small in my entire life.

Something's happening in this town — something involving Trina, the Church, and me, somehow. Someone else is going to die, no one believes me.

And I'm afraid time is running out.

The front porch light isn't on. I take one of the new keys out of my pocket and unlock the door. Henry did a good job installing the locks. At the very least, they'll keep Trina out.

I go through the house as I make my way to check on Mom, turn on lights, check dark corners, and process the past few hours as much as I'm able.

I'm not crazy. The note from the private investigator is real. Everyone's seen it. Touched it.

I peek inside my bedroom, turn on the lights. The dolls are still on my dresser. My go bag still hangs on my chair. As far as I know, Caitlin's note and cryptic page are still there, and Emmie saw all of it. How could she possibly think . . .

A stale sigh escapes me. I should have known better than to think I could come home and *actually* come home. Home changes. People change. I've changed.

Mom's bedroom door is shut tight. I didn't leave it like that.

"Mom?" I hold my breath and open her door. She's sitting upright in bed, but before I can relax and let out the breath I'm holding, her expression strikes me all wrong.

Her eyes are wild, darting back and forth, and her breath is hard, fast. Her hand flutters on top of her flower-print bed sheet, dancing like a trapped moth — constant, futile movement.

"Momma?" I grab her hand, squeeze her fingers, and she finally meets my gaze. She taps her throat.

"What's wrong?"

She's not talking. Again, she taps her throat.

"Your voice is gone?"

Quick nod, then she's clutching my hand as if I'm somehow her rope.

"Okay, let's calm down. Just breathe. You've been asleep for the better part of a day."

She frowns, her gaze skimming the room — sharp, restless. Her grip tightens, like she's bracing for a storm. "Trina gave you some tea and melatonin, but I think it had another sleep aid in there."

Her frown quickly turns razor-sharp.

"Maybe this is just laryngitis?"

She shakes her head back and forth, slow and steady.

"Okay. Deep breaths," I say, more for me than her. "I'll get you some water, then we'll figure this out." I squeeze her hand again and leave the room.

The lights in the kitchen reflect against the window glass, obscuring the view outside. Given my day, I don't like it. It feels like the dark is staring back. I quickly fill a glass with water and head back to Mom's room, all the while questions swirl around my head. Did I do something wrong? Miss some sign? Was this even a symptom of Mom's disease?

Or did Trina do this?

I can't exactly call her to ask if she's somehow hurting my mother, but I don't have anyone else I can call and discuss her symptoms. My options are severely limited. And like Emmie said, I have no proof other than I don't like Trina's medical decisions. I have no real reason to keep Trina away from my mother . . . other than gut instinct and the photos of Trina's room on my phone.

I stop at Mom's bedroom doorway. Her head is turned away, and the thin sheet covering her isn't enough to hide her frail bones.

"Here you go, Mom," I say, and she slowly turns her head toward me. Tear tracks stain her cheek, but her eyes are dry. I've never seen her cry, but the evidence remains.

She's scared.

I hand her the glass, and she takes a sip, then gives it back to me.

"Can you stand? Do you need to use the restroom?"

She shakes her head and lifts one finger.

"You need to go number one?"

She rolls her eyes and makes a writing motion with her hand. That, I can understand. I dig out a pencil and notepad from her nightstand drawer, which she yanks from me as soon as I'm in grabbing distance.

She might be scared, but she's also frustrated.

1? at a time.

"Right. Sorry."

She pats my hand, and I can almost hear her practical words dismissing my apology.

"Can you stand?" I repeat.

In answer, she sits up and swings her legs out of bed, but the movement costs her. She rests at the edge of the bed, eyes closed, taking deep breaths.

I bring over her walker and sit next to her, waiting until she catches her breath. She struggles to her feet and grips tightly to the metal bars, but she does it. She stands on her own.

I follow her to the bathroom, but she bats me away. Message received. She may not be able to talk, but she can damn well use the toilet by herself.

For now, at least.

CHAPTER TWENTY-FOUR

After Mom is settled with her journal and some soft music playing in her room, I retreat to mine. Trina's diary lays hidden in an old shoebox in my closet. I pull it out, open it to the first page, and start skimming.

Most of it is irrelevant or borderline sycophantic about the Church — Pastor Abe in particular. Abe's older than Trina, by a good two decades, but it seems in her youth she was obsessed with the then middle-aged pastor.

> *Pastor Abe's sermon today spoke directly to my heart. Faith, love, dedication. It was as if he were speaking only to me.*

> *Church today. Pastor Abe got a new tie — it brings out the blue in his eyes. I hope one day, I can find a man of faith like him.*

> *Pastor Abe called me to his office after Wednesday Bible study! Said he'd noticed my devotion to the Church, and wanted to invite me to receive the Blessing of the Chosen! I don't know what that is, but I asked around . . . only a few other girls were invited!*

Tonight's the night! The Feast is happening again, and it's special this year. This year, I become a full Church member through initiation! And receive the Blessing of the Chosen!

Then it stops.

For months.

The dates on the daily entries skip from May to August.

When Trina starts writing again, something's changed. The tone of voice, the slant of her writing, as if she's in a hurry to get the words out.

It didn't work. I'm not Chosen. There must be another way. This can't be it . . .

The rest of the diary is blank, except for that last page. The page of the girl on the altar, knees spread.

Is *that* the blessing? It can't be. My mind reaches for another explanation, but comes up empty. Something in my chest twists, kinks, tangles beyond comprehension.

Are girls being raped by Pastor Abe?

Surely, if so, word would have gotten around town. Girls talk. There would have been talk.

I rub at the dull pain behind my forehead. I have more questions than answers and no time to figure them all out. I dig out the mysterious note from the private investigator and study it again.

It's happening again. Come home before she dies, too.

It has to refer to the Feast — the 'it's.' It's the only thing that's happening again. Every six years, the Feast returns, and it's always a big deal. A new batch of young adults initiates into the Church, swelling its numbers. I haven't been to one since I was about seven years old. It's a faint memory, but the scent of charred wood, smoke, and incensed prayers from the Light the Night bonfire still hits me every once in a while.

147

The only girl that I know of who died mysteriously in our town is Caitlin. The message has to refer to her. It has to.

Because if it doesn't, I have nothing. No ideas, no clues, no way to move forward. Whoever sent me this message must have believed I could stop another girl from dying.

I breathe out through my nose, frustrated, and pull out Caitlin's coded paper.

Tomorrow, I'll visit COES and the library. I'm going to figure out what she tried to tell me all those years ago and maybe have a chance at stopping another death.

* * *

I find Mom upright in bed the next morning, scribbling away in her journal. She looks better, more alert, but still, her voice is gone.

"Tea, Mom? And would you like to move to the living room?" She nods yes to both, barely taking her eyes from her writing. I make her some tea, and as I set it on the coffee table in the living room, there's a soft knock at the front door.

I open the door to Trina, dressed in her Sunday best, though it's Thursday, a baby blue suit complete with a matching bag and a lacy hat. The only thing messing up her ensemble is the medical bag slung over her shoulder.

"Morning, Darla. Thought I'd check on Suzanne." Her tone is too cheery.

Does she notice the new locks? I'm not ready for that confrontation, not before coffee.

"Yeah, um. She woke up last night, unable to talk." I watch Trina's face for any sort of tick, twitch, twinge, anything that would give her away. "But she's in full control of her mental faculties," read that one online, "could this be a stroke? Her disease advancing?" Despite my aversion to Trina, my concerns fly out of my mouth faster than a horse fly on fresh meat, and I force myself to slow down, take a breath, not panic. "She seems weak, but she can sit up and stand on her own, and use a pencil to write things."

"She lost her voice?" Her question doesn't end in confusion, but trills up at the end, and a flicker of emotion flits across her face, gone so fast I could have imagined it.

"Does that mean something to you?" I prod, but Trina ignores me, her gaze fixed over my shoulder.

Mom inches her way into the room, her eyes locked on Trina. Trina, in turn, goes straight to Mom. She helps her to the couch, helps her ease into her favorite spot, tucks a blanket around her, and I try very, very hard not to be hurt that Mom still accepts her help, and resists mine.

"Let's take a look, shall we?" Trina pulls out a stethoscope and a penlight, and checks Mom's heart rate, her breathing, her pupils. "When did you first realize you lost your voice?" She rubs Mom's throat, checking for I'm not entirely sure what.

Mom shrugs then holds up her fingers. Seven last night? She'd been struggling for an hour before I got home. Why didn't she alert Henry? He'd been in the house, hadn't he?

But she'd been so weak. Maybe she couldn't. God, how terrifying. I sink to the chair opposite the couch and rest my head in my hand. I need to do better, need to be home more, set alarms through the night to check on her, need to—

Trina pats my shoulder, interrupting my spiral. "Darla, Suzanne's trying to tell you something."

I meet Mom's gaze, and it's like falling into a pool of worry, but not worry about herself. Worry about me. She simply shakes her head and smiles.

A sob catches in my throat, and I shift my position from the chair to the couch and wrap my arm around her. "I'm sorry. I'll do better."

Trina clears her throat. "From what I can see, you might have suffered a minor stroke. Are you experiencing any pain?"

Mom wiggles her hand back and forth and shakes her head.

"So, no more discomfort than usual?"

She nods.

"Okay then." Trina pats her knees and stands. "I'll set out some pills that'll make you comfortable, though I know you won't take them. But try just one, all right?"

"About that . . ." I cross my arms, and next to me, I can feel Mom stiffen. "Did you give Mom something more than melatonin? Because she slept for twenty-four hours straight."

Trina's face reminds me of an evening primrose, all fragile innocence. "If she slept that long, she must have needed it. Could be another symptom of a stroke. This is end-of-life care, Darla." She shrugs. "We don't go looking for answers to every ache and pain."

I do a quick check on Mom, but her expression is nothing but acceptance.

Trina stands. "I'm about to miss praise team practice so I'll leave you two ladies to your day. Gotta be in tip top tune shape for the Feast." She ends in a sing-song. "Speaking of, will you join us at the Feast tomorrow?" Her gaze lasers into mine.

"I shouldn't leave Mom alone," I respond, and inch a little closer to her.

Trina nods, walks to the door, then turns back around and dips her chin, ever so slightly. "Kat's doing fine today, just so you know. No need to check on her." Her gaze lingers on mine, then she makes her exit.

Message received.

The door clicks shut behind her, and I turn to Mom. "I have to take care of a few things today. Should I call someone over to sit with you or—"

She rolls her eyes and swats at me.

"I shouldn't be gone long, but I'll put a sandwich in the fridge in case you get hungry."

Mom sighs and goes back to her journal.

And with that, I've been dismissed. She's always been a little too independent for her own good. Some might say it runs in the family.

CHAPTER TWENTY-FIVE

A slight breeze drifts through my cracked car window as I wait for the librarian to show up. She's not one to be early, that's for sure. The hour hand hits nine on the clock above the library entrance, and an old sedan turns into the parking lot.

I give her a few minutes to get the door unlocked, turn on the lights, do whatever it is that librarians do to open a library, then march through the front door.

"Hello, may I help—"

"Where would the history of the town be kept? Possibly a census or something that lists the families?"

She jerks her head back because I've come on too strong.

"Sorry. I'm sorry. I left my sick mother at home and am in a hurry to get back to her."

Her expression softens. "Of course, dear. Town records will be in our local history section. I'll show you."

She leads me to a back corner of the library, where three shelves contain books with titles like *The Atakapa of East Texas* and *Bluebonnets and More — Welcome to The Piney Woods*.

"This section holds old records of the town and geneal-ogy information. Founding families, census records, notable events, etcetera."

151

"What about old Yellow Pages?"

She raises one eyebrow.

"Just in case someone I'm looking for isn't in the genealogy records."

"There might be some in storage. Not many requests for those."

"Would you mind looking? Anything in the past forty years?"

"Forty—" she sputters. "Darlin', you're gonna have to narrow it down a bit."

"Early nineties?" I throw out. Should be long enough ago to be relevant to Caitlin's era.

She gives me a look, like I'm already not her most favorite patron of the day. "I'll see what I can do." And spins on a thick heel.

"Thank you," I call after her, but I'm fairly certain it's too late to get on her good side.

I grab all the genealogy binders, find a nearby table, and spread out the blank sheets of paper, colored pencils, and highlighters I've brought. Caitlin's pages have so many dotted lines, wiggly lines, straight lines, and doubled lines that cross over and under and around each other, it's hard to figure out where each one goes.

Typical family trees use solid vertical lines to indicate offspring. Solid horizontal lines to indicate either siblings or, in some examples I found online, marriages. Though marriages are more commonly shown with a double line. The dotted lines, if this were a typical family tree, would be used to show divorce. But looking at Caitlin's abstract use of symbols, I'm starting to seriously doubt this is a family tree.

I start at the top, with the J.S. initials, and make a column on a spare sheet of paper. Underneath it, I start recording the initials that J.S. connects to with a doubled, solid line. If there's another initial connected to that one, I mark it in parenthesis.

Before the librarian returns, I have a list of four initials, three connected to another initial via a vertical line.

She thumps down a few thick books full of yellow pages, and a musty cloud of dust rises from them. "Anything else?"

"No, thank you. I appreciate the help." The smile on my face is forced — not because I'm not thankful but because I'm finally doing something about Caitlin's code — and she can tell.

She hums and click-clacks off to the front desk.

I start with the genealogy binders. If J.S. is Abe's father or grandfather, it'd be the easiest place to start. And given that the Smiths founded COES, they have to be mentioned in the genealogy records.

Book one, I hit the jackpot. It's a book dedicated entirely to the Smiths of Trinity Falls, Texas, though the dates it covers show that it hasn't been updated since before Tristan's birth. No matter; I keep going.

There's a list of contributors under the title page. Karen Smith is listed as the main contributor, along with other family names I recognize from around town, like the Williams family, who contributed newspaper articles or the Martin family, who contributed photographs. But it looks as if Karen Smith ran this project. Abe isn't listed as a contributor, even though it's about his family.

"Typical Karen," I mutter, and trace down the contributor names, to see if any initials match the ones on Caitlin's sheet. A few hits here and there, but what I really want to do is cross-reference the hits from my town research with the Church membership directory. Because whatever this is has to do with COES.

I make notations as I go through the record book, more and more certain that J.S. is indeed John Smith II, Abe's father. There are too many matches for the initials to refer to the original John Smith or his wife, Mary Smith. By the time I get through the book, I've got possible matches for each of my four initials, some with multiple.

"If any of you match the Church records, I'm writing you in pen," I tell them, then look around to make sure no one overheard me talking to myself . . . or rather to a piece of paper.

"Miss . . . Librarian?" I call out as I get up and head to the front desk. Should have gotten her name.

She just raises her eyebrow at me again.

"Do you happen to have records about COES? Like membership directories?"

She smiles her first true smile. "Of course, dear. We have a special section dedicated to COES. Why, the Church is one of our biggest donors."

She leads me to a section not far from the local history section. "Here, you'll find records of church registries since we started recording, back in 1901. But no addresses or phone numbers are listed. Just names mind you. We don't need to make those damn solicitor's jobs any easier." She smiles another beatific smile and leaves me be.

I run my finger across the black bindings, looking for 1990 in the gold lettering. It's not a thick volume, but COES isn't a megachurch. Even less so in the nineties. I take it back to my table and flip past the pictures of Church services and events, past the goals and missions accomplished for the year, to the back. To the membership directory.

It's like an adult yearbook, but with family pictures instead of individuals. I turn to the B's and find Brown and Baker.

The Brown family has two entries. One picture of an older couple. Edward Brown and Elizabeth Brown. The second entry is of a family. Eddie Brown, Eloise Brown, and their two children, Sabrina and Robin. Edward, Elizabeth, Eddie, or Eloise — the same Eloise who dropped food off for Mom last week — could be the ones connected to John Smith.

"This doesn't make any sense, Caitlin," I whisper, annoyed at her for not being clearer. How hard would it have been just to write it all down?

I continue on to the next family, with much the same result. Nothing. My head hurts. I check the time . . . one hour gone.

I gnaw on my lip, and keep going through the exercise with John Smith's double lines. I flip to the Martin family, and before I even realize what I'm looking at, my fingertips tremble, and a chill erupts from my wrists all the way up my arms.

Trina Martin.

"It can't be." But it can, it is. I try to zoom in on her picture with my fingers, remember that this is paper, not a screen. My thoughts are twisted, tumbled, turning inside out.

Trina is connected to John Smith.

I go back to Caitlin's page. There's a scribbly line going from Trina's initials, all the way down the page. It's the only line like it. And it connects to C.R.

"Caitlin?" I whisper. Trina is Caitlin's aunt, so it makes total sense, but . . .

There's another line — a solid, vertical one.

Just like the line under A.S. connecting to T.S. Abe Smith and his son, Tristan Smith.

But this one is under Caitlin's initials and leads to a question mark.

"She was pregnant," I breathe.

* * *

I sit back in the uncomfortable library chair, gaze frozen on the taped sheet of paper in front of me.

She was pregnant.

My heart turns to stone, plummets to my lap. Unanswered questions pile, thick and unmoving, in my mind. What happened to her baby? When was she pregnant? Bile burns at the back of my throat, and a shudder starts at my bellybutton and ricochets through my body.

Could she have been pregnant when she died?

I feel dizzy. The library goes fuzzy around me. Too many ifs, too few hows.

"I need a break," I whisper. I need to go home, check on Mom, maybe grab something to eat, and give all this new information a minute to process.

I gather my things and make my way to the front desk.

The librarian's talking to someone on the black desk phone, but excuses herself and tilts the mouthpiece toward her neck. "Yes?"

"I need to get back home. Can I get a new library card? I'd like to check out the books I was looking at."

She's shaking her head before I finish talking.

"Historical records are not allowed to be checked out. They must be viewed exclusively in the library." She crinkles her nose up as she says this, like I should have known better.

"Oh. Right. I'll be back later then. After lunch. Would you mind holding these for me behind the desk?"

She inclines her head toward the counter, where I place my stack of books. "Of course, dear. But if anyone else asks for them, I can't refuse their request."

I nod, push my bag back up my shoulder. "See you in an hour."

She just raises her eyebrows and goes back to her conversation, but I can feel her eyes on my back the entire way to the front door. Likely, she's hoping I won't come back.

I hold my bag close. The notes I've taken, Caitlin's code, the flyer, Trina's journal . . . they're all inside. I've developed a fear in the past day or so, maybe an irrational fear, that if I leave them unprotected, they'll disappear. Like they never existed.

When I get home, Mom's where I left her on the couch, but she's slumped over, blanket drawn up to her neck, asleep. Her sandwich is in the fridge, untouched, and her glass of water is just as full as when I left this morning.

I prod her awake, get her to eat and drink a little bit, but her voice is still gone. No miraculous improvement in the short time I've been away.

"I need to go out again. I'll probably be a few more hours. Do you need anything before I go?"

She shakes her head, then holds a finger up for me to wait, struggles to stand with her walker, and hobbles down the hallway to the bathroom.

Yeah. I don't want her moving around the house unsupervised either.

I wait until she's back, settled with her journal, her phone, and the TV remote within easy reach, and wait a bit longer until she's so annoyed with my fussing she shoos me toward the door.

I lock the front door behind me and double-check that it's bolted shut. No ice pick will get through this lock. I give the plants on the porch a squirt of water and, for a moment, allow myself to miss who I was becoming. Master gardener, my own person, just . . . me. Me without all the weighted history of being here, being home. I miss the scent of rich soil, the quiet of the greenhouse, the peace in knowing I was safe, and the not knowing that everyone I left behind wasn't. One way or another, they aren't safe. Mom's not safe from disease, my old friends aren't safe from the Church, and a girl in town has a target on her back.

I don't get the luxury of not knowing any more, of feeling safe. Caitlin made sure of that, intentional or not.

My roots are woven deep into this ground. There's no getting away, no matter how far I toss my seeds into the wind. I'm here, for better or for worse.

The drive back to the library seems to take seconds. I walk through the front door, but my librarian friend is nowhere to be seen. I peek behind the counter, but the books I'd set there are gone. From the little I picked up on her personality, she likely reshelved everything.

I cast my gaze around the small building, but don't see anyone. She must be in the storage room or taking a break somewhere. I settle myself back at my same table and walk over to the Church records section.

The shelves are empty.

My muscles turn rigid. A knot lodges in my throat, and my stomach calcifies. Am I in the wrong section? I blink, take a step back. There aren't many sections. I can't be in the wrong section. What happened to the records?

"Miss?" I call out, an edge to my voice I distantly recognize as panic. "Miss?"

I hurry to the front, to the storage room — she's not here — and electricity is zinging up and down and through my chest. Something's wrong.

A door creaks closed at the back of the library. "Hello?"

"Coming," a familiar voice calls out, and the librarian walks briskly around the corner. Her friendly smile is sharp as an agarita bush and just as dangerous to walk into. A strong scent of smoke trails from her, and I have my answer. Cigarette break.

"Where are all the records?"

"The ones you were looking at?"

I nod.

"Behind my desk. I haven't moved them."

"They're gone. They are *all* gone."

Either she's practiced the expression, or she truly is shocked. She rushes to the back of the library and stands still in front of the empty shelves. "I don't understand . . ." She turns back to me. "Sometimes Karen, you know, Pastor Abe's wife? Sometimes she takes them to update the records, but usually she lets me know . . . I was only outside for fifteen minutes . . ."

"Does the Church have copies of everything?"

She nods. "Yes, yes, of course. They have the originals, dating back to nineteen hun—"

I don't wait for her to finish. I rush to my car, she sputters to life, and for the first time in only God knows how long, I go to church.

CHAPTER TWENTY-SIX

My chest tightens with every mile that passes, a woodworking vise that compresses, compresses, compresses until I feel my lungs will pop.

The last place I want to be is this church.

I turn into the parking lot, which is half full, likely with Church members volunteering for the Feast. I look for a sign that says *Office* and park as close as I can to the door. Why would Karen remove all the records the day I was looking at them? My brain wheels over possible explanations. Unless . . .

I stop breathing.

Unless she knows.

I pull Caitlin's code back out of my bag, find Karen's initials, double-check them against the other names I've unveiled.

"She's the only one connected to a child with a dotted line," I whisper. Why would she be the only woman connected to her child with a dotted line?

The answer is there; I can feel it on the tip of my mind's tongue. I shove Caitlin's page back into my bag, get out, and lock the car door, and make my way into the office.

There are flowers everywhere. It looks like the aftermath of a funeral, and the overpowering scent of lilies makes it smell like one, too. Even the secretary's desk is covered in vases and bouquets. The click-clack of typing comes from behind the floral barrier. "Be right with you," a voice says.

There's a final click, punched with satisfaction, and a graying head appears above the flowers.

"Drat these flowers. I'm coming, I'm coming." Eloise comes from around the desk, then stops when she sees it's me. "Darla? Is everything okay? Is your Momma—"

I hold up a hand. "She's okay. At home, resting. Trina thinks she had a minor stroke. She's struggling to talk right now."

Eloise places a hand on her heart. "Oh my. We'll update the prayer list. I'll try to get by to see her later this week. After the Feast is over, we'll all have a little more time."

I shake my head. "It's fine. I'm actually here looking for the records of the Church's membership."

Eloise tilts her head and scrunches her nose. "Why on God's good earth would you want those?"

"Genealogy project. Mom and I are working on it." I came up with the flimsy excuse on the way over. "We have a couple of ancestors that we believe were members, but need to confirm."

"Hmm, sounds like a boring project, but I guess that anything that keeps the hands busy is good work. Right over here." She leads me to an upright bookcase in the corner of the lobby and a waist-high glass case that shows the timeline of the Church. A black-and-white photo of John Smith is on the far left, amid a backdrop of painted forest. His wife, Mary Smith, is at his side, hands clasped in front of her waist, a serious stillness to her slight smile, and her dark eyes stare deeply into the camera.

The timeline follows John Smith's life, the construction of the first church building and his expanding family; then John Smith II takes over, has Abe Smith, who then has Tristan Smith. Tristan's listed on the timeline already, not as head pastor but as associate pastor. The succeeding pastor's wives are smiling next to them — Lydia Smith, Karen Smith, and Shelly Smith — there to support each and every accomplishment.

There are no other children mentioned. Just a history of a single male child who takes over the throne. But if Caitlin connected the Smiths to other families, does that mean the Smiths have had illegitimate children with other Church members?

"I can't let you borrow these, mind you, but you're welcome to that chair as long as I'm here." Eloise's voice brings me back to the office. She casts her gaze around and lets out a martyred sigh. "Which will be another few hours by the looks of it." She sits back down behind her flower jungle.

I snatch the year I'd been researching in the library and flip back to the members page. "Eloise, do you know if John Smith, Abe's father, had any other children?"

"Good heavens, no. They wanted a litter, but the good Lord knew what He was doing and gave them Abe instead. My oh my, he was a handful when he was younger. I used to sit with him during the service to keep him from wriggling too much."

I close the book, keeping my finger in to mark my place. "So, you know the Smiths quite well."

She looks around a giant vase and shrugs. "As well as anyone can, I suppose. Been working here since I graduated high school. Helped look after Abe, then Tristan. Helped Karen out when she had all those awful miscarriages."

My grip on the book tightens. "Miscarriages?"

"Oh yes, she had the worst time getting pregnant and staying that way. Tristan's their miracle child."

My heart is thumping harder, faster, and I'm having a hard time keeping my voice normal. "I didn't know. That's tough."

She nods in agreement, then dips back behind the flowers. I flip through the records book and stop on a photo. A photo of four young women, with a caption that reads *The*

161

Blessed Chosen Class. Four young women: Jenny Baker, Clarice Williams, Elizabeth Baker and . . .

Trina Martin.

My mouth has gone dry, and if Eloise can't hear my heart pounding, then she needs hearing aids. "Did the Church always do the Blessing of the Chosen ceremony?" I croak.

She pokes her head back out, a concerned look on her face.

"We found a note about it in an old photo album," I lie, my pulse fluttering in my throat. "I was just wondering if it's a practice that went back to the founding of the Church."

She shrugs. "Dunno. My mother was, but I never got invited, which let me tell you was a sore spot for a number of years. But I've proven my worth since then." She raises her chin.

"Eloise, have you called the fire department yet?" A distant voice calls from the hall behind Eloise, coming closer as she speaks. "We need to make sure that—" Karen appears around the corner and sees me. "Darla?" Her mouth morphs into a gaping *O*, and her gaze darts from me to the records book in my hand. "How can we help you?"

"She's working on her family history with Suzanne," Eloise chimes in.

"I was looking at the books in the library, but they disappeared while I was gone for lunch." I keep my voice steady, my gaze trained on Karen. "The librarian thought you may have borrowed them. But with you so busy with the Feast . . ." I let my doubt echo through the overabundance of lilies.

Eloise looks from me to Karen, back to me, then to the bookshelf, her confusion slowly fading to uh-oh.

"Strange." Karen hums thoughtfully. "Well as you pointed out, we are very busy with preparations and I'd hate for Eloise to have to stay later tonight because of extra distractions." She steps forward, effectively blocking my view of Eloise. "I'm sure we'll be happy to show you these records next week. As it is, this is not a good time."

"Oh, of course." I let my tone cascade up as if I hadn't thought of it like that before. "I'll get out of your hair." I turn my back to them and pick up my bag, hiding my movements as I stuff the records book into my backpack. "Have a good Feast," I blurt and half-run out the door to my car. I don't even stop to buckle my seatbelt but turn the key in the ignition, send up all the prayers that she starts without a hitch, and speed out of the parking lot and back onto the main road.

I don't think I breathe until I pull into our driveway. I lock the car doors and sit in the heavy silence, my breaths coming fast, shallow, as if I've just outrun something. I yank the record book out of my bag, fish around for Caitlin's code, and scan the initials tied to the doubled lines next to John Smith. Every single one belongs to a member of the Blessed Chosen class.

Tristan's grandfather wasn't just connected to the children of other families. He was connected through the Blessing.

And they are all girls.

***

The only sound in the car is my breathing. I'm not sure how long I've sat here, but the heat is building, and if I stay any longer, I'll be one of those idiots on the news who died in their car due to heatstroke.

I walk inside the house, check on Mom — asleep — lather my arms, shoulders, and the back of my neck with sunscreen, and head to the back garden. I need to think, to put my thoughts in order with each scrape of dirt. I need what I'm thinking to not be true.

It's happening again. The Blessing. The Blessing is happening again.

Before she dies, too. Like Caitlin. Who went through the Blessing. Who was pregnant. Who died.

I dig the aerator back into the hard clay, and give it a firm twist.

Kat's going to go through the Blessing like Trina did. Like Caitlin.

My stomach churns. Does that mean Trina was raped? Caitlin? Does this mean the pastors of COES — Tristan's father, grandfather, great-grandfather — have been raping girls for generations?

The thought hovers. Heavy. Still.

It can't be. It's too horrific to be true. But . . .

There are no other explanations.

What I can't figure out is why none of them would talk. Why wouldn't Caitlin tell me? But flashes of Caitlin — of who she was back then — course through my mind. Her almost complete inability to talk about the Church or about what happened in her Bible studies — a big mystery shadowing every part of her life that had to do with the Church. I break apart more dirt, and the rage simmering within me doesn't calm, doesn't settle. It transforms into something fiery, something that will burn.

"Because COES is a fucking cult," I growl to no one. And it's the only explanation I need. I give the dirt one final twist, throw the tool across the garden, and get back in my car.

I'm not thinking straight, my hands tremble against the steering wheel, I don't even know exactly where I'm going until another question upends my mind. Did Tristan know?

Was he a part of it?

Nausea threatens to overtake me, heat cascades from my stomach, up my arms, my neck, and it's like having morning sickness all over again. The steering wheel wrenches under my hands, and before I know it, I'm heading toward the magazine-worthy cottage that Tristan and Shelly share. Perched on a hill behind the Church, prime observation landing to watch the entire town.

My brakes screech as I pull in front of their house, knocking over one of the flowerpots expertly placed at intervals along the semi-circle drive, and I don't remember how I got to the front door, how I'm banging on the doorknocker, ringing the bell, but I am.

Shelly flings open the door, eyes wide. "Darla? What the hell?"

"Where's Tristan?"

She folds her arms, spreads her legs, blocks the doorway. "He's putting the girls down for a nap. Why?"

Tristan appears at her shoulder. "What's going on?"

"Did you know?" I want to yell the words, to punch something — *him* — as I spit them, but my voice comes out low, slow, heated.

They exchange glances. "Know what, Darla?" Shelly says, and I can hear her attempt to be soothing.

I ignore her, focusing on Tristan. "Your father. Your grandfather." The words come out from between my teeth, I can't seem to unclench my jaw. "*Caitlin.*" Her name breaks my voice, and one hot tear runs down my cheek.

Tristan pulls Shelly out of the way while keeping his eyes trained on mine. "What about them?"

"They raped her, Tris. They raped them all. The Blessing." A sob interrupts me, but I push through. "Did. You. Know?"

Tristan freezes.

In the background, I hear Shelly on the phone, giving someone their address.

And then Tristan's shoulders relax. His expression goes from shocked to . . . pity?

"Darla, Emmie called us. Please tell us what's going on. Can we help?"

I shake my head, backing away. "No, don't do this."

"You need therapy, Darla. I don't know what life has done to you, but this," he gestures at me, "isn't the Darla we used to know. You must realize this behavior is not normal." In place of Tristan's face, I only see the picture-perfect pastor — saintly, sympathetic, selfless.

I keep backing away. "You're just like them. Aren't you?"

His expression doesn't change.

"*Aren't you*?!" I scream, and finally, finally, he flinches. Looks behind me. I follow his gaze over my shoulder and see a cop car heading in our direction from town.

A laugh escapes my throat. "You called the cops? On me? That's rich, Tris." I get back in my car, coax her to life, and take the back roads back into town.

He knew.

Tristan's just as guilty as the rest of them. And Shelly's letting him do it.

CHAPTER TWENTY-SEVEN

I don't know if the cops are after me, but I don't hear sirens, and my gut tells me that Shelly called them as a scare tactic to get me away from her family. Still, I take every back road that I know and come into town from a side street that leads into the alley behind the bistro.

My closest friends think I'm crazy. Yet, one of them knows more than they're letting on. One of them gave me the other half of Caitlin's message. And if I rule out Emmie, Tristan, and Shelly, that only leaves Karl and Ivan.

I park behind the dumpster, my car half-hidden from a normal glance, and sneak into the bistro's kitchen.

Lola is hard at work, chopping heads of lettuce and yelling out instructions over her shoulder. I feel bad, but I duck behind the counter and crouch-walk through the kitchen and into the bistro.

It feels like stepping into a church fellowship hall after a Sunday service — laughter a little too loud, chairs too close together, and an imagined whiff of powdered donuts and bad coffee hanging in the air. It's a half-full house, and the COES vibe is strong, and I can't decide if that works in my favor or not. From the looks, there are out-of-towners visiting families, COES families playing host, COES volunteers taking a break, all getting revved up for the Feast tomorrow.

Kat's at a table, server pad in hand, apron tied around her waist. Her hair is in a tight, French braid, and she looks more put together than I've ever seen her.

I intercept her on the way back to the kitchen, grab her by the elbow, and usher her into the empty group room. "Need to talk to you."

"Get off m—" she starts to yell, but I slap my hand over her mouth.

"*Please*. Just give me one minute." Taking a play out of Shelly's book, I attempt to soothe. Like with me, I don't think it's working. But Kat, eyes wide, nods, and I let her go.

"You can't go to the Blessing."

She narrows her eyes and crosses her arms. Whatever she thought I was going to say, this wasn't it. "Why?" she finally counters.

"They rape girls there, Kat. They've been doing it for years."

She's silent for a moment, and her face loses a shade of color. "No." She shakes her head. "They give us the blessing of the Church."

"And what is that, exactly? Did they tell you?"

She falls quiet again.

"There's a reason they're not telling you. Who else is in your Chosen class?"

She shrugs, that teenage you're-making-a-big-deal-out-of-nothing aura radiating off her in waves, but her eyes won't meet mine. I've rattled something. "You wouldn't know them."

"Tell me."

"It's just kids from school."

"All girls, right?"

She scoffs, but her fingers fidget with the frayed edge of her server's apron. "So? Boys have unclean thoughts. They can't be in the class."

168

"Names, Kat." I grab her server pad and pen from her. "Now."

Her gaze darts for the exit to the room, but I'm blocking her. She's not getting past me without causing a scene, and while it's something she probably should do, social rules dictate. She sighs. "Emily Jones and Jessica Worth."

I write down the names, tear off the paper, and hand her pad back to her. "Thank you. Okay, next plan," I breathe out slowly, trying to still my racing heart.

"I gave you your minute." She grabs the pen from my hands. "I need to get these orders in." She shoves past me back into the din of the bistro.

"Wait, Kat. You can't go home after your shift. Come to mine."

She scrunches up her nose. "Why?"

"Because . . ." I scramble. I know Trina is wrapped up in all this, somehow, but I don't have proof. "She'll make you go to the Initiation, to the Blessing. She's been through it before."

"You're saying my mom was raped? By someone at the Church?"

"By the previous pastor. Ask her."

"Then why would she want me to go through the same thing?"

Good question. But I know what I saw in Trina's room. Trina's first love is that Church, and she'll do what they ask. "You said your mom is COES's biggest cheerleader," I offer instead. "I think they've screwed with her mind. Brainwashed her. Maybe she doesn't view the Blessing as rape. But, Kat, it is. Come to mine. I'll keep you safe."

"What in Tarnation is the hold-up out there?" Lola's voice bursts through from the kitchen.

Kat uses the distraction to hurry out of sight. I take a deep breath and rub at my forehead.

A minute later, heavy footsteps thump out of the kitchen. Lola rounds the corner and props her hands on her hips at me.

169

"You are not supposed to be here, and you are definitely *not* supposed to be harassing my one and only server."

I hold my hands up. "I'm leaving. It was important."

"Out," Lola commands, pointing to the door.

By now, people are staring, but it doesn't matter. I hurry out the front door and jog around the block back to my car.

Kat doesn't believe me. If she doesn't believe me, what options do I have — kidnap her? I can't do that. And there are two other girls out there who are about to go through the same thing.

I pick up speed, breath coming harder, feet hitting pavement with sharp, uneven slaps.

Bottom line: I cannot let the Blessing occur tomorrow night. Whatever it takes, I have to stop it.

* * *

I go home. Where else can I go? I've burned every bridge, more completely than I did the first time by leaving. The one bridge I haven't burned, the one bridge that seems unburnable, is my mother.

She's awake when I unlock the door. She rubs at her throat, as if it's hurting her, so I make her some honey and lemon tea, sit next to her while she sips at it, and don't say a word. How does one go about stopping an event from happening when everyone else thinks she's nuts?

I could present my evidence to the police, but Emmie's right — I very well could have made it all up. And with my track record of running and lying, I'm not exactly the most reputable source.

It goes back to what I've been lacking since returning home. Actual evidence. Physical proof that these girls are being harmed; have been harmed.

I pat Mom's hand and leave her to her journal, dive into my go bag in my room, and pull out the stolen records book. There has to be more in here, something I'm missing. I go back into the living room, curl up on the armchair next to Mom, open to page one, and start reading.

I've barely started page three when the front door rattles. I suck in a breath and hold it, certain it's Trina out there, uncertain that Henry's locksmith skills are enough to keep her out. Mom looks up from her notebook, a confused look on her face.

"I changed the locks," I tell her, keeping my voice low. "I know you trust her, but I don't."

I can't decipher the look on her face, and I'm just glad no one from town has talked to her in the past day or two. If she heard my so-called friends' side of the story, this — me changing the locks and keeping her inside and everyone else out — would not look good.

Trina tries her key in the lock, then knocks at the front door. "Darla? Are you in there?"

The handle rattles again, then Trina's shadow appears at the front porch window. Even though the blinds are closed, I feel exposed.

"I talked with Emmie. And Tristan. And then Kat called me a few minutes ago."

Shit. There's absolutely no chance they haven't convinced her that I'm out of my mind.

She knocks on the door and tries the handle once more. "Darla, if you're in there, I need to give Suzanne her medicine." Her voice pitches a bit higher with something I can't quite pinpoint — irritation? Panic? Worry?

I check how Mom is taking this, but she's got a vacant look in her eye as if she's not quite processing.

Trina's shadow disappears from the front window. I hear her footsteps walk away, down the steps, and I take a deep breath. My phone rings from its perch on the kitchen table, and the solid surface seems to amplify the tone through the house and its paper-thin windows.

"Dammit," I whisper and tip-toe-run to my phone, switch it to silent, but I'm afraid it's too late. Footsteps creak outside the back door.

A few breaths later, the handle jiggles. "Darla, I just heard your phone ring so I know you're in the house. If you don't answer, I'll have to assume you're not well. My next step is to call the paramedics and have them take down this door." Her knocks morph into bangs.

I clench my hands into fists so hard my ragged nails bite into my palms. Acid fills my throat and my chest, threatening to drown my breaths, which have gone uneven. Trina's *bam bam bam* matches me step for step as I pick my way to the back door.

"I'm here. Not feeling very well. We're just resting." I attempt to make my voice sound like I'm actually sick. It's not that hard. I feel nauseous. Powerless. "Can you come back later?"

She huffs out a breath. "Darla, everyone is very worried. Please think of your mother. Suzanne needs to stay on her med schedule. Now open the door, please."

"She doesn't want the medicine. You know that, Trina. Besides, if she needs anything, I can give it to her." Reasonable enough — she can't argue with that.

Trina falls silent, but I can just about hear her thoughts, twisting and tumbling over her options.

"No, I'm sorry. You are not medically authorized to administer this medicine, and it's my license on the line if something goes wrong. Please unlock the door."

I lean against the door frame, the cracked wood cool against my forehead. I'm out of options. "I'm sorry, Trina, but I can't." I pull aside the lacy curtain that covers the back door window so she can see my face. "You've gone against my mother's wishes. You will not come into this house again without my permission and supervision."

Trina's face pales, her lips thin, and the blacks of her eyes seem to swell. "Your mother gave me power of—"

"Show me the paperwork. I haven't seen it. All I have is your word."

She presses her lips together. The bones in her neck pop out as if she's clenching every muscle in her body. "I'll call the sheriff. He's a personal friend — I've sat next to him in Bible study for years."

I shrug. "So call him. I'm not letting you in here until the law makes me." I let the curtain swing back into place and don't bother softening my departing steps.

"You have to leave sometime, Darla," Trina shouts. "You can't stay in there forever."

I don't answer because I have my answer. Whatever Trina's been up to, I don't trust it. Her concern for my mother is a pretense — so why does she really want to get in here?

She bangs on the back door again, and I have to admire my dad's craftsmanship. Unlike Trina's flimsy new construction doors, this one doesn't budge. I go back to the living room, half-expecting a rock to come flying through the glass, but a few moments later, the crunch of Trina's bicycle reaches me, rolling away down the packed-dirt drive.

CHAPTER TWENTY-EIGHT

I help Mom to bed, but she doesn't want me to leave, so I cuddle up next to her, and at some point, we both fall asleep. When I next wake, it's very late, and the light of the moon is low in the window.

Mom shifts in the bed next to me, her bony elbow connecting with my collarbone. "Darla?" she whispers, her voice like static on the radio.

I flip over, reaching for the bedside light.

Mom blinks at the sudden brightness, then connects her gaze with mine.

"Your voice is back?" I try not to shriek, but the shrillness bubbles out anyway.

She swallows, gestures for her water, and I quickly hand it over. "Hurts," she says after taking a gentle sip.

"It hurts to talk?"

She nods.

"Okay, then let's take it easy."

She nods again and casts her gaze around the room before leaning against the headboard, and I slide out of the bed to give her more room. "Can I make you some hot tea? Maybe with honey in it?"

She presses her fingers to the space above her nose and nods with her eyes closed.

The clock on the oven reads 4:03 a.m. and the tea kettle whines as the water heats. But a resounding chorus of *what the hell* reverberates through my mind. Mom's voice is back. Is that typical for a stroke victim?

The pop of the tea kettle jerks my attention back to the task at hand. I make her tea and carry it back to her, half-expecting her to be asleep by the time I return. She's not.

I place her *Everything's Bigger In Texas* mug in her hands, and she takes a slow sip as I sink to the chair by her bedside. After a few quiet moments, I gather enough courage to ask, "Do you trust Trina?"

Mom takes her time, sipping at her tea. "She was all I had."

I nod, even though my windpipe feels like it's in a trash compactor. I should have been here. I should never have left.

The quiet of predawn seeps into the bedroom. The darkness changes ever so slightly outside the thin curtains, and there's a lightness that comes with it, as if the night has a weight. Between the low lamplight and the scent of Mom's tea, it almost feels like I'm at confession. She leans against the headrest, her white nightgown slipping off one skeletal shoulder, and I get a sinking feeling all of a sudden that we don't have much time — that she doesn't have much time.

"Did you know Trina went through Initiation?"

Her eyes widen, her lips thin, and one hand clutches at the blanket at her hips, but she nods.

"And the Blessing of the Chosen?" I'm watching her — closely, too closely maybe — but something's off. I study her for any twitch, any flicker, anything to explain why she suddenly looks so afraid.

Instead of answering, she points to the memory box on her dresser, where she's always kept her special trinkets locked away. I grab the shoebox-sized wooden box, the edges rounded and worn smooth from the years, and bring it to her. She clasps the small key on her necklace and unlocks the box.

She pushes the unlocked box back at my hands, leans back, and closes her eyes without saying a word. I've never seen the inside. She'd sometimes open it and show me a memento or two, but I was never allowed to look inside before.

It's warm from her hands, and the open lock feels crusty under my fingertips. I gently slide it off the latch and place it on the bedside table, keeping one eye on Mom in case she changes her mind. Her eyes are still closed as if this is the part of the movie she can't watch, but her hand still clenches the blanket tight.

I open the lid. Linen paper lines the inside, an old-fashioned design that has become brittle, curling in on little cracks running between the paper and the glue. Littered on the inside are years of keepsakes, things I made for her when I was little, letters from Dad, an old charm bracelet, and at the very bottom, covered up by all these other expressions of love, a yellowed newspaper article, and a small book.

Panic surges through me, and I don't know why. But there is no turning back from this moment; no more running away. I feel Mom's eyes on me now, and they're intense with some emotion I'm not sure how to define.

I gently lift the fragile paper out of the box. On it is an article from the Church, announcing the year's Chosen class.

Three girls. In dresses with white collars and knee-high socks. The caption reads, *Pastor Abe and wife, Karen, with this year's Chosen class, Gabriela Martinez, Marlene Waters, and Suzanne Adams.*

My heart is nothing but lead weight, and despite the heat in the ever-warm house, everything inside me goes frigid.

"Mom?" Tears bead in my eyes — not falling but burning — and I slowly make eye contact with her.

Her shining eyes match mine, and she nods for me to continue.

I don't want to, but I'm not a little girl who needs protecting anymore, and the time for ignorance has long passed. I lift the book out from under its buried space. The gilded lettering contrasts sharply with the faded black on the spine. The worn corners. Her name scrawled on the inside cover. And there, in the back, a small envelope inviting her to a sacred ceremony to receive the Blessing of the Chosen.

"You were . . ." I can't say the words.

There are tears in her eyes, but they don't fall. She's still as stone, and even though it's me at her feet, it feels as if she's the one begging for forgiveness.

"Like, Trina?" I confirm, but she shakes her head.

"We weren't raped," she chokes out. "We were inseminated."

Inseminated? I can only mouth the word.

She takes another sip of her tea. "It's all . . . here . . ." And pats her journal. "They wanted," she breaks into a coughing fit, "virgin births."

"That's insane." The words are sharpened sticks flinging from my lips. "And Caitlin?" Her name is a broken whisper, but Mom gently shakes her head.

"I don't know," she whispers. "Things changed after that."

"So, Tristan's father . . ."

She stays still again, letting me work through it all.

"No wonder you hated that we dated."

She doesn't say anything but stares at me, not breaking eye contact, and I try to piece the jigsaw together.

Caitlin's code flies into my mind.

I'd listed myself as one of the potential initials, but there'd been other options, and besides, my mother was Suzanne Caraway, not the S.A. initials that the D was linked to.

Except she wasn't always Suzanne Caraway. I look back at the article in the box. *S.A.*

Suzanne Adams.

"Mom . . ."

She shakes her head gently as if she doesn't want me to figure it out, even though I have to. But I can't.

"I was from the virgin birth?"

She holds her lips together, just barely, and her chest is heaving harder, faster.

177

"Whose sperm, Mom?"

Those tears that had been waiting to fall do so now. Only they don't just fall; they cascade.

"Who is my father?" I'm standing; I don't remember standing, but I'm looming over her, and as frail as she is, I want to shake the truth from her. The truth I should have been told long ago, before . . . before . . .

Tristan.

"Is my father Abe Smith?" The words taste like acid, like bile, like a thousand regrets that don't hold a candle to this one despicable truth.

She's not answering.

"I had sex with my half-brother? I got pregnant with . . ."

She presses her lips together and reaches out to me, but I'm backing away, seeing nothing, nothing, and that cry. That one little cry that has haunted me.

She was never supposed to be born.

Every feeling I've ever experienced is balling up in my chest, forcing its way out my throat, and a slashing, tearing, rending scream wrenches through me, through the house, through our lives.

I don't make it to the bathroom. I'm sick, right there, on Mom's floor, in front of her bed. She's too weak to get up, but she's saying my name over and over and over again, and I can do nothing but crawl away. I have nowhere to go. No escape. There's no escaping this. I'm a mouse in a maze, a demented experiment that I've been a part of since before I was born.

Did Tristan know?

My stomach threatens to empty itself again.

Oh my God, what if he knew? What if he always knew exactly what he was doing?

I dig my fingernails into the thin carpet, hold on to the fragile fibers, and do my best to breathe, breathe between sobs, between screams, breathe between my whole life resetting. Everything, everyone, nothing, no one . . . was any of it real?

Somehow, I'm on my feet. I'm fumbling with the dead-bolt on the front door. I'm at the car. My purse, somehow with me. My keys buried at the bottom. Life's happening in flashes, all the extraneous cut out. And once again . . .

I'm running.

CHAPTER TWENTY-NINE

I'm two hours out of town before I'm aware I've left East Texas, left home. Again. My heart beats like war drums deep in my ears, my fingers shake, and deep exhaustion sweeps through me. I look to Percy—

My breath catches at the back of my throat. "I left him."

I swerve over to the side of the highway, cars and semi-trucks zooming past fast enough to make the car vibrate. I rest my head against the hot steering wheel, take a breath, another, in through my nose, out through my mouth.

Percy's just a plant. I would hate it, but I could leave him.

Kat's not, though. Neither are the two other girls.

I look over the steering wheel, the oncoming traffic on the other side of the concrete median coming at me like multi-colored thoughts, all grease and heat and deadly steel, and I can't leave. Not yet.

I have to go back.

The nausea roiling in my stomach threatens to make a reappearance with each turn of the steering wheel, but I pull back onto the highway, take the next exit, turn around, and two hours later, cross the bridge over Suicide Rock for the second time in a week.

It's mid-afternoon by the time I turn onto Main Street. The sun shines directly in my eyes, and I raise a hand to shadow my view. Crowded with vendor trucks for the Feast, I see Main Street for what it truly is — a distraction, a thick, gaudy icing on a cake to hide all the cracks. To keep people from seeing what's really happening in this town.

I drive past the turn-off to my house without looking in its direction. I'm not ready to see her right now. She should have told me, should have—

My knuckles find their way to my mouth. I bite down. Utter a muffled scream. *Focus, Darla*. I don't have time for the breakdown that is coming. That can come tomorrow, or later tonight when I've stopped this. When I've finally done what Caitlin needed me to do all those years ago.

I need to find Kat and the other two girls who are part of her Chosen class.

I rub at the bite marks on my hand, pull off onto a side street near Old Reed Lane, and park the car. Bessie makes that sound again that Karl was worried about, but I can't give it any of my energy. I grab one of my gardening hats from the backseat, pull it low over my face, and make my way through the yards and the trees to Trina and Kat's house.

I still don't know why Trina — and maybe Kat — cleared their rooms out. But it stands to reason that they know what is happening in this town, and the paraphernalia they are hiding is somewhere on the property. Evidence that I can bring to the police and prove to Emmie I'm not nuts. Maybe that journal that has my picture in it. I need to find what they're hiding, what part they think I play in all of this, and I need to find Kat and convince her that she's safer with me. That Trina doesn't have her best interests at heart.

That Trina might not even be her mother.

The thought aches like a splinter buried deep — sharp, stubborn, impossible to ignore. Trina wasn't pregnant, but I was. Trina delivered my baby, didn't let me see her, took her away before I could hold her. And that cry — I *heard* her cry. My hands curl into fists without meaning to.

Then I left town. Then Trina left town. Then Trina came back. Six years ago. At the time of the last Feast. With a teenage daughter.

Kat could be mine.

Adrenaline buzzes through my brain, and it feels like even the shadows are sharp. The trees give way to Trina and Kat's skinny side yard, their wonky fence barricading the way into the backyard. I creep around to the front. The driveway is empty, and Trina's bike is gone from its place by the front door.

I knock on the door, ring the doorbell, and hold my breath. No one answers. I check under the flowerpot, but the spare key is gone. I almost growl in frustration. *Of course it is*. The back door is a no-go, not with the security pole in place. I chew on my lip while I survey my options, then eye the window into Trina's room.

This is crazy. I don't even have Percy to bounce this idea off. But I'm out of time, out of options; I need to get into this house, find the proof I need, find Kat, and stop the Blessing.

I pick the pot up, happy to find it's as heavy as it looks, and throw it at Trina's single pane window. A loud crack pierces the air, and the flowerpot explodes into shards that fall all over the shrubs. A spiderweb of cracks splinters through the middle of the window, but it's not broken. I jiggle it to see if maybe I've dislodged it enough to slide it open past the lock, but it doesn't move. I pick up one of the larger shards from the pot and throw it as hard as I can, and this time, the window shatters inward.

I tear off a piece of my shirt — it had holes in it anyway — and clear off the jagged edges before gingerly climbing in.

My eyes take a second to adjust to the dark.

Her crucifixes are back along with the Jesus above her bed. I hold my breath, listening for any sounds that indicate someone in the house, but it's quiet except for the ticking of the wall clock by Trina's door. I didn't notice it last time, but the time is off by a good five hours, and there's a black mark on the glass above twelve. I turn on the lights and take a closer look. Trina's drawn a cross over the glass, a cross with a bird on one side and a jagged circle on the other.

I don't know what it means, just that it must tie back to the Church. Trina's clock says there are only five hours to midnight. Five hours from now is 10:14. I grab my phone, flip through my photos to the flyer I found in Trina's nightstand.

10:14 p.m. B101.

A countdown to Kat's Blessing?

My heart slides into second gear, and I hastily pull up the Church website on my phone and check the schedule for the Feast. The Light the Night bonfire is scheduled for then. As well as the Sanctified Men's Offering.

I press my lips together and move on. Trina's nightstand still has her COES bible and purple toy, but anything associated with the Feast has been removed. The box of dolls under her bed is still missing, and there's no trace of the *Her Savior* journal with my picture on the first page.

I open her door and the push lock pops. She'd locked her bedroom again. I can only guess at why.

I turn back around to take another look — the clock, the Jesus, the desk clear of everything except her latest batch of soap. The vase of oleander cuttings, no blooms, which is odd. "It's August," I mutter. Prime blooming season for oleander.

I stop and pick up one of the twigs. There's still water in the vase, and the cuttings are supple — still alive. "But where are the blooms?"

The beautiful, toxic blooms.

"Oh no . . ." My gaze snaps to Trina's soap. The soap she uses on her patients, on Mom, on Kat. The soap with that floral and spice aroma I couldn't quite place.

Orange, like Trina said. Orange.

And oleander.

I never recommend oleander to my clients with families or pets. Oleander causes rashes when in contact with the skin.

When ingested, dizziness, nausea, lethargy, headache and, in big enough quantities, coma and death. It's not a family-friendly plant.

Weakness shoots through my legs, and I find myself leaning against the doorframe for support, but I manage to pop a bar of soap out of Trina's silicone mold. I empty the vase out the window and use the bottom to smash the still-curing soap.

The soap breaks into small pieces, and I bash it again, again, until it's nothing but moist crumbs.

And oleander flower petals.

Trina's been poisoning Mom and Kat through her soap, through her tea? "Why?" I breathe. Why care for Mom and poison her at the same time? Why hurt Kat?

My mind flips through everything I know about oleanders. Used in witchcraft, the name rooted in mythology, the plant's association with charm and romance. "None of that fits." I stare at the soap as if I can divine answers from the destruction.

Oleander used to be thought to have air-purifying properties. In a Zen Garden, oleander represents spiritual cleansing.

Could that be it? Trina's been spiritually cleansing Mom and Kat?

I cast another gaze around Trina's room and leave. There's no sense in covering my tracks this time. I've left imprints the size of a giant's, and there's no hiding them.

Kat's room is still devoid of the crib, but I spot one of her yearbooks on the shelf next to her bed and take a few moments to snap pictures of Emily Jones and Jessica Worth, the other two girls in her Chosen class. They'll be at the Feast with Kat tonight. If I can't get Kat to listen to me, maybe one of them will.

I search the rest of the house, including closets, the pantry, cupboards, nothing. There's only the garage left.

I open the door to the connected garage and fumble for the light switch. A dim, yellow light turns on and reveals a hoarder's paradise.

Furniture is stacked on top of furniture. Books are scattered around the floor like paving stones. And in the corner of the garage, closest to the door and on top of a battered bookshelf, is the crib.

CHAPTER THIRTY

I open a message to Emmie and start filming a video. "See, Ems, I'm not crazy. Maybe a criminal, but I'm not crazy." I pan across the garage and focus on the crib, then walk back through the house to Trina's room, making sure to get the living room Emmie studied in the shot and record the creepy Jesus, the soap, the oleander. "She's been poisoning my mom and Kat. Call me when you get this."

It's a large file, and my data limit isn't, but I hit send on the video. I'm not sure if it'll go through, but I have to try. Sweat prickles in my elbows, slicks my fingers. My heart pounds — fast, erratic, desperate. I need Emmie back on my side.

I leave through the front door and lock the handle from the inside before shutting it closed.

The heat crashes into me as soon as I'm outside. It seems to have thickened since I broke through Trina's window, and the air feels heavy and dense. The trees are so tall and thick that it's hard to see the horizon, but if I had money to bet, I'd bet on a storm rolling in. Sometime soon.

According to the Church's website, the Feast is set to begin any minute, and as much as I don't want to be there,

I have to be. There's no sense in going back for my car — parking will be limited at the Church, and I don't want to be stuck getting out of a parking lot later. Despite the heat and the potential for a storm, my best option is to walk.

Families are out all throughout town. Most are hiding from the sun under oversized golf umbrellas. Kids are dressed in casual Sunday wear, sundresses for the girls, long shorts with suspenders and white shirts for the boys. Most of the adults are dressed similarly but in more drab colors.

It's tradition for the Feast, to come as we once were. Simple cut homemade dresses, bonnets. Old-fashioned trousers held up by suspenders. The town looks like a movie set for a historical film. I'm out of place with my gardening hat, jeans, and Simpsons t-shirt, but I'm not the only one. Many of the teens are dressed as they'd be on any normal day, too cool to take part in the tradition. But Kat and the rest of her Chosen class?

They will be in all white.

Everyone is headed in one direction, greeting each other as they come upon friends and fellow Church members, and I feel a bit like a black sheep being herded down Main Street. Ahead, the Church looms on the hill, and a myriad of colors fill the field between the graveyard and the Church parking lot. Large white tents are ordered in military rows, each dedicated to food or drink or religious crafts or t-shirt sales, all to raise money for missions, of course. On the edge, a Ferris wheel has been constructed, and other carnival games are splattered around. Closer to the Church, a large stage has been erected, complete with professional lights and a sound system, and in the clearing just beyond the Church, between the graveyard and the forest, is a large pile of wood for the Light the Night bonfire.

As is tradition, part of the forest has been cleared for the bonfire over the years. Each tree was selectively cut down and left to dry, then carved with the insignia of the Church. From this far away, it looks like nothing more than a pile of sticks, but up close, the engineering feat of building a fire with eight-foot-tall pieces of wood is more apparent.

The Feast is the Church's event, but it's also the town's event. A local spectacle for any curious about the Church or for anyone needing to fill a Friday night.

It's still early, but a bluegrass band starts playing hymnals on stage, and the deceptively easy notes trickle through the dense heat. It's a party, a feast for the senses, and also a feast for the spiritual heart. It's a time to celebrate the blessings bestowed upon the Church through the past six years, and more significantly, for this Feast celebration, a time to acknowledge the two-hundred-year history of the Church.

I push my way through the growing crowd, aiming for the stage. I'm not sure where the leaders or the initiates — the girls — are being kept until showtime, but my guess is somewhere near the heart of the action.

"Darla? What are you doing here?"

His voice, which has always caused me tremors, sends a 6.6 magnitude of nausea through me. I turn to face Tristan.

"Did. You. Know?" I repeat the same question I asked at his house, but there's more venom in my voice this time, more layers of meaning.

He sighs like I'm annoying him. Like he needs to placate me. "Know what?"

"That you're my half-brother."

A hush falls on the world around us, as though it's just the two of us trapped in a bubble.

"That's insane," he whispers, but gray undertones leech into his tanned skin.

"Is it? Ask your parents what they actually do to the Chosen girls. What they did to my mother." I hold his gaze, and I'm certain he knows me well enough to know I'm telling the truth. I just don't know him well enough to know if his reaction is a lie. "Where are they keeping Kat, Emily, and Jessica?"

He shakes his head slowly, side to side, as if he's still processing or in shock.

"Tristan!" I yell his voice like it's a physical slap, and it bursts our quiet bubble. He looks at me then. So does everyone else. I grab his arm, and he immediately jerks away. "Where are they?"

"There's a . . . a tent." He licks his lips as if his mouth has gone dry. "Behind the stage. Women only. Shelly should be there—"

I don't wait for him to finish. He's not my concern. I spin on my heel, jog toward the stage, pushing past people when they don't move quickly enough. I don't know if he believes me. I almost don't care. It doesn't matter right now. What matters is getting to the girls. Convincing them to run away.

Surely, they haven't been inseminated yet. It's too early. Trina's note said 10:14 tonight. The clock in her room is counting down to 10:14 tonight. They wouldn't inseminate them in a tent. Not in public, where anyone can walk in. I'm not too late.

I *can't* be too late.

A few more breaths and I'm at the stage. The bluegrass band is playing a peppy version of some classic hymn, and the speakers blast into my ears as I run past. It's less crowded by the stage, with fewer attendees and more staff, many of whom give me wide-eyed stares as I hurry behind the stage. A temporary chain link fence has been erected and behind it is a white tent completely closed up. My head swivels left, right; there's got to be a gate.

"Excuse me, miss?" A voice calls out from behind me, but I ignore it. They can't arrest me. I don't think.

To the left, directly behind the stage, is the gate. I dart to it.

"Miss, it's not safe for you back here. Cords and equipment and such."

I place my hand on the latch, look back. A security guard has followed me. He holds one arm out, inviting me to follow him. His other hand rests on his baton.

"She's with me," a voice calls out, and the guard turns.

Tristan rounds the corner, his color still not right, but he faces the guard with a white-toothed, everything's-fine smile.

The guard looks between us, a note of disbelief tuning his expression, but he nods and leaves us be.

I wait, poised to run, to fight, to do what I have to do, hand on the latch.

Tristan walks toward me, hands raised.

"The men of the Church, the sanctified ones?" He begins, and I nod for him to go on. "We give an offering every Feast. It's supposed to symbolize a piece of our soul that we dedicate to the Church and to God, a symbol of our devotion to growing the Church and spreading its message."

"And?" I do not have time for this.

"It's our seed, Darla." Tristan's face has gone from pale to bright red. "Semen. They burn it at the Light the Night bonfire. Or at least, they're supposed to."

Everything in me turns to stone. "You are an idiot."

Whatever he thought I was going to say, that wasn't it.

"You never asked questions? It didn't occur to you that that's, oh, I don't know, a *fucking weird* practice?"

"I . . . I've always . . . it's just what we grew up doing, being told," he stammers, but I can see the shock in the white of his eyes, the way he's rewriting his life. "The way it's taught, it seemed . . . it seemed right." His voice is thin, dazed — like a child who's just discovered Santa isn't real.

"Does it still seem right to you?" The gate's latch warms under my too-tight grip. The metal bites into my palm, but I can't let go. I can't trust him.

He slowly swings his head back and forth. "I've got to find Dad. Ask about this."

"Good plan. Meanwhile, I need to find the girls. So they don't get *blessed* with your offering." Ice and heat feed my every word, and Tristan flinches with each syllable. I don't wait for him to respond, to move, I'm already through the gate, looking for the opening to the tent.

It's on the opposite side, facing away from the festival, zipped up tight with a padlock threaded between the two

190

zippers. I press my ear to the plasticky canvas and hear nothing. I jiggle the padlock. It doesn't budge.

"Sorry, Dad," I whisper and pull his gardening scissors out of the side leg pocket of my pants. He'd roll over in his grave if he knew I was about to use them on non-plant material, but in this instance, he might understand. I unfold the metal blades, lock the handles into place, squat next to the corner of the tent, and start cutting.

The material is thick, but I keep Dad's scissors sharp. Heat billows out of the opening I'm cutting, and the scent of hot plastic and something else, something bitter, seeps out. I make the opening just big enough for me to crawl through, hoping if anyone is in there, no one's noticed.

The light that seeps through the canvas is dim, but it's enough to see that the tent is empty. I look around for clues as to where the girls may have gone if they were ever here in the first place. What is this tent used for?

There's a small folding table set up on the side, along with three chairs. Half-used candles have been placed on tall candelabras around the tent, and something about it reminds me of Trina's drawing in her diary. The table itself is covered with a banner of the Church, and a cooled pot of some liquid takes up the center. Next to the pot are three large glasses. There are lip prints on the sides and a bit of liquid left in the bottoms. I pick one up, smell it, and confirm the source of the bitter odor. Next to the pot is a ladle. I dip it into the pot. It's mostly empty, but some sludge is left at the bottom. I scrape it out, pour it onto the table, turn on the flashlight on my camera, and take a better look.

Discolored blossoms and pieces of some vegetable matter swim in the sludge. I pick one of the blossoms up, rub it between my fingers, and smell it. "Not oleander," I mutter, which is a small blessing. But the bitter odor, the chunks of tough, green material, and the blossoms remind me of a cactus. Some cacti are edible; some are hallucinogenic, and some are poisonous.

I scoop a little onto my finger, touch it to my tongue, and recognize it immediately.

"Peyote," I growl.

They gave the girls peyote tea.

It takes between one to three hours for peyote to take effect. The effects? Hallucinations, euphoria, altered perception of space and time, all of which can last up to twelve hours. The girls won't understand what's happening to them.

They won't be able to say no.

CHAPTER THIRTY-ONE

I sneak out the way I came in, duck my head through first, and make sure no one's watching. The field between the tent and the Church is clear, with most everyone on the other side of the fence. It's quiet, other than the faint sound of the bluegrass band's music, but from where I stand, at a distance behind the stage, the sound has distorted.

It's about a dozen yards to the Church entrance, less than a football field, and the Church is the next logical place where the girls might be secluded.

A full hour has already galloped by. Four hours until 10:14, and I still don't know what I'll do once I find the girls. It's not like I can pick them up and carry them out, and in their drugged state, they won't be capable of listening to reason. Right now, the most important thing is finding them.

I jog across the field, avoiding taller patches of sticky grass and keeping an eye out for sneaky fire ant beds, and enter the Church through the old sanctuary. It's been left as it was built, with wooden pews lining the small, cathedral-shaped room and tall yet simple windows on either side. Since the construction of the larger sanctuary on the other side of the Church building, I doubt it's used often, maybe for smaller events and ceremonies, but I check the room anyway.

The preacher's pulpit at the front is the original. It's dinged and dented from the years — the stained wood faded in spots. John Smith the First taught his first sermon from here two hundred years ago to the day, planting the seeds of what this town has become. I run my hand over the smooth surface, shivering at the thought that he's — has always been — my ancestor.

There's no sign that this room has been used lately, and I have an entire church to search. I open the door behind the pulpit that John Smith would enter through and pass into a narrow hallway lined in dark wood. It's musty in here, and I find myself holding my breath as if to stop from breathing in an infectious disease. A swinging door at the end of the hallway is obviously from a more modern era, and I push through into the main church building at the end of one of the corridors.

It's quiet except for the white noise of the air conditioner, and I have a sense that I'm completely alone. Not just in the building but everywhere. As if I've entered a new dimension where I'm the only one who exists.

B101. Tristan had said in Emmie's text messages that room didn't exist at the Church, but I can't trust anyone right now. The stakes are too high. The lights are off, but there is enough ambient light that I can read the names of the rooms — *Love, Joy, Peace, Patience, Kindness, Goodness, Faithfulness, Gentleness, Self-Control.* "The Fruits of the Spirit hallway," I mutter as I come to the beginning, which opens into a small room that holds a coffee machine, a few tables, and the stale scent of old donuts.

There are two other corridors to clear. I take the one on the right and enter a stretch of rooms labeled with names like *Wisdom, Grace, Blessed, Light, Cherished . . .*

Chosen.

I stop. It can't be this easy. But still, I open the door.

It's a simple room. A few chairs gathered in an imperfect circle. A standard window on the opposite side, a whiteboard

194

hanging on the right wall. On the other wall, a quote from John Smith has been stenciled and painted.

Only through our unity and devotion can we be shielded from the darkness that seeks to consume us.

Under the quote is a table with stacked pamphlets. *The Hallmarks of Darkness. Steps to Spiritual Cleansing. What It Means To Be Chosen.*

I pick up the last one and flip through the propaganda. Nowhere in the pamphlet does it mention being drugged. Being inseminated. It's all about preparing one's mind and body to receive the blessing.

"Dead end," I mutter and leave the room.

The last hallway leads to the Church offices. They're locked, of course, and with sturdier locks and doors than Trina's place. I'm about to blow through it and into the main sanctuary when I stop.

The bookshelf. The one with all the Church records and membership directories. Next to the table with the visual model of the Church's history. It's empty.

And suddenly, my mind makes that last connection that I've been missing. The reason why Caitlin focused her research on the Smith family, the true family only a few knew about, and not the Church. It was never about the Church.

The secrets lie with the family.

* * *

Pastor Abe's house is a five-minute walk from the Church if you go by the sidewalk. Three minutes if you take the old dirt road that follows the curve of the forest.

I duck behind a shrub that borders the Smiths' backyard. This used to be a handy way to sneak Tristan in and out of his house back when he still lived here with his parents. Back when I didn't know.

But did he?

The question burns white-hot in my mind, a brand that'll leave its mark for the rest of my life. His reaction seemed real enough, but that's not enough.

I've only been inside the Smith home a few times. It's a giant colonial, a registered historical home denoted by a cast iron plaque, officially called the John Smith Manor. A wrap-around porch commands one side of the home, a Victorian-styled turret on the other side. It's painted a soft yellow and, from the sidewalk, looks every bit the charming, welcoming home one would expect from a pastor's family.

The back is much the same — the manicured lawn, the gazebo where Tristan asked me to prom, the deck with patio furniture. But all the curtains are closed, even the downstairs ones where I know there to be a living room and a kitchen, so I can't tell if Abe and Karen are still home.

I'm going to have to take my chances. Either the Chosen girls are in there right now, or the proof of what the Smiths are doing.

I shove my phone into my back pocket, check to make sure Dad's scissors are still in my side cargo pant pocket, and creep through their backyard.

The shrubs are fuller and taller than when I was here last. Whoever their gardener is, I'm grateful for their fertilizer — the foliage provides the perfect cover.

I'm also grateful that so much of the house is still the same — the old windows, the large live oak with the thick branch that reaches toward Tristan's old room, and especially, the steps nailed into the tree from Tristan's childhood. I sneak closer, and it looks as if they've been repaired or replaced, likely for the grandchildren's safety.

On the lower branches of the tree, a tree house has been built. It's painted granddaughter pink, with purple and blue flower decals on the sides. I'm sure the inside is a fairytale dream, but I'm not interested in the inside. I'm interested in knowing whether the roof is sturdy.

I check again that the curtains are all closed and no one is peeking out, and lift myself on top of Tristan's kids' treehouse. The branch he used to climb onto from his window is just above the treehouse roof. I grab hold, check that it's healthy and strong, clamber on top. The bark scratches my skin, the rough knobs and little twigs prick at my knees, and I quickly conclude that climbing trees is not for adults.

Tristan's bedroom window never locked, and I'm hoping it hasn't been fixed. I scoot closer to the house, and the tree limb bends under my weight just enough to make me hold on tighter. Tristan's window is within reach, and I hold my breath as I place one palm flat on the dirty glass and push up.

It doesn't budge. I let my breath out slowly, tighten my core and squeeze the branch with my thighs, place both hands against the window and try again.

There's a loud squeak, and a small opening appears at the bottom of the window, just enough for me to cram my fingers under and lift. From the creaking and groaning and the start-stop progress, I can tell it hasn't been opened in a while, and I can only hope that the sounds can't be heard through the rest of the old house because there is no turning back now. I have no quick escape from this position.

With the closed curtains and the lights off, I have zero chance of seeing if the room has been rearranged and, more importantly if anything is blocking the window that I'm going to knock over. I get it open enough to squeeze through and pull myself from the branch into the house, head and shoulders through the window, covered by the dusty curtains, legs dangling against the side of the house.

The windowsill digs into my hands, and the corpses of long-dead June bugs crunch under my palms. I pull myself in, brace my hands on the floor, and wiggle the rest of the way into the room. The curtains slide from my head, down my back, my hips, and finally, I'm free.

I blink, adjusting to the low light, expecting dust-covered trophies and high-school memorabilia.

It's pink.

A lot of pink.

Tristan's room has been transformed into a nursery. A changing table stands on one side, a crib on another, and toys litter the floor. A whooshing sound comes from the corner of the room, but it's the soft breathing coming from the crib that has me frozen.

Tristan's youngest is fast asleep in the crib. She's toddler-sized and has dried snot crusting her nose. Her breathing comes out in soft snores, and sweaty, golden curls cover half her little face.

I can't help it. My feet take over, and I'm at the crib, watching her little chest rise and fall, her eyelids flutter as she dreams. The urge to stroke her cheek is almost unbearable, but I can't. She's not mine, and mine shouldn't have been born.

But even still, knowing that, the something I thought was broken forever deep inside, it breaks again, shatters, cuts up my insides with a million sharp shards.

I should leave, immediately, but I'm already here, and I've got no other ideas. I pull myself away from Tristan's sleeping daughter, tiptoe across the room, open the door as quietly as I can, and slip into the hallway.

The house is silent, but there's no way I'm alone. Karen wouldn't leave her granddaughter napping alone in the house. I stand still, listening for a few seconds, but there's nothing other than the soft whooshing from the room behind me. I pull the door to almost closed, leaving just a slip so I can sneak out the way I've come in, and tread on the soft carpet runner to deaden my footfalls.

Karen and Abe's bedroom is down this hall to the right, in what would be the turret on the side of the house. The stairs leading down to the front hall are to the left. There are other doors in this hallway, and one at the very end that could be a utility closet or stairs to the attic.

I don't have a clue where to start or what to look for, but there has to be evidence in this house that the Smiths are getting young girls pregnant. Maybe not physical rape, but it's a rape just the same. Convincing them that it's God's will for them to give a virgin birth, and what for? To create a pure generation of COES members? It's the only reason I can come up with. Maybe there's a manifesto in the house. Or some sort of procedural manual. I need *something* I can take to the police today, before it happens again.

The downstairs office would be too obvious. If they don't want anyone to know what's going on, or at least only a select few to know what's going on — the Chosen — the information would be hidden.

My gaze slips to the door at the end of the hall again. If that is an attic, maybe there are some hidden skeletons.

I hurry down the hallway, checking to make sure any open doors are nothing but empty rooms as I pass. The sound of running water escapes Abe and Karen's room, the door cracked. The shower? Whoever is home won't be in there forever. I open the door at the end of the hallway, and a set of stairs leads up. I close the door behind me, holding it tight so the latch doesn't click, and climb the ten or so steps to the next floor. Another door blockades the top of the stairs.

A door with an electronic keypad over the doorknob.

CHAPTER THIRTY-TWO

My heart skitters against my chest, and my mouth has gone dry. Who the hell puts an electronic lock on their attic door? I don't know what's behind this door, but whatever it is will be enough to take down the Smith family and stop this procedure before any other girls are assaulted. I'm sure of it.

I strain my ears to hear anything at the bottom of the steps, anything that might indicate they know I'm here. I jiggle the doorknob, but the door doesn't budge. It's newer than the rest of the house and looks industrial. No ice pick is getting through this thing. I'll need to enter a code.

My chest tightens, then releases with the realization. Code? *B101*

It's not a room. It's the only reason Trina would have written it on the back of the Feast flyer. It's a code.

I hold my breath and enter it. The soft beeps reverberate through the small space. What if this sends a notification to the Smiths that someone's entered the code? Is this contraption that advanced?

There's no way to know, and there's no choice but to keep moving forward. I press enter.

With a soft click, the door unlocks.

The knob twists easily under my hand, the door swings open, and my lungs finally release my held breath. The room is dark. No windows. A mechanical whir comes from somewhere on the other side of the attic. I fumble at the threshold, searching along the wall for a light switch until my hand bumps across the switch and a soft lamp light floods the attic.

It's decorated like a living area. Cream-colored rugs on the floor, a puffy chair in the corner, and silk greenery along the walls. And if it wasn't for the exam table in the middle of the room, it would have been quite cozy.

I whip my phone out of my back pocket, open the message to Emmie, and record another video. The first still hasn't been sent, but it's all I can do. No more photos that can be taken out of context. I scan the room, taking it all in: the table with the stirrups at the end, the deep freezer at the side of the room, the source of the whirring sounds, and the decor.

"I'm in Pastor Abe Smith's attic. They create virgin births here, Emmie, inseminating young girls in this room after drugging them. This is our proof."

I continue walking around the attic, capturing all the details, before stopping in front of an old secretary's desk. The bottom is burled wood with a key inserted into a lock. But the top is glass. Tall, wooden doors with large lead-rimmed squares that hold antique, wavy glass. Large jars are stacked on the inside, but it's hard to make out their contents through all the layers of ancient glass. I hit stop on the video and send what I have so far to Emmie, but the signal is poor — I'll have to try again later. I shove the phone back in my pocket and unlatch the doors.

Six jars take up three shelves. Six large jars of varying sizes with metal lids. Six jars that cannot contain what they look to contain.

I slide one out, hands trembling, and kneel with it on the ground. It's the size of a commercial-sized pickle jar, the kind you see behind concession stands at ball games. My mind slides to the practical, to the logical, to the things I can make sense of. The cool weight of the jar. The yellowed and hand-printed label with a forty-year-old date. The slow slosh of the clear liquid inside.

The baby suspended in the liquid, translucent eyelids closed, floating as if it's made of air.

"No, no, no, *no*," and it's all I can get out. I gently place the baby on the floor and pull out another one, another one, another one, all in various stages of advanced development.

Eloise said Karen had miscarriages, but these couldn't possibly be hers, could they? Or . . .

I pull out the last one. This jar is more modern, and the label isn't handwritten but printed by a label maker.

January 17, 2002

My breath sucks backward in a strangled scream, and it sounds like glass breaking, high and fragile and not mine. But it is mine. The jar . . . mine, too.

It's her.

I clasp her to my chest, curl around her, and do my best to keep her safe and still, but I've already failed. I failed her sixteen years ago. I bring my forehead to hers through the glass. Trina had said she was deformed. A lie — she's perfect. What happened to her? Why is she here?

What did Trina *do*?

I have a thousand questions and no answers, but my heart is here, right where I left it, with her. Trapped inside glass and preserved in some sort of liquid. She should be buried, not kept like this.

My body feels like it's not mine, but instead, I'm wearing it. It's heavy and clumsy, hard to move. I don't have access to the controls. My hands clench around the jar, but I can't feel it. I'm numb. My fingers, my lips, my cheeks. Tears fall to my lap and stain the jar, but I can't feel them fall. I'm not here. This isn't happening. This isn't real.

I don't know how long I stay there. How long I cannot move. But it's long enough to feel that too much time has passed.

Long enough to hear the click of the attic door opening.

CHAPTER THIRTY-THREE

Karen stands on the other side of the room, dressed in a loose, cream-colored linen dress, hair still damp from her shower. She clutches a small gun in one hand, pointed at me, and her cell phone against her ear in the other. "Put my granddaughter down."

My body refuses to cooperate. Instead, I hear what sounds like my voice whisper, "Why is she in a jar?" My hands tremble, sweating around the jar as I hold tighter.

Karen's gaze softens, and she looks over at the jars I've placed on the floor with an expression similar to a new mom looking at her baby. "She's sleeping. Don't worry, she's safe in there. Preserved."

"Preserved?" I repeat, the word harsh and acidic at the back of my throat.

Karen nods. "She'll wake up soon. Once the Savior returns. Now put her down. Gently." She gestures with the gun, and finally, I find the energy to move, to do as she says.

"Good. Now step away. Over there please. Ten steps." She gestures, once again with her gun, toward the exam table. "No, I got this," she says into her phone, then hangs up and puts it into one of her dress pockets. She refocuses on me.

"Karen, that's my daughter. And she's dead." It hurts to say it, more now than it ever has in the past, but I have to reason with her.

Karen lets out a little laugh. "You really have no idea what's happening here, do you?"

"Tell me." I hold out my hands. "Help me understand."

She shakes her head. "You will. Soon enough. There are materials we need under that table. Grab them. Keep your eyes on me."

I don't. I stay where I am. She's not going to kill me. She can't. She's the pastor's wife. Tristan's mom. I've known her since I was in diapers.

"I do not want to shoot a bullet into your leg and risk waking up my granddaughter downstairs, but I will. Do it." Her hand is steady as she speaks, and I have no doubt that she knows how to use that gun.

I swallow against the lump in my throat, reach blindly under the table, and fumble against the cold metal until I run across rough, thick fabric, my eyes never leaving Karen's. I knock it all to the ground.

"Pick them up. Sit on the table."

"Excuse me?"

There's a loud crack. I scream, duck; the lamp across the room explodes.

Karen doesn't even flinch. She simply re-aims the gun at me and waits, silent.

Electricity shoots from my fingertips to my spine. I grab the things off the floor, sit on the table, and look down at what Karen made me collect. In my lap are two black bands with yellow buckles and a pair of black wrist restraints that look like they came straight from the supply closet at the super-max prison on the other side of the lake.

"If Esme wakes up, she is really going to throw us off schedule, and you do *not* want that. Put them on. Bands on your ankles and thighs. Then the wrist restraints."

Once again, I do as she says. I wrap the black bands around my ankles, thread one end through the other at the buckle, and cinch it tight. The strap around my thighs goes right around my side pants pocket. I dart a glance at Karen, but she hasn't broken eye contact. I pretend to fumble with the strap, slip my hand inside my pocket, and palm Dad's folded scissors before tightening this strap too. They won't be able to cut through this fabric, but if I can manage to unfold them without her noticing, they're sharp enough to do some damage.

I push my hands through the wrist restraints. "Please," I say before I tighten the band around my wrists. "Whatever this is, we can go downstairs. Talk about it."

She doesn't say a word, just cocks her head and slides her finger to the safety on the side of the gun.

My hands tremble so hard that it takes a few tries, but I thread the plastic in and pull it tight around my wrists with my teeth, keeping the small rectangle of metal hidden inside my hand. Only when I show her that I'm bound does she walk over, keeping the gun on me at all times. She kneels at my feet and tightens the ties even further. She moves to check my wrists, and my heart is a steel-toed boot kicking mercilessly deep in my throat. If she sees the scissors, I lose all my chances.

She reaches around and tightens the wrist restraints, her eyes on the buckles, not my clenched hands.

"There now. That's better, isn't it?" She pats my head, steps back, and stares at me with an expression that's one part proud, the other part undefinable. Behind her, the deep freezer clicks.

"Do you know what this place is?" She steps away from the table and gazes at the freezer.

"A den of iniquity?" I spit. Maybe not the best tactic to be sarcastic with a woman holding a gun while I'm tied up and helpless, but the rage simmering in my bones needs an outlet.

She shakes her head, a beatific expression on her face, the gun relaxed at her side, still in her hand. "A vault. The future of the Church. This receptacle," she places a hand on the freezer and caresses the top, "contains generations of souls destined for purity. It is our insurance — the purity of the

Church will continue, and we will succeed against the forces of evil."

"You're insane."

"No more than Noah when he built the ark. Or Abraham being willing to sacrifice his own son. Or even Joan of Arc who followed visions from the Lord and helped win a war. I am doing the Lord's will."

"What's in the freezer?"

Behind the exam table on the other side of the room, the attic door clicks open. Someone enters. Karen's eyes flit to the other side of the room, and I use the opportunity to unfold Dad's scissors, handles in, blade out. "I told you I had this under control."

"I heard you—"

Trina.

"—But I don't trust you," she continues, making her way across the room. "Or your methods." She gestures at the shattered lamp across the room, and despite the situation, despite the very real fact that Trina is deeply involved with all of this, I feel a slight relief. Trina's a nurse. Nurses swear oaths. Oaths like *do no harm*.

But she did poison my mother.

She stops at my side, looks into my eyes. "Are you okay, Darla?"

I lift my handcuffed hands in response, keeping the blades pressed between my prayered palms. She pats my hand, and her palm is cool and dry.

I ask my question again. "What's in the freezer?" Though I think I know.

Neither of them answers. Instead, they have a silent conversation with their eyes, and then Trina takes a breath, runs her hand along the exam table. "As did Mary, so do we."

I look from Karen to Trina, but they are on the same page in a different book.

"You were conceived, right here," Trina says. "At the time, we only had Pastor Abe's father's and grandfather's offerings. Since then, other sanctified men have come forth. Every Feast, we take in new offerings, and we are able to further expand our population of children derived from virgin births. In just a few generations, we will have set out to do what Mary Smith envisioned. A pure Church."

"Mary Smith?"

"The mother of the Church." Karen takes over. "She leads us from the beyond, directing each new pastor's wife so that one day, the Savior will be born. It is not the men who lead the Church, but the women. Every Feast, we collect the offerings of the men we have selected. They have no knowledge of what we do here."

All those pictures of the pastors' wives through the years, at his side, silent and demure, and I have no doubt that she's telling the truth.

"So that freezer . . ."

"Holds the offerings of Chosen men."

"Sperm?" I clarify.

Karen crinkles her nose at this.

"Let me get this straight. You drug teenage girls and then force them to get pregnant with sperm you keep in a freezer in your attic?" I let every ounce of disbelief, doubt, and condemnation seep into my tone.

A saccharine smile spreads across Karen's face. "We do not *force* anyone. The girls volunteer. Their parents give permission and sign a contract of support. Everything we do here is completely legal."

Legal? My legs shift against the restraints, as if my muscles believe I can make a run for it. "There's no way any of this is legal. What about the peyote?"

She shrugs. "The use of peyote as a religious aid is well documented. The age of consent in Texas is seventeen. Besides, there is no sexual intercourse. The procedure is completely pure."

"How many?" I croak. My voice is almost gone. "How long have you been doing this?"

Trina clears her throat, stopping Karen from answering.

207

I try a different tactic. "Is Abe my father?" My words come out scratchy and hoarse, and I'm not sure they hear me until Karen shakes her head.

"John Smith the First is your father. You were the only child to be born of that offering. A very special child indeed." Karen strokes my hair. "In a way, you're Tristan's great-aunt. You can see why I didn't want you two to date, but there is no reasoning with young people." She sighs and throws the comment away, as though unknowing incest is a boring topic.

Meanwhile, I grip the scissors harder, transferring the sick feeling in my throat to the clench of my hands. Hoping that I'm keeping my expression hard, seemingly unaffected by this news.

Trina's watch beeps with an alarm. "Karen," she says and shows Karen her watch, "there is still much to do."

Karen gives a slight nod and steps away while Trina fiddles with something at her side. Out of the corner of my eye, I watch as she drags a needle and a vial out of her bag.

So much for her nurse's oath; do no harm, my ass.

I wait until she gets close, pretend I don't see anything, slide the blades past the tips of my fingers, and swing my arms up hard — aimed straight for her face. I hit something solid, and from Trina's shriek, I'm guessing it landed.

Karen jumps to Trina's aid, gun in hand, too close to my face. "Drop them."

It takes every bit of willpower I have to do what she says. But in gardening scissors versus gun, gun wins. The blades clatter to the floor, and Trina comes into my field of vision, her hand clasped against her cheek, blood trickling down her chin. And a full needle in her hand.

"If you weren't you, there'd be something much different in this needle."

She plunges it into my restrained arms, and everything fades to gray, then black.

CHAPTER THIRTY-FOUR

Something sharp, cold, and wet, cuts into my cheek and into my hip. A loud rushing noise, like a strong wind blowing through the trees, bleeds into my senses. Pine and wet riverbank and the bitter scent of peyote creep in the more I wake, and something else — orange; lavender.

Oleander.

My eyelids are lead weights. I force them to open, but the world is bleary, blurry, full of shadows. A massive headache throbs behind my eyes, my skin itches from head to toe, and I try to move, but my hands . . . .

Right. The wrist restraints.

A warm light flickers in the distance, but it's a few more moments before I find the strength to sit up, before things clear.

Water rushes around both sides of me. My hair is soaking wet, as is the sheer, sleeveless white shift dress I'm wearing. Where are my clothes? My arms, legs, and hands are covered in red scratches and small bumps, and I know Trina has scrubbed me with her soap. In her eyes, I've been spiritually cleansed.

Trees tower overhead, and the river disappears into the shadowy distance. The first star appears in a darkening sky, and I recognize its position. I recognize the curve of the river, the tree with the thick vine that hangs on the opposite side, and the riverside beach where I've had too many beers.

I'm tied to Suicide Rock.

Black dots pollute my vision, and my breaths come short, fast, uneven. I pull against my restraints, but they don't budge. The restraint around my thighs has been removed, but chains descend from the bands around my wrists and ankles, descend into the river. I can't stand. I can't jump in. I can't swim away.

A low hum of a song can be heard above the panicked gasps of the river. The campfire on the bank of the river is low, coals burning red hot. People-shaped shadows move at the edge, but I can't tell who's there. Or how many of them there are.

Behind me, a motor approaches, purring softly.

The nose of a flat-bottomed fishing boat glides into view alongside Suicide Rock. Perched on its bow is a large camping lantern, and the bright white glow bounces off the river. The motor turns off. There's a splash of something heavy dropped into the water — an anchor? The boat continues to float forward, following the downstream flow of the river, until it softly jerks to a stop in front of me, reaching the end of its tether.

I raise my gaze from the boat to its captain.

Trina sits in the sole pedestal chair at the back of the boat, her hand resting on a small trolling motor, a large bandage covering her right cheek. Behind her, distant lightning flashes, and the first star disappears behind darkening clouds. The heat increases, becoming a physical force pressing down on us all.

And in the base of the boat are the girls.

My pulse flutters, falters. Dressed in white linen dresses to match mine, but with yellow lifejackets buckled around their chests, they gaze vacantly skyward, each holding one glass jar from the attic.

"Trina, let me go, let *them* go, there's still time," I plead, my words nothing more than broken vowels and the occasional consonant. I hold out my hands, but I can't stretch my arms straight. She doesn't look at me, doesn't acknowledge that I've said anything.

"Think of Kat," I say. "You don't want this for Kat."

Trina tilts her head, looking at Kat, not once at me. "Kat is a believer, through and through. Like you, she was born in purity."

Born in purity? The question mark on Caitlin's coded message. "She's Caitlin's daughter?" My voice rises.

Trina looks at me then, the light of the lantern bouncing unnaturally off her profile, her gaze dark and full of holes. "Caitlin wasn't the Savior. It's why I had to bring you home." Her voice is toneless, cold, and she looks away from me like I no longer exist.

The pieces start locking into place — slow, sick clicks in the back of my mind.

"You sent the private investigator?"

She stands without answering me, clears her throat, and faces the campfire. In her hands is her journal. The journal titled, *Her Savior.* The journal with my picture on the inside. She opens it to the middle, where I can see that she has pieces of paper taped inside as if she's prepared a sermon.

"Lunasa is the day that we celebrate and remember Tailtiu, our Great Mother, who sacrificed herself so that her people could prosper."

The chatter and songs around the campfire diminish, and only the whine of the mosquitoes interrupts the silence.

"This Lunasa is uniquely special, and yet our men have forgotten this day and her sacrifice. They have stopped giving honor to the divine feminine who gives of her body to bring life. Instead, they celebrate their accomplishments. What accomplishments do they have that cannot be traced back to the Mother?"

A few voices from the beach shout, "That's right."

"Two hundred years ago, our Mother Mary prophesied these words, declaring that the woman who fits inside these words would be Tailtiu reborn, the Savior of the true Church. Our Church!" She raises her voice at the last. Trina flips a few pages back and then recites.

"She walks two worlds, straddling the line between our land and theirs. Her father was false, and her mother, voiceless. Her firstborn took one breath, and then no more. She is born in purity of the first blood. Like previous Saviors, she has been doubted, cast aside by her peers, and walks a lonely path. Yet still, she perseveres. Chosen Sisters, I submit before you this candidate for our Savior. She fits these words and has been prepared. Do you accept her candidacy?"

There's a chorus of ayes from the shoreline.

"From the womb comes both life and loss. Let us restore loss as we bless life."

At those words, she prods the girls to stand, and one by one, still holding their jars, they dip themselves into the river and float downstream until a rope tied to their lifejacket holds them in place. Once they're off the boat, Trina steps onto Suicide Rock, something silver glinting in her hand.

"Trina, please. Let us go, don't do this." Tears burn their way down my cheeks, and I can't stop the terror bubbling in my chest. "What happens when the babies don't wake up?" Tears flow down my cheeks. "What then?"

"It just means our Savior has not appeared. We will try again. There will be other candidates. We have faith." Her eyes flick to Kat; then she fumbles with the chains fastened to my wrists. I'm pulled as she tightens the chains, pulled until I'm lying on my back, arms outstretched.

"Is this what you did to Caitlin?" I whisper. My words broken; they hurt. "What you'll do to Kat?"

Trina looks me in the eyes, something akin to compassion in them. "Caitlin was not the Savior. Kat is a believer," she says again, her voice taking on a chanting cadence as if she's said the words so many times to herself that they've become a mantra. Thunder breaks loose above us, and the lightning flashes again, closer.

"Kat is an impressionable girl who has been fed these lies her entire life. She doesn't have a true choice. You have to stop this. You have to—"

Trina's watch alarm goes off, and suddenly, I know. I know what happens at 10:14 p.m. It's happened before, and it's happening again.

Come home before she dies, too.

It's me.

I'm the girl in the message.

I'm the one who dies.

"As did Mary, so do we," Trina whispers, placing a knife against my arm.

She plunges it in.

Electric, white pain erupts in front of my eyes, and a scream tears through my throat, but Trina doesn't stop. She drags the knife down to my wrist, stopping just above the restraints, searing pain following the blade. Blood pours from my arm in rivulets, puddling onto the rock and streaming into the river where the girls float.

"This will be easier for you if you don't struggle." She starts on my other arm, digging the knife in deep.

I feel it. Every millimeter. Every layer of skin, muscle, and nerve that she tears through. It's all I can see, feel, hear. My entire world has snapped to these few inches, this flesh that cannot be mine, this cannot be happening, this cannot be me.

My blood pours out, and I can imagine the river turning red. I'm going cold, numb. Trina switches her position and moves to my legs, and I hear myself muttering, "No." She makes another cut, and I can feel the blade, but the pain is distant, not real. I no longer have the energy to struggle.

A blur moves in my periphery. Not from the beach. From the other side of the river. The tribe's land.

Something sails through the air, clunking into the boat with a crash. Trina jerks away from my leg. Her eyes widen as she looks for the source and finds it.

"Jonathan Abraham!" She screams. "No. Go back."

213

Another something flies through the air, hits Trina with enough force to fling her into the river. Then something's splashing in the water, growing nearer, but they're too late. It's all happening too late. My eyes drift open and close. Red and white lights compete with the lightning. The river is falling on my face, someone sits beside me, breathing heavily, and presses something into my hand.

"Darla!" A distant scream, a voice I recognize, and then, it's all gone.

CHAPTER THIRTY-FIVE

"I'm just fine, *mmhmm*. Now, you tend to my daughter."

I try to move, to open my eyes, but my body feels like it's cased in clay. "Mom?" I groan, or rather try to groan, but nothing comes out. I lick my lips and try again. "Mom?"

Shuffling noises at my side, then a warm weight on my forehead. "Right here, baby girl. I'm right here."

But this can't be my mom. The last time I saw her, she couldn't get out of bed. She can't be here.

I try again to open my eyes. They're dry and feel sealed shut, but I manage to open them enough to see.

The room is white, bright. There's a television mounted to the wall and a whiteboard just under it with three faces drawn in three colors. One smiling, one not, one frowning. The words *How is your pain today?* are written underneath.

"Nurse, she's waking up, *mmhmm*," Mom shouts, and I'm able to open my eyes a little more. Move my head.

One side of the room is nothing but a glass wall with a curtain pulled open. The other side has a window, and outside that, I recognize the parking lot.

I'm in the hospital.

A woman walks in, wearing scrubs, followed by my mom — steady on her walker, each step deliberate but strong.

I can't take my eyes off her. Her skin holds more color now, less gray and sunken. There's life in her eyes, not much, but enough to catch the light. She still looks sick — frail, fragile — but not like death is her best friend.

"Imagine meeting you here," the nurse says, and I recognize her. She's Janie, the nurse from the bar.

"I thought you worked in maternity," I croak. She shines a light in my eyes, holds my wrist below some rather thick bandages, and checks the monitor as she checks my pulse.

"Switched departments. Figured a diet of vodka hold-the-tonic wasn't a healthy lifestyle choice." She grins, then fiddles with something to my side. I follow her movements and watch as she adjusts the IV that flows into my arm. "You're looking a sight better than you did when you were admitted, though you'll need to take it easy for a while." She glances at the door to the room. "I'll hold them off for as long as I can." She winks at me, pats my shoulder, and intercepts someone at the door, closing it behind her.

Mom sinks to a chair next to my bed. "Now I know the worry you went through when I wouldn't wake up."

"How long have I been—" A coughing fit takes over.

"Asleep? 'Bout sixteen hours. They had to give you blood. Surgery to fix the tendons. What I wouldn't give to git my hands on that woman." Mom's face twists into angry bear mode, and I see a glimpse of the Mom I used to know.

"How are you better?"

"Someone dropped by to let me know what happened to you. They came in, saw my state, got me here. Docs hooked me up to some medicine and flushed the poison outta my system. Trina's been drugging me. Still got the disease, but it ain't gonna kill me tomorrow."

"The tea. Oleander."

She frowns. "How did you know?"

"Found it in the soap at her house. What happened?"

"Not rightly sure. Everyone seems a bit mystified. The ambulance fellows found this clutched in your hand." She digs

216

in her bag and passes over a wooden figure. "Gossip says Karen and Trina were up to some sort of witchcraft?"

I take the doll from her. The wood seems old, the finish faded, but what's most striking is the girl's hands, stretched out into a T shape, horsehair dangling from her wrists. A large knot of wood is fastened to her back, and if she were lying down instead of standing up, and splashes of red have been spattered over it.

"It's Caitlin," I whisper and turn the figure over so the doll is balanced on the knot of wood. "He saw her tied to Suicide Rock." My thoughts are fuzzy, but I remember those last moments. Trina distracted, being hit by something, falling into the river, then someone next to me until help came, who put this in my hand.

"Trina called out a name — Jonathan Abraham. Do you know who that could be?"

Mom's mouth forms an *O*. "She said he died . . ." She whispers, her voice trailing off into a distant memory.

I try to sit up, but even with the painkillers they're giving me, my arms and my leg hurt too much. "Who died?"

"Trina had a son. She named him Jonathan Abraham, after the COES pastors. Said he died when he was about four years old."

"He came from the direction of the tribe land. Gave me this." I rub my thumb over Caitlin's face, the time-worn wood smooth.

"Well, whaddya know," Mom laughs quietly. "The witch-child is Trina's long-dead son."

There's a knock on the door, and my nurse comes in, followed by a whirlwind that is Emmie.

"Oh my God, Darla, I'm so so, so, so, *soooooo* sorry. I should have listened. I know you're not crazy, but then there were all those crazy things and they just couldn't be true and I got your videos." She takes a breath. "I'm sorry. This is all my fault."

"How on earth is this your fault?"

"Well, if I'd have believed you, you wouldn't have felt the need to find all that evidence."

I just raise my eyebrows. They're one of the few things that don't hurt.

"Okay, maybe you still would have, but I would have helped. You wouldn't have been alone."

"It's okay, Ems."

"No, no, it's not. I did put the call out to all our friends trying to find you. Ivan's the one who finally did."

I can feel my face crinkle. "Ivan?"

"Yeah. Somehow, he knew exactly where you'd be. Called the ambulance and told them to meet us there. Actually, that's kind of weird, isn't it?"

A pair of police officers appear in the doorway, kicking Mom, Emmie, and the nurse out of the room. I tell them everything I know. From the Smiths' attic to the women's cult, to the journal Trina kept, even the private investigator who first delivered the message that brought me home. I give them the doll and tell them about the witch-child, supposedly Jonathan Abraham, who may or may not live on the Atakapa reservation, who may or may not have witnessed Caitlin's murder. In turn, they inform me what happened after.

The girls were brought to the hospital. They hadn't been inseminated. That was apparently planned for after their 'blessing' in the river. Trina was found downstream, unconscious, with a lump on her head. She woke up when the rescue team found her and proceeded to babble-confess everything. The babies were recovered from the river as well and were being taken to the morgue for post-mortems. Both Karen and Trina were arrested for kidnapping, assault, and using illicit drugs on minors. Karen was charged due to storing human remains in her house. Neither named any of the other women who were at the river.

The officers leave, and I take what feels like the first unhindered breath since I arrived in East Texas. This still isn't home, and maybe it won't ever be again, but at the very least, I'm starting to understand Dad's wisdom all those years ago.

You gotta cut away the dead for a chance at life.

Now I understand what happened to my daughter, and to Caitlin. Both sacrificed in service of a delusion two centuries in the making. And now that I know, maybe I can finally let them go.

Maybe I finally get to have my chance at life.

***

A few days later, the hospital releases me. I'll need physical therapy and months of recovery, but all said, I was lucky. Luckier than Caitlin.

A nurse wheels me into the lobby, where Emmie waits to take me home. Only her gaze is locked on something across the room, hands clenched at her side.

"You've got a lot of nerve showing your face here." Her words are deep and fiery.

I follow her gaze and land on Pastor Abe, who's standing at the door, blocking my exit. He ignores Emmie, instead landing his focus on me.

The nurse wheels me closer, and Emmie steps between me and Abe. Her eyes glint and her body is completely tense like she's ready to fight. "We need a security escort out of the hospital." She tells the nurse, and the nurse starts to stammer.

I hold up a hand, even though it shoots pain all the way through my arm. "What do you want, Abe?"

I've never seen him like this. His button-up shirt is wrinkled, and he's sporting at least two-day-old stubble. A hat is pulled low over his face, and dark sunglasses cover his eyes. If I didn't know better, I'd say he'd been on a bender.

"Karen is innocent." He stabs his finger at me. "Confess to your lies or I'll make sure you never set foot in this town again."

Emmie takes a breath to speak, but I stop her. "Still on that old threat?"

He sputters.

"I'm not lying, Abe, and neither are the rest of the witnesses. Karen was knee-deep in some crazy shit, and no amount of denial is going to make that go away."

He smiles and shakes his head as if I'm a child to be pacified. "You're wrong. Time will out the truth. Your days are limited here, girl."

"Actually," Emmie speaks up, "I believe it's your time that is limited. From what I hear, the COES board met and unanimously approved your immediate removal as lead pastor."

His skin grays, his smile fades, and his shoulders lower, as if she's pricked a hole in him, and he's losing hot air.

A security guard arrives. "Is there a problem here, Pastor?"

Emmie and I exchange glances. Great, a COES member. I draw in a breath, ready to correct the guard, to tell him we're the ones who need the escort — not Abe. But before I can get a word out, the guard takes another step toward Abe. "Sure would hate to throw you out of the hospital and call the police, what with all your recent troubles."

Abe holds both his hands up and it strikes me that he's not as tall as I remember him being. "I'm leaving." He backs away. "Remember my words, Darla. You've been a thorn in this town since you were a child. But around here, thorns have a way of getting burned out."

A tangle of fear wraps around my heart. I have no doubt that Abe can follow through on his threat.

"Thanks, Pastor," Emmie chirps cheerfully, then waves her phone about and presses the screen. Abe's voice fills the lobby, repeating his threat word for word. "Audio is super clear, don't you think? We'll submit this as part of our statement to the police after we leave here." She steps back and places a hand on my wheelchair, more effective than a muscled bodyguard.

Abe spins on his heel and stomps out of the hospital. A minute later, he speeds out of the parking lot in his midnight blue sedan.

With our escort, Emmie wheels me outside to her waiting car, humming "Another One Bites the Dust."

CHAPTER THIRTY-SIX

Four Months Later

I groan as I stand and stretch out my calves, taking extra care with my left leg — which has mostly healed but is still weak and achy — and clap the dirt off my gloves. There are a few pumpkins left in the garden, but I leave them for the week-end. My small gardening stand is only open on Saturdays and Sundays. The winter vegetables are flourishing, and I pick a few more baskets of pole beans for Kat, Mom, and me to clean and freeze later tonight after the funeral. We should have enough to fill the shelves on the stand this weekend and put a little more toward our goal of renting one of the buildings downtown for a real store.

After Mom sold the rights to her story to a production studio, we had the money to climb out of debt and have a small amount of financial wiggle room for dreams.

"Think the frost will hold off for another month or so?" I ask Percy, who's enjoying his new home, firmly planted in the soil near the gardening shed. I think Dad would have liked him.

A cloud scuttles across the sun, and the diffused light casts the garden, the field, and the forest in a misty sort of scene. I pull the light jacket I wear back around my wrists, covering the bright-pink scars on my arms. They still ache from time to time, and I still find myself dropping more things than I hold, but it's getting better. I'm getting better.

I head inside to wash up. "Kat!" I yell down the hall toward the bathroom. "Hurry up!"

She moved in after a stay at a mental health facility. *Just until graduation, then I'm outta here*, she says. I'm just thankful that her life's mission is no longer to raise a family for the Church.

An hour later, Kat and I wheel Mom down our driveway and toward the cemetery. Karl is still working on our car, but it doesn't matter. With Mom's new need for a wheelchair, we're going to have to find an alternative to get her to doctor visits.

"See Ivan lately?" Mom asks.

I can't help the tightening of my hands around her wheelchair nor the fluttering in my belly. "Not since last week. He said he'll be back sometime next week to fix the porch."

Ivan had taken to fixing up the house. We didn't ask him to, and he refuses money. If I had to guess, it's guilt driving him. Guilt over what, I'm not sure, but I have guesses — guesses like his mother, in the same Chosen class as my mother, was likely one of the women at the river.

Cars, and a local news camera crew, are parked outside the cemetery when we arrive, but it's to be expected. They've made weekly appearances in town since the news broke about the Mary Smith Cult, as it has come to be known. Emmie's café is making bank as a result, and my take-home tips have tripled, so at least one good thing has come of this.

We make our way toward the newer side of the cemetery. Henry and Ems see us coming and help clear a path through the crowd. As one of the babies' mothers, I'll be front and center next to the graves. A perfect headline news photo to add to my collection.

Two other women had come forward, claiming two more of the babies that Karen had in her attic. The others are thought to be Karen's, but she's not here. She's spending time in a mental health facility before being transported to a women's prison in North Texas. Trina's in prison, awaiting sentencing after confessing to Caitlin's murder.

The post-mortem results on the full-term babies were inconclusive. It'd been too long, and the chemicals they'd been kept in had destroyed any potential evidence. Stillborn or murdered? I'm not sure I'll ever know.

On the hill above town, Tristan and Shelly's house watches over the cemetery. Shelly skipped town, leaving her daughters with Tristan, and no one's been able to locate her. I can't tell if Tristan's heart is more broken over her leaving, her betrayal, or what his Church has done to this town.

"How are my baby girls?" Eloise wraps an arm around me and Kat, then pats Mom on the shoulder. She retired from the Church, adopted us, and has become a powerhouse sales-woman in the gardening stand.

Kat hugs her back, but I continue forward, leaving Mom with Eloise. Six tiny holes have been dug in the ground, with six tiny caskets waiting to be lowered. Henry stands at the head of the graves, and more flowers than can fit on the graves back him up. He shows me where to stand — next to my daughter's casket. It's a glossy mauve color and so very small. Before this past week, I didn't know they made caskets this small.

Emmie starts singing an old hymn, and we follow along, the crowd coming together. There aren't many tears. We all said our goodbyes a long time ago. The caskets are lowered into the graves, and a prayer is said. Not a COES prayer, but an Irish one, led by Henry.

"Eternal rest grant unto them, O Lord, and let perpetual light shine upon them. May the souls of all the faithful departed, through the mercy of God, rest in peace. Amen."

We walk back after the funeral, after smiling and saying thank you to too many strangers. Many of the townspeople were there as well, but I still don't know who was at the river that night. And the way some of the women let their gaze slide over me as if I'm made of slippery glass makes me wonder. It keeps me on edge.

We wheel Mom up the new ramp Ivan built.

"Looks like your boyfriend left another present," Kat says.

"Not my boyfriend." The words are a reflex, but I ignore her. My stomach tickles as I bend down and pick up the doll, running my fingers over every inch. The time it must have taken to do this . . .

"Is it you?" Mom asks.

I nod, speechless. Jonathan Abraham, the town's mysterious witch-child. Born without the ability to talk, Trina had given him to the tribe. Eventually, he'd shown the police where he buried Caitlin after rescuing her body from the river. He is Caitlin's cousin, after all. And all this time, he'd been trying to tell his story, and Caitlin's story, through the dolls left to people in the community.

He'd caught me in my essence. Kneeling on the ground, hands in the earth, plants blooming all around. It's made from a solid piece of wood, but the plants are real. Little blossoms that fit into tiny holes all around me. It's a blossom flower vase. It's art.

"Put these inside with the others?" I ask Mom, and she takes it from my hand.

"For sale at the shop?" She examines it as if she's trying to assign a price.

I shake my head. "No. This one is mine."

Kat flicks her gaze to mine, and it's the same expression Caitlin used to give me when I didn't make sense to her. Now that I know, I see Caitlin in her every move. Don't know how I couldn't see it before.

"We'll see you later, Mom. Meeting Emmie."

Mom unlocks the door and wheels herself inside. I wait until the deadbolt flips over, and she's safe. We've all become a lot more cautious over the past few months.

It's a twenty-minute walk to the river, but even though it's early December, it feels like a crisp autumn day. Emmie had offered to drive, but today, I'd wanted to walk. To have time to answer all of Kat's questions about Caitlin. About her mother.

"Favorite food?" she asks. It's a warm-up question before we get to the deeper ones.

"Bean burritos."

She nods like, yes, this makes sense. "Favorite book?"

"*CosmoGirl*."

Kat snorts.

I've answered all these questions before, but the answers have become a comfort blanket of sorts for Kat, grounding her after the earth crumbled under her feet.

She's a few minutes before her next, and her words come out soft and hesitant. "Would she have loved me?"

I stop, turn to her, taking her face in my hands. Say to her exactly what I would have told my own daughter. "More than words can possibly express."

Kat's eyes fill with tears, as do mine. I stroke her cheek and give her a let's-be-brave smile before we continue on.

Emmie's car, along with Karl's beater and Ivan's Jeep, are already parked when we arrive. Tristan's truck is there, too, and my heart clenches in my chest. I've tried to avoid him over the past few months. I think he's also tried to avoid me.

Kat and I enter the footpath and make our way through the bare trees. A breeze blows through, rattling branches and kicking up leaves.

I haven't been back since that night, and it has an air of abandonment. Even the teens stopped using the beach after the story broke.

Branches litter the ground, and clear prints of animal tracks are embedded in the soft sand by the river. The gang already has a fire blazing, and Emmie stands once she sees us. She wraps Kat in a big hug — she'd warmed up to her after she became *unbrainwashed*, as Emmie put it.

Karl comes up and gives me a hug. Ivan too.

Tristan hangs back, wearing a new Trinity Falls Real Estate shirt, clearly uncomfortable, and that's just fine with me. Maybe he didn't know. Maybe he had nothing to do with his mom's and his wife's plans, but I still haven't forgiven him. Maybe with time. But not now — not yet.

On the other side of the riverbank, bushes rustle, and Jonathan Abraham emerges. He's in worn jeans and a loose button-up shirt. His long hair is typical of the Atakapa, but his balding spot isn't.

I raise a hand and wave to him, my stomach fluttering. He ducks his head.

"He showed," Kat breathes.

"I hoped he would," I say as Emmie passes out the little paper boats with candles on them. Each boat has something on it that reminds us of Caitlin. Mine is the picture of all of us here, back when we were almost innocent. Kat's is the inside page of their shared Initiation book, with both their names on it.

Ivan starts singing Caitlin's favorite song, "It's My Life," lights his candle and places it in the river. The water catches the small boat and carries it downstream.

We all join in, lighting our candles and placing our boats in the water. By the time we get to the chorus, the twinkling lights of the boats have disappeared around the bend. I look across the river, but Jonathan Abraham is gone.

We turn back to the fire, and one by one, we all take a seat, Kat wedged between Emmie and me. The heat of the flames brushes my shins, and for the first time in what feels like forever, my breath comes easy. There's a flutter in my belly — light, quiet — like little butterflies dancing.

We go round the circle, each of us telling Kat our own stories of her mother. I've never seen Kat smile so big, so true.

Another flutter stirs low in my belly, impossible to ignore. I gasp, cover my stomach, wait.

"Darla, are you okay?" Kat places a hand on my shoulder, and I look into her green eyes.

I flip back through my mental calendar, the times I attributed my missed period to the extreme stress my body had been through. At the Feast, the Chosen girls, Kat, weren't given Mary Smith's blessing.

But — my heart matches the pace of the stirring in my belly.

Was I?

THE END

ACKNOWLEDGMENTS

Stories don't grow in isolation. They take root in quiet conversations, scribbled notes, sleepless nights — and in the people who make space for them to emerge.

This one began with an old family tale, and blossomed into a story that, at its heart, is about family.

To my husband: thank you for your steadiness, your patience, and your willingness to hold the real world together while I slip into the shadows of another one.

To my two patooties: thank you for being my cheerleaders, my biggest supporters, and for reminding me — always — why stories matter.

To Julie Glover and Rob Eveling — thank you for the honest reads, the tough questions, and the steady guidance through each revision. You helped this story become what it was meant to be.

To Justine Covington — thank you for that first brainstorming session, and for your invaluable insights into the unsettling world of cults.

To the Scribblers — Rob (again!), Steve Griffiths, Chris Nunn, Genny Haines, Doris Hogan, and Rosie Greenhalgh — thank you for the thoughtful critiques and for helping me stay brave on the page.

To my Granny, who provided the foundation of family and showed me what it means to lift others up, even while carrying the weight of your own life.

To my parents, for always encouraging creative obsession, even when it looked a little strange from the outside.

To my agent, Michelle Grajkowski — thank you for your fierce support and wise counsel. I'm so grateful to have you in my corner.

To Kate Lyall Grant — thank you for discovering my work, and for helping shape this book into something sharper, darker, and more true.

To the extraordinary team at Joffe Books: thank you for the care and craftsmanship you bring to each part of the process.

And to the reader — thank you for following the quiet unease of this story wherever it led. I hope it lingers, just a little, after you turn the last page.

Christina Delay

THE JOFFE BOOKS STORY

We began in 2014 when Jasper agreed to publish his mum's much-rejected romance novel and it became a bestseller.

Since then we've grown into the largest independent publisher in the UK. We're extremely proud to publish some of the very best writers in the world, including Joy Ellis, Faith Martin, Caro Ramsay, Helen Forrester, Simon Brett and Robert Goddard. Everyone at Joffe Books loves reading and we never forget that it all begins with the magic of an author telling a story.

We are proud to publish talented first-time authors, as well as established writers whose books we love introducing to a new generation of readers.

We won Trade Publisher of the Year at the Independent Publishing Awards in 2023 and Best Publisher Award in 2024 at the People's Book Prize. We have been shortlisted for Independent Publisher of the Year at the British Book Awards for the last five years, and were shortlisted for the Diversity and Inclusivity Award at the 2022 Independent Publishing Awards. In 2023 we were shortlisted for Publisher of the Year at the RNA Industry Awards, and in 2024 we were shortlisted at the CWA Daggers for the Best Crime and Mystery Publisher.

We built this company with your help, and we love to hear from you, so please email us about absolutely anything bookish at feedback@joffebooks.com.

If you want to receive free books every Friday and hear about all our new releases, join our mailing list here: www.joffebooks.com/freebooks.

And when you tell your friends about us, just remember: it's pronounced Joffe as in coffee or toffee!